COLETTE

Claudine at School

TRANSLATED FROM THE FRENCH BY
Antonia White

VINTAGE

4 6 8 10 9 7 5

Vintage
20 Vauxhall Bridge Road,
London SW1V 2SA

Vintage Classics is part of the Penguin Random House group of companies
whose addresses can be found at global.penguinrandomhouse.com.

Penguin
Random House
UK

Copyright © Martin Secker & Warburg Ltd 1956

First published in France as *Claudine à l'école*, attributed to Willy, in 1900
This translation first published in Great Britain by
Martin Secker & Warburg in 1956
First published by Vintage Classics in 2001

www.vintage-books.co.uk

A CIP catalogue record for this book is available
from the British Library

ISBN 9780099422471

Printed and bound in Great Britain by Clays Ltd, Elcograf S.p.A.

Penguin Random House is committed to a sustainable future
for our business, our readers and our planet. This book is
made from Forest Stewardship Council® certified paper.

MIX
Paper from
responsible sources
FSC® C018179
FSC
www.fsc.org

COLETTE

Colette, the creator of Claudine, Cheri and Gigi,
and one of France's outstanding writers, had
a long, varied and active life. She was born in
Burgundy in 1873 into a home overflowing with
dogs, cats and children, and educated at the local
village school. At the age of twenty she moved
to Paris with her first husband, the notorious
writer and critic Henry Gauthiers-Viller (Willy).
By locking her in her room, Willy forced Colette
to write her first novels (the *Claudine* sequence),
which he published under his name. They were
an instant success. Colette left Willy in 1906 and
worked in music halls as an actor and dancer.
She had a love affair with Napoleon's niece,
married twice more, and had a baby at 40
and at 47. Her writing, which included novels,
portraits, essays and a large body of autobio-
graphical prose, was admired by Proust and
Gide. She was the first woman President of the
Académie Goncourt, and when she died, aged
81, she was given a state funeral and buried in
Père Lachaise Cemetery in Paris.

ALSO BY COLETTE

Fiction

Claudine in Paris
Claudine Married
Claudine and Annie
Gigi
The Cat
Chéri
The Last of Chéri
Chance Acquaintances
Julie de Carneilhan
The Ripening Seed
The Vagabond
Break of Day
The Innocent Libertine
Mitsou
The Other One
The Shackle

Non-fiction

My Apprenticeships and Music-Hall Sidelights
The Blue Lantern
My Mother's House and Sido
The Pure and the Impure

PREFACE

I have told in *Mes Apprentissages* how, some two years after our marriage, therefore about 1895, Monsieur Willy said to me one day:

'You ought to jot down on paper some memories of the Primary School. I might be able to make something out of them . . . Don't be afraid of racy details.'

This curious and still comparatively unknown man, who put his name to I know not how many volumes without having written a single one of them, was constantly on the look-out for new talents for his literary factory. It was not in the least surprising that he should have extended his investigations as far as his own home.

'I was recovering from a long and serious illness which had left my mind and body lazy. But, having found at a stationer's some exercise-books like the ones I had at school, and bought them again, their cream-laid pages, ruled in grey, with red margins, their black linen spines, and their covers bearing a medallion and an ornate title *Le Calligraphe* gave my fingers back a kind of itch for doing "lines", for the passivity of a set task. A certain watermark, seen through the cream-laid paper, made me feel six years younger. On a stub of a desk, the window behind me, one shoulder askew and my knees crossed, I wrote with application and indifference . . .

'When I had finished, I handed over to my husband a closely-written manuscript which respected the margins. He skimmed through it and said:

'"I made a mistake, this can't be of the slightest use . . ."

'Released, I went back to the sofa, to the cat, to books, to silence, to a life that I tried to make pleasant for myself and that I did not know was unhealthy for me.

'The exercise-books remained for two years at the bottom of a drawer. One day Willy decided to tidy up the contents of his desk.

'The appalling counter-like object of sham ebony with a crimson baize top displayed its deal drawers and disgorged bundles of old papers and once again we saw the forgotten exercise-books in which I had scribbled: *Claudine à l'école*.

'"Fancy," said Monsieur Willy. "I thought I had put them in the waste-paper basket."

'He opened one exercise-book and turned over the pages:

'"It's charming . . ."

'He opened a second exercise-book, and said no more – a third, then a fourth . . .

'"Good Lord," he muttered, "I'm an utter imbecile . . ."

'He swept up the exercise-books haphazard, pounced on his flat-brimmed hat and rushed off to a publisher . . . And that was how I became a writer.'

But that was also how I very nearly missed ever becoming a writer. I lacked the literary vocation and it is probable that I should never have produced another line if, after the success of *Claudine à l'école*, other imposed tasks had not, little by little, got me into the habit of writing.

Claudine à l'école appeared in 1900, published by Paul Ollendorff, bearing Willy's sole name as the author. In the interval, I had to get back to the job again to put a little 'spice' into my text.

'Couldn't you,' Willy said to me, 'hot this – these childish reminiscences up a little? For example, a too passionate friendship between Claudine and one of her schoolmates . . . And then some dialect, lots of dialect words . . . Some naughty pranks . . . You see what I mean?'

The pliancy of extreme youth is only equalled by its lack of scruples. What was the extent of Willy's collaboration? The manuscripts furnish a partial answer to a question that has been asked a hundred times. Out of the four *Claudine* books, only the manuscripts of *Claudine en ménage* and *Claudine s'en va* have been saved from the destruction which Willy ordered Paul Barlet to carry out. Paul Barlet, known as Paul Héon – secretary, friend, Negro and extremely honourable man – suspended the execution, which had begun to be carried out, and brought me what remained, which I still possess.

Turning over the pages of those exercise-books is not without interest. Written entirely in my handwriting, a very fine writing appears at distant intervals, changing a word, adding a pun or a very sharp rebuke. Likewise one could also read (in *Claudine en ménage* and *Claudine s'en va*) two more important re-written passages pasted over the original which I am omitting in the present edition.

The success of the *Claudine* books was, for the period, very great. It inspired fashions, plays, and beauty-products. Being honourable, and above all indifferent, I kept silent about the truth, which did not become known till very much later. Nevertheless, it is today for the first time that the *Claudine* books appear under the single name of their single author. I should also be glad if, henceforth, *La Retraite sentimentale* – a pretty title suggested by Alfred Vallette – were considered as the last book in the *Claudine* series. The reader will find this far more satisfactory from the point of view of both logic and convenience.

COLETTE

MY NAME IS CLAUDINE, I live in Montigny; I was born there in 1884; I shall probably not die there. My *Manual of Departmental Geography* expresses itself thus: 'Montigny-en-Fresnois, a pretty little town of 1,950 inhabitants, built in tiers above the Thaize; its well-preserved Saracen tower is worthy of note . . .' To me, those descriptions are totally meaningless! To begin with, the Thaize doesn't exist. Of course I know it's supposed to run through the meadows under the level-crossing but you won't find enough water there in any season to give a sparrow a foot-bath. Montigny 'built in tiers'? No, that's not how I see it; to my mind, the houses just tumble haphazard from the top of the hill to the bottom of the valley. They rise one above the other, like a staircase, leading up to a bit château that was rebuilt under Louis XV and is already more dilapidated than the squat, ivy-sheathed Saracen tower that crumbles away from the top a trifle more every day. Montigny is a village, not a town: its streets, thank heaven, are not paved; the showers roll down them in little torrents that dry up in a couple of hours; it is a village, not even a very pretty village, but, all the same, I adore it.

The charm, the delight of this countryside composed of hills and of valleys so narrow that some are ravines, lies in the woods – the deep, encroaching woods that ripple and wave away into the distance as far as you can see . . . Green meadows make rifts in them here and there, so do little patches of cultivation. But these do not amount to much, for the magnificent woods devour everything. As a result, this

1

lovely region is atrociously poor and its few scattered farms provide just the requisite number of red roofs to set off the velvety green of the woods.

Dear woods! I know them all; I've scoured them so often. There are the copses, where bushes spitefully catch your face as you pass. Those are full of sun and strawberries and lilies-of-the-valley; they are also full of snakes. I've shuddered there with choking terror at the sight of those dreadful, smooth, cold little bodies gliding just in front of my feet. Dozens of times near the 'rose-mallow' I've stopped still, panting, when I've found a well-behaved grass snake under my hand. It would be neatly coiled up, like a snail-shell, with its head raised and its little golden eyes staring at me: it was not dangerous, but how it frightened me! But never mind all that: I shall always end by going back there, alone or with my friends. Better alone, because those girls are so young-lady-ish that they annoy me. They're frightened of being scratched by brambles; they're frightened of little creatures such as hairy caterpillars and those pretty heath-spiders that are as pink and round as pearls; they squeal, they get tired — in fact, they're insufferable.

And then there are my favourites, the great woods that are sixteen and twenty years old. It makes my heart bleed to see one of those cut down. No bushy undergrowth in *them* but trees like pillars and narrow paths where it is almost night at noon, where one's voice and one's steps resound in a disturbing way. Heavens, how I love them! I feel so much alone there, my eyes lost far away among the trees, in the green, mysterious daylight that is at once deliciously peaceful and a little unnerving because of the loneliness and the vague darkness . . . No small creatures in those great dark woods; no tall grasses; but beaten earth, now dry, and sonorous, now soft on account of the springs. Rabbits with white scuts range through them, and timid deer who run so fast that you can only guess their passage. Great heavy pheasants too, red and golden, and wild boars (I've never seen one) and wolves. I heard a wolf once, at the beginning of winter, while I was picking up beech-nuts — those nice, oily little beech-nuts that tickle your throat and make you cough. Sometimes storm-showers surprise you in those woods; you huddle under an oak that is thicker than the others and listen to the rain pattering up there as if on a roof. You're so well-sheltered that when you come out of those depths you are quite lost and dazzled and feel ill at ease in the broad daylight.

And the fir-woods! Not very deep, these, and hardly at all mysterious. I love them for their smell, for the pink and purple heather that grows under them and for the way they sing in the wind. Before you get to them, you have to go through dense forest; then suddenly you have the delicious surprise of coming out on the edge of a lake; a smooth, deep lake, enclosed on all sides by the woods, far, far away from everything! The firs grow on a kind of island in the middle; you have to straddle bravely across on a fallen tree-trunk that bridges the two banks. Under the firs, you light a fire, even in summer, because it's forbidden; you cook any old thing, an apple, a pear, a potato stolen from a field, some wholemeal bread if you've nothing better. And there's a smell of acrid smoke and resin – it's abominable but it's exquisite.

I have lived ten years of wild rovings, of conquests and discoveries, in those woods; the day when I have to leave them my heart will be very heavy.

Two months ago, when I turned fifteen and let down my skirts to my ankles, they demolished the old school and changed the Headmistress. The long skirts were necessitated by my calves; they attracted glances and were already making me look too much like a young lady. The old school was falling into ruins. As for the Headmistress, poor good Madame X, forty, ugly, ignorant, gentle, and always terrified in the presence of the Elementary School inspectors, Doctor Dutertre, our District Superintendent of Schools, needed her place for a protégée of his own. In this part of the world, what Dutertre wishes, the Minister wishes too.

Poor old school, dilapidated and unhygienic, but so amusing! The handsome buildings they are putting up now will never make me forget you!

The rooms on the first floor, the ones belonging to the

masters, were cheerless and uncomfortable. The ground floor was occupied by our two classrooms, the big girls' and the little girls'; two rooms of incredible ugliness and dirtiness, with tables whose like I have never seen since. They were worn down to half their height by constant use and, by rights, we ought to have become hunchbacks after six months of sitting over them. The smell of those classrooms, after the three hours of study in the morning and in the afternoon, was literally enough to knock you down. I have never had schoolmates of my own kind, for the few middle-class families of Montigny send their children as a matter of course to boarding-school in the main county town. Thus the school's only pupils were the daughters of grocers, farmers, policemen, and, for the most part, of labourers; all of them none too well washed.

The reason I find myself in this strange *milieu* is that I do not want to leave Montigny. If had a Mamma, I know very well that she would not have let me stay here twenty-four hours. But Papa – *he* doesn't notice anything and doesn't bother about me. He is entirely wrapped up in his work and it never occurs to him that I might be more suitably brought up in a convent or in some Lycée or other. There's no danger of my opening his eyes!

As companions therefore, I had – and still have – Claire (I won't give her surname) who made her First Communion with me, a gentle girl with beautiful, soft eyes and a romantic little soul. She spent her time at school becoming enamoured (oh! platonically, of course!) of a new boy every week and, even now, her only ambition is to fall in love with the first idiot of an assistant-master or road-surveyor who happens to be in the mood for 'poetical' declarations.

Then there's the lanky Anaïs who, no doubt, will succeed in entering the portals of the school at Fontenay-aux-Roses, thanks to a prodigious memory which takes the place of real intelligence. She is cold, vicious, and so impossible to upset that she never blushes, lucky creature! She is a positive past mistress of comedy and often makes me quite ill with laughing. Her hair is neither dark nor fair; she has a yellow skin, no colour in her cheeks, and narrow black eyes, and she is as tall as a bean-pole. Someone quite out of the ordinary, in fact. Liar, toady, swindler, and traitress, that lanky Anaïs will always know how to get out of any scrape in life. At thirteen, she was writing to some booby of her own age and making assignations with him; this got about and resulted in gossip which upset all the girls in the school except herself. Then there are the Jauberts, two sisters – twins actually – both model pupils. Model pupils! Don't I know it! I could cheerfully flay them alive, they exasperate me so much with their good behaviour and their pretty, neat handwriting and their silly identical flat, flabby faces and sheep's eyes full of maudlin mildness. They swot all the time; they're bursting with good marks; they're prim and underhand and their breath smells of glue. Ugh!

And Marie Belhomme, a goose but such a cheerful one! At fifteen, she has as much reasoning power and common sense as a rather backward child of eight; she overflows with colossally naïve remarks that disarm our maliciousness and we are very fond of her. I'm always saying any amount of disgraceful things in front of her because, at first, she's genuinely shocked and then, the next minute, she laughs wholeheartedly, flinging up her long, narrow hands as high as they'll go. 'Her midwife's hands' Anaïs calls them. Dark, with a matt complexion, long, humid black eyes, and an innocent nose, Marie looks like a pretty, timid hare. These four and myself make up an envied set this year; from now on we rank above the 'big girls' as aspirants to the elementary School Certificate. The rest, in our eyes, are mere scum; lower orders beneath contempt! I shall introduce a few more of my schoolmates in the course of this diary for it is definitely a diary, or very nearly one, that I am about to begin . . .

When Madame X received the notice of her dismissal, she cried about it for an entire day, poor woman – and so did we. This inspired me with a strong aversion for her successor. Just when the demolishers of the old school made their appearance in the playground, the new Headmistress, Mademoiselle Sergent, arrived. She was accompanied by her mother, a fat woman in a starched cap who waits on her daughter and admires her and who gives me the impression of a wily peasant who knows the price of butter but is not bad at heart. As for Mademoiselle Sergent, *she* seemed anything but kindly and I augured ill of that redhead. She has a good figure, with well-rounded bust and hips, but she is flagrantly ugly. Her face is puffy and permanently crimson and her nose is slightly snub between two small black eyes, deep-set and suspicious. She occupies a room in the old school which does not have to be demolished straight away and so does her assistant, the pretty Aimée Lanthenay who attracts me as much as her superior repels me. Against Mademoiselle Sergent, the intruder, I keep up a fierce and rebellious attitude. She has already tried to tame me but I've jibbed in an almost insolent way. After a few lively skirmishes, I have to admit that she is an unusually good Headmistress; decisive, often imperious, with a strength of purpose that would be admirably clear-sighted if it were not occasionally blinded by rage. If she had more command over herself, that woman would be admirable. But, if one resists her, her eyes blaze and her red hair becomes soaked with sweat. The day before yesterday I saw her leave the room so as not to throw an inkpot at my head.

At recreation-time, since the damp cold of this wretched autumn doesn't make me feel in the least inclined to play games, I talk to Mademoiselle Aimée. Our intimacy is progressing very fast. Her nature is like a demonstrative cat's; she is delicate, acutely sensitive to cold, and incredibly caressing in her ways. I like looking at her nice pink face, like a fair-haired little girl's, and at her golden eyes with their curled-up lashes. Lovely eyes that only ask to smile! They make the boys turn and look after her when she goes out. Often, when we're talking in the doorway of the little crowded classroom, Mademoiselle Sergent passes by us on the way back to her room. She doesn't say a word but fixes us with her jealous, searching looks. Her silence makes us feel, my new friend and I, that she's furious at seeing us 'hit it off' so well.

This little Aimée – she's nineteen and only comes up to my ears – chatters, like the schoolgirl she still was only three months ago, with a need for affection and with repressed gestures that touch me. Repressed gestures! She controls them from an instinctive fear of Mademoiselle Sergent, clutching her cold little hands tight under the imitation fur collar (poor little thing, she has no money like thousands of her kind). To make her less shy, I behave gently (it isn't difficult) and I ask her questions, quite content just to look at her. When she talks she's pretty, in spite of – or because of – her irregular little face. If her cheekbones are a trifle too salient, if her rather too full mouth, under the short nose, makes a funny little dint at the left side when she laughs, what marvellous golden-yellow eyes she has to make up for them! And what a complexion – one of those complexions that look so delicate but are so reliable that the cold doesn't even turn them blue! She talks and she talks – about her father who's a gem-cutter and her mother who was liberal with her smacks, about her sister and her three brothers, about the hard training-college in the country-town where the water froze in the jugs and where she was always dropping with sleep because they got up at five o'clock (luckily the English mistress was very nice to her), about the holidays at home where they used to force her to go back to housework, telling her she'd do better to cook than to sham the young lady. All this was unfolded in her endless chatter; all that poverty-stricken youth that she had endured with impatience and remembered with terror.

Little Mademoiselle Lanthenay, your supple body seeks and demands an unknown satisfaction. If you were not an assistant mistress at Montigny you might be . . . I'd rather not say what. But how I like listening to you and looking at you – you who are four years older than I am and yet make me feel every single moment like your elder sister!

My new confidante told me one day that she knew quite a lot of English and this inspired me with a simply marvellous idea. I asked Papa (as he takes Mama's place) if he wouldn't like me to get Mademoiselle Aimée Lanthenay to give me lessons in English grammar. Papa thought the idea a good one, like most of my ideas, and to 'clinch the matter', as he says, he came with me to see Mademoiselle Sergent. She received us with a stony politeness and, while Papa was explaining *his* idea to her, she seemed to be approving it. But

7

I felt vaguely uneasy at not seeing her eyes while she was talking. (I'd noticed very quickly that her eyes always tell what she is thinking without her being able to disguise it and I was worried to observe that she kept them obstinately lowered.) Mademoiselle Aimée was called down and arrived eager and blushing. She kept repeating 'Yes, Monsieur', and 'Certainly, Monsieur', hardly realizing what she was saying, while I watched her, highly delighted with my ruse and rejoicing in the thought that, henceforth, I should have her with me in more privacy than on the threshold of the small classroom. Price of the lessons: fifteen francs a month and two sessions a week. For this poor little assistant mistress, who earns sixty-five francs a month and has to pay for her keep out of it, this was a windfall beyond her dreams. I believe, too, that she was pleased at the idea of being with me more often. During that visit, I barely exchanged a couple of sentences with her.

The day of our first lesson! I waited for her after class while she collected her English books and off we went to my home! I'd arranged a comfortable corner for us in Papa's library – a big table, pens, and exercise-books, with a good lamp that only lit the table. Mademoiselle Aimée, extremely embarrassed (why?), blushed and said with a nervous little cough:

'Now then, Claudine, you know your alphabet, I think?'

'Of course, Mademoiselle. I also know a little grammar. I could easily do that little bit of translation . . . We're cosy here, aren't we?'

'Yes, very cosy.'

I asked, lowering my voice a little as I did when we were having our gossips:

'Did Mademoiselle Sergent mention my lessons with you again?'

'Oh, hardly at all. She told me it was a piece of luck for me – that you'd give me no trouble if you were only willing to work a little – that you could learn very quickly when you wanted to.'

'Was that all? That's not much! She must have been sure you'd repeat it to me.'

8

'Now, now, Claudine, we're not working. In English there is only one article . . . etc., etc.'

After ten minutes of serious English, I questioned her again.

'Did you notice she didn't look at all pleased when I came with Papa to ask to have lessons with you?'

'No . . . Yes . . . Well, perhaps. But we hardly spoke to each other that evening.'

'Do take off your jacket, it's always stifling in Papa's room. How slim you are – one could snap you in two! Your eyes are awfully pretty by this light.'

I said that because I thought it and also because it gave me pleasure to pay her compliments – more pleasure than if I had received them on my own account. I inquired:

'Do you still sleep in the same room as Mademoiselle Sergent?'

This proximity seemed odious to me but how could she do otherwise? All the rooms had already been stripped of their furniture and the men were beginning to take off the roof. The poor little thing sighed:

'I have to, but it's too tiresome for words. At nine o'clock I go to bed at once – quick, quick – and she comes up to bed later on. But it's unpleasant all the same, when the two of us are so ill-at-ease together.'

'Oh, I do feel so frightfully sorry for you! It must be maddening for you to have to dress in front of her in the morning! I should loathe to have to show myself in my chemise to people I don't like!'

Mademoiselle Lanthenay started as she pulled out her watch.

'Really, Claudine, we're not doing a thing! We simply must work!'

'Yes . . . Did you know they're expecting some new assistant-masters?'

'I know. Two. They're arriving tomorrow.'

'That'll be amusing! Two admirers for you!'

'Oh, be quiet, do. To begin with, all the ones I've seen were so stupid that I wasn't a bit tempted. And, besides, I know the names of these two already. Such ludicrous names – Antonin Rabastens and Armand Duplessis.'

'I bet those two idiots will go through our playground twenty times a day. They'll make the excuse that the boys' entrance is cluttered up with builder's rubbish . . .'

'Listen, Claudine, this is disgraceful. We haven't done a stroke today.'

'Oh, it's always like that the first day. We'll work much better next Friday. One has to have time to get going.'

In spite of this convincing reasoning, Mademoiselle Lanthenay felt guilty about her own laziness and made me work seriously to the end of the hour. Afterwards, I accompanied her down to the bottom of the street. It was dark and freezing and it upset me to see this small shadow going off into that cold and that blackness to return to the Redhead with the jealous eyes.

This week we've enjoyed some hours of pure bliss because they've been using us big ones to clear the loft and bring down all the books and the old lumber with which it was crammed. We had to hurry: the builders were waiting to pull down the first storey. There were mad gallops through the attics and up and down the stairs. At the risk of being punished we ventured, the lanky Anaïs and I, right on to the staircase leading to the masters' rooms, in the hope of at least catching a glimpse of the two new assistants who had remained invisible since their arrival . . .

Yesterday, in front of a door left ajar, Anaïs gave me a shove. I stumbled and pushed the door right open with my head. Then we burst into giggles and stood rooted to the spot on the threshold of this room, obviously a master's and, luckily, empty of its tenant. Hastily, we inspected it. On the wall and on the mantelpiece were large chromolithographs in commonplace frames: an Italian girl with luxuriant hair, dazzling teeth, and eyes three times the size of her mouth; as a companion-piece, a swooning blonde clutching a spaniel to her blue-ribboned bodice. Above the bed of Antonin Rabastens (he had stuck his card on the door with four drawing-pins) hung entwined pennants in the French and Russian national colours. What else? A table with a wash-basin, two chairs, some butterflies stuck on corks, some sentimental songs lying about the mantelpiece, and not a thing besides. We stared at all this without saying a word, then suddenly we escaped towards the loft at full speed, oppressed by an absurd fear that Antonin (one simply *can't* be called Antonin!) might be coming up the stairs. Our trampling on those forbidden steps was so noisy that a door opened on the ground-floor – the door of the boys' classroom – and someone appeared, inquiring in a funny Marseilles accent:

'What on earth's going on? For the last half-hour, have I been hearing *hosses* on the staircase?'

We had just time to catch a glimpse of a tall, dark youth with healthy ruddy cheeks . . . Up there, safe at last, my accomplice said, panting:

'Just suppose, if he knew we'd come from his room!'

'Well, suppose he did? He'd be inconsolable at having missed us.'

'Missed us!' went on Anaïs with icy gravity. 'He looks like a tough chap who couldn't be likely to miss you.'

'Go on, you great slut!'

And we went on with the clearing-out of the loft. It was fascinating to rummage among the pile of books and periodicals to be carried down and that belonged to Mademoiselle Sergent. Of course, we had a good look through the heap before taking them down and I noticed it contained Pierre Loüys' *Aphrodite* and several numbers of the *Journal amusant*. Anaïs and I regaled ourselves excitedly with a drawing by Gerbault entitled *Whispers behind the Scenes*. It showed gentlemen in black evening clothes occupied in tickling charming Opera dancers, in tights and ballet-skirts, who were twittering and gesticulating. The other pupils had gone downstairs; it was getting dark in the attic and we lingered over some pictures that made us laugh – some Albert Guillaumes that were far from suitable for young ladies.

Suddenly, we started for someone had opened the door and was asking in a garlicky voice: 'Hi! who's been making this infernal row on the staircase?'

We stood up, looking very serious, our arms loaded with books and said, very deliberately: 'Good morning, Sir,' fighting down an agonizing desire to laugh. It was the big

11

assistant-master with the jolly face we'd seen just now. So then, because we're both tall and look at least sixteen, he apologized and went away, saying: 'A thousand pardons, young ladies.' So we danced behind his back in silence, making devilish faces at him. We arrived downstairs late and were scolded. Mademoiselle Sergent asked me: 'What on earth were you doing up there?' So I ostentatiously put down the pile of books at her feet with the daring *Aphrodite* and the numbers of *Journal amusant* on top, folded back to display the pictures. She saw them at once; her red cheeks turned redder than ever but she recovered herself at once and remarked: 'Ah! Those are the Headmaster's books you have brought down. Everything gets so mixed up in that loft we all use. I'll give them back to him.' And there the sermon ended; not the least punishment for the two of us. As we went out, I nudged Anaïs whose narrow eyes were crinkled with laughter.

'Hmm, the Headmaster's got a broad back!'

'Claudine, can you *imagine* that innocent collecting bits of dirt! I wouldn't be surprised if he believes babies are found under gooseberry bushes!'

For the Headmaster is a sad, colourless widower. One hardly knows he exists for he only leaves his classroom to shut himself up in his bedroom.

The following Friday, I took my second lesson with Mademoiselle Aimée Lanthenay. I asked her:

'Are the new masters pursuing you already?'

'Oh! As it happens, Claudine, they came yesterday to "pay their respects". The nice boy who swaggers a bit is Antonin Rabastens.'

'Known as "the pearl of the Canebière"; and the other one, what's *he* like?'

'Slim, handsome, with an interesting face. He's called Armand Duplessis.'

'It would be a sin not to nickname him "Richelieu".'

She laughed.

'A name that's stick to him all through the school, you wicked Claudine! But what a savage! He doesn't say a word except Yes and No.'

My English mistress seemed adorable that night under the library lamp. Her cat's eyes shone pure gold, at once malicious and caressing, and I admired them, not without reminding myself that they were neither kind nor frank nor trustworthy. But they sparkled so brilliantly in her fresh face and she seemed so utterly at ease in this warm, softly-lit room that I already felt ready to love her so much, so very much, with all my irrational heart. Yes, I've known perfectly well, for a long time, that I have an irrational heart. But knowing it doesn't stop me in the least.

'And *she*, the Redhead – doesn't she say anything to you these days?'

'No. She's even being quite amiable. I don't think she's as annoyed as you think to see us getting on so well together.'

'Pooh! *You* don't see her eyes. They're not as lovely as yours, but they're more wicked . . . Pretty little Mademoiselle, what a darling you are!'

She blushed deeply and said, with complete lack of conviction:

'You're a little mad, Claudine. I'm beginning to believe it, I've been told so so often!'

'Yes, I'm quite aware that other people say so, but who cares? I like being with you. Tell me about your lovers.'

'I haven't any! You know, I think we shall see plenty of the two assistant-masters. Rabastens strikes me as very "man of the world" and Duplessis will follow in his footsteps. By the way, did you know that I shall probably get my little sister to come here as a boarder?'

'I don't care a fig about your sister. How old is she?'

'Your age. A few months younger, just on fifteen.'

'Is she nice?'

'Not pretty, as you'll see. A bit shy and wild.'

'Sucks to your sister! I say, I saw Rabastens in the loft. He came up on purpose. He's got a Marseilles accent you could cut with a knife, that hulking Antonin!'

'Yes, but he's not too ugly . . . Come along, Claudine, let's get down to work. Aren't you ashamed of yourself? Read that and translate it.'

But it was no good her being indignant: work made no progress at all. I kissed her when we said good-bye.

The next day, during recreation, Anaïs was in the act of dancing like a maniac in front of me, hoping to reduce me to pulp and keeping a perfectly straight face all the while, when suddenly Rabastens and Duplessis appeared at the playground gate.

As we were there – Marie Belhomme, the lanky Anaïs, and myself – their lordships bowed and we replied with icy correctness. They went into the big room where the mistresses were correcting exercise-books and we saw them talking and laughing with them. At that, I discovered a sudden and urgent need to fetch my hood, which I had left behind on my desk. I burst into the classroom, pushing open the door as if I had no idea that their Lordships might be inside. Then I stopped, pretending to be confused, in the open doorway. Mademoiselle Sergent arrested my course with a 'Control yourself, Claudine' that would have cracked a water-jug and I tiptoed away like a cat. But I'd had time to see that Mademoiselle Aimée Lanthenay was laughing as she chatted to Duplessis and was setting herself out to charm him. Just you wait, my hero wrapped in Byronic gloom! Tomorrow or the day after there'll be a song about you or some cheap puns or some nicknames. That'll teach you to seduce Mademoiselle Aimée. But . . . all right, what is it? Were they calling me back? What luck? I re-entered looking very meek.

'Claudine,' said Mademoiselle by way of explanation. 'Come and read this at sight. Monsieur Rabastens is musical but not so musical as you are.'

How amiable she was! What a complete changeover! *This* was a song from *The Chalet*, boring to tears. Nothing reduces my voice to a shred like singing in front of people I don't know, so I read it correctly but in an absurdly shaky voice that became firmer, thank heavens, at the end of the piece.

'Ah, Mademoiselle, allow me to congratulate you. You sing with such *forrce*!'

I protested politely, mentally sticking out my tongue (my

tonngue, he'd say) at him. And I went off to find the *otherrs* (it's catching) who gave me a welcome like vinegar.

'Darling!' the lanky Anaïs said between her teeth. 'I hope you're in everyone's good books now! You must have produced a smashing impression on those gentlemen, so we shall be seeing them often.'

The Jauberts indulged in covert, sneering giggles of jealousy.

'Let me alone, will you? Honestly, there's nothing to foam at the mouth about because I happened to read something at sight. Rabastens is one hundred and fifty per cent a southerner and that's a species I detest. As to Richelieu, if he comes here often, I know quite well who the attraction is.'

'Well, who?'

'Mademoiselle Aimée, of course! He positively devours her with his eyes.'

'Own up,' whispered Anaïs. 'It's not him you're jealous of, so it must be her . . .'

That insufferable Anaïs! That girl sees everything and what she doesn't see, she invents!

The two masters re-entered the playground; Antonin Rabastens expansive and smiling at us all, the other nervous, almost cowed. It was time they went away; the bell was on the point of ringing for the end of recreation and their urchins in the neighbouring playground were making as much noise as if the whole lot had been simultaneously plunged in a cauldron of boiling water. The bell rang for us and I said to Anaïs:

'I say, it's a long time since the District Superintendent came. I shall be awfully surprised if he doesn't turn up this week.'

'He arrived yesterday. He's sure to come and poke his nose in here.'

Dutertre, the District Superintendent of Schools, is also the doctor to the orphanage. Most of the children there attend the school and this gives him double authorization to visit us. Heaven knows he makes enough use of it! Some people declare that Mademoiselle Sergent is his mistress. I don't know if it's true or not. What I am prepared to bet is that he owes her money. Electoral campaigns cost a lot and this Dutertre, who hasn't a penny, has set his heart, in spite of persistent failure, on replacing the dumb, but immensely rich old moron who represents the voters of Fresnois in the Chambre des Députés. And I'm absolutely certain that passionate redhead is in love with him! She trembles with jealous fury when she sees him pawing us rather too insistently.

For, I repeat, he frequently honours us with his visits. He sits on the tables, behaves badly, lingers with the older ones, especially with me, reads our essays, thrusts his moustache in our ears, strokes our necks and calls us *tu* (he knew us when we were *so* high), flashing his wolf's teeth and his black eyes. We find him extremely amiable but I know him to be such a rotter that I don't feel in the least shy with him. And this scandalizes my schoolfriends. It was our day for the sewing-lesson. We were plying our needles lazily and talking in inaudible voices. Suddenly, to our joy, we saw white flakes beginning to fall. What luck! We should be able to make slides; there'd be lots of tumbles; we'd have snowball fights. Mademoiselle Sergent stared at us without seeing us, her mind elsewhere.

Tap, tap on the window-panes! Through the whirling feathers of the snow, we could see Dutertre knocking on the glass. He was all wrapped up in furs and wore a fur cap. He looked handsome in them, with his shining eyes and the teeth he is always displaying. The first bench (myself, Marie Belhomme, and the lanky Anaïs) came to life; I fluffed up my hair on my temples, Anaïs bit her lips to make them red and Marie tightened her belt by a hole. The Jaubert sisters clasped their hands like two pictures of First Communicants: 'I am the temple of the Holy Ghost.'

Mademoiselle Sergent leapt to her feet, so brusquely that she upset her chair and her footstool, and ran to open the door. The sight of all this commotion made me split with laughter. Anaïs took advantage of my helplessness to pinch me and to make diabolical faces at me as she chewed charcoal and india-rubber. (However much they forbid her these strange comestibles, all day long her pockets and her mouth are filled with pencil stubs, filthy black india-rubber, charcoal,

16

and pink blotting-paper. Chalk, pencil-lead and such-like satisfy her stomach in the most peculiar way: it must be those things she eats that give her a complexion the colour of wood and grey plaster. At least I only eat cigarette-paper and only one special kind of that. But that gawk Anaïs ruins the store from which they give out the school stationery. She asks for new 'equipment' every single week to such an extent that, at the beginning of term, the Municipal Council made a complaint.)

Dutertre shook his snow-powdered furs – they looked like his natural hide. Mademoiselle Sergent sparkled with such joy at the sight of him that it didn't even occur to her to notice if I were watching her. He cracked jokes with her and his quick, resonant voice (he speaks with the accent they have up in the mountains) seemed to warm up the whole classroom. I inspected my nails and let my hair be well in evidence, for the visitor was directing most of his glances at us. After all, we're big girls of fifteen and if my face looks younger than my age, my figure looks eighteen at least. And my hair is worth showing off, too. It makes a curly flying mass whose colour varies according to the season between dull chestnut and deep gold, and contrasts, by no means unattractively, with my coffee-brown eyes. Curly, as it is, it comes down almost to my hips. I've never worn plaits or a chignon. Chignons give me a headache and plaits don't frame my face enough. When we play prisoners' base, I gather up my heap of hair, which would make me too easy a victim, and tie it up in a horse's tail. Well, after all, isn't it prettier like that?

Mademoiselle Sergent finally broke off her raptured conversation with the District Superintendent and rapped out a: 'Girls, you are behaving extremely badly!' To confirm her in this conviction, Anaïs thought it helped to let out the 'Hpp . . .' of suppressed hysterical giggles without moving a muscle in her face. So it was at me that Mademoiselle shot a furious glance which boded punishment.

At last Monsieur Dutertre raised his voice and we heard him ask: 'They're working well, here? They're keeping well?'

'They're keeping extremely well,' replied Mademoiselle

17

Sergent. 'But they do little enough work. The laziness of those big girls is incredible!'

The moment we saw the handsome doctor turn towards us, we all bent over our work with an air of intense application as if we were too absorbed to remember he was there.

'Ah! Ah!' he said, coming towards our benches. 'So we don't do much work? What ideas have we in our heads? Is Mademoiselle Claudine no longer top in French composition?'

Those French compositions, how I loathe them! Such stupid and disgusting subjects: 'Imagine the thoughts and actions of a young blind girl.' (Why not deaf and dumb as well?) Or: 'Write, so as to draw your own physical and moral portrait, to a brother whom you have not seen for ten years.' (I have no fraternal bonds, I am an only child.) No one will ever know the efforts I have to make to restrain myself from writing pure spoof or highly subversive opinions! But, for all that, my companions – all except Anaïs – make such a hash of it that, in spite of myself I am 'the outstanding pupil in literary composition.'

Dutertre had now arrived at the point he wanted to arrive at and I raised my head as Mademoiselle Sergent answered him.

'Claudine? Oh, she's still top. But it's not *her* fault. She's gifted for that and doesn't need to make any effort.'

He sat down on the table, swinging one leg and addressing me as *tu* so as not to lose the habit of doing so.

'So you're lazy?'

'Of course. It's my only pleasure in the world.'

'You don't mean that seriously! You prefer reading, eh? What do you read? Everything you can lay hands on? Everything in your father's library?'

'No, Sir. Not books that bore me.'

'I bet you're teaching yourself some remarkable things. Give me your exercise-book.'

To read it more comfortably, he leant a hand on my shoulder and twisted a curl of my hair. This made the lanky Anaïs turn dangerously yellow; he had not asked for her exercise-book! I should pay for this favouritism by sur-reptitious pin-pricks, sly tale-telling to Mademoiselle Sergent, and being spied on whenever I talked to Mademoiselle Lanthenay. She was standing near the door of the small classroom, that charming Aimée, and she smiled at me so tenderly with her golden eyes that I was almost consoled for not having been able to talk to her today or yesterday except in front of my schoolmates. Dutertre laid down my exercise-book and stroked my shoulders in an absent-minded way. He was not thinking in the least about what he was doing, evidently . . . oh, *very* evidently . . .

'How old are you?'

'Fifteen.'

'Funny little girl! If you didn't look so crazy, you'd seem older, you know. You'll sit for your certificate next October?'

'Yes, Sir, to please Papa.'

'Your father? What on earth does it matter to him? But you yourself, you're not particularly eager at the prospect?'

'Oh yes, I am. It'll amuse me to see all those people who question us. And besides there are concerns in the town then. It'll be fun.'

'You won't go on to the training-college?'

I leapt in my seat.

'Good heavens, no!'

'Why so emphatic, you excitable girl?'

'I don't want to go there any more than I wanted to go to boarding-school – because you're shut up.'

'Oho! Your liberty means as much as all that to you, does it? Your husband won't have things all his own way, poor fellow! Show me that face. Are you keeping well? A trifle anaemic, perhaps?'

This kindly doctor turned me towards the window, slipped his arm round me and gazed searchingly into my eyes with his wolfish stare. I made my own gaze frank and devoid of mystery. I always have dark circles under my eyes and he asked me if I suffered from palpitations and breathlessness.

'No, never.'

I lowered my lids because if felt I was blushing idiotically. Also he was staring at me too hard! And I was conscious of Mademoiselle Sergent behind us, her nerves tense.

'Do you sleep all night?'

I was furious at blushing more than ever as I answered:

'Oh, yes, Sir. All night long.'

He did not press the point but stood upright and let go my waist.

'Tcha! Fundamentally, you're as sound as a bell.'

A little caress on my cheek, then he went on to the lanky Anaïs who was withering on her bench.

'Show me your exercise-book.'

While he turned over the pages, pretty fast, Mademoiselle Sergent was fulminating in an undertone at the First Division (girls of twelve and fourteen who were already beginning to pinch in their waists and wear chignons), for the First Division had taken advantage of authority's inattention to indulge in a Witches' Sabbath. We could hear hands being smacked with rulers, the squeals of girls who were being pinched. They were letting themselves in for a general detention, not a doubt of it!

Anaïs was suffocated with joy at seeing her exercise-book in such august hands but no doubt Dutertre did not find her worth much attention for he passed on after paying her a few compliments and pinching her ear. He lingered some minutes by Marie Belhomme whose smooth, dark freshness attracted him but she was promptly overwhelmed with shyness. She lowered her head like a ram, said Yes when she meant No and addressed Dutertre as 'Mademoiselle'. As to the two Jaubert sisters, he complimented them on their beautiful handwriting, as might have been foretold. At last, he left the room. Good riddance!

We still had ten minutes to go before the end of class; how could we use use them? I asked permission to leave the room so that I could surreptitiously gather up a handful of the still-falling snow. I made a snowball and bit into it; it was cold and delicious. It always smells a little of dust, this first fall. I hid it in my pocket and returned to the classroom. Everyone round me made signs to me and I passed the snowball round. Each of them, with the exception of the virtuous twins, bit into it with expressions of rapture. Then that ninny of a Marie Belhomme had to go and drop the last bit and Mademoiselle Sergent saw it.

'Claudine! Have you gone and brought in snow again? This is really getting beyond the limit!'

She rolled her eyes so furiously that I bit back the retort 'It's the first time since last year', for I was afraid Mademoiselle Lanthenay might suffer for my impertinence. So I opened my *History of France* without answering a word.

This evening I should be having my English lesson and that would console me for my silence.

At four o'clock, Mademoiselle Aimée appeared and we went off happily together.

How nice it was there with her in the warm library! I pulled my chair right up against hers and laid my head on her shoulder. She put her arm round me and I squeezed her supple waist.

'Darling little Mademoiselle, it's such ages since I've seen you!'

'But . . . it's only three days . . .'

'What does that matter? . . . Don't talk, and kiss me! You're very unkind; time seems short to you when you're away from me . . . Do they bore you frightfully, these lessons?'

'Oh, Claudine! On the contrary, you know you're the only person I can ever really talk to and I'm only happy when I'm here.'

She kissed me and I purred. Then, suddenly, I hugged her so violently that she gave a little shriek.

'Claudine, we *must* work!'

I wished English grammar to the devil! I much preferred to lay my head on her breast while she stroked my hair or my neck and I could hear her heart beat breathlessly under my ear. How I loved being with her! Nevertheless, I had to take up a pen and at least pretend to be working! But really, what was the point? Who could possibly come in? Papa? Nothing less likely! Papa shuts himself up like a hermit in the most uncomfortable room on the first floor, the one where you freeze in winter and roast in summer and there he remains blindly absorbed, deaf to the noises of the world, busy with . . . But, of course . . . you haven't read, because it'll never be finished, his great work on the *Malacology of the Region of*

21

Fresnois and you'll never know that, after complicated experiments and anxious vigils that have kept him bending for hours and hours over innumerable slugs enclosed in little bell-glasses and wire cages, Papa has established the following epoch-making fact: in one day, a *limax flavus* devours as much as 0.24 grammes of food whereas the *helix ventricosa* only consumes 0.19 grammes in the same time! How could you expect that the budding hope of such discoveries would leave a passionate malacologist any paternal sentiment between seven in the morning and nine at night? He's the best and kindest of men – between two orgies of slugs. Moreover, he watches me live – when he has time to – with positive admiration. He's astonished to see me existing 'like a real human being'. This fact makes him laugh, with his small deep-set eyes and his noble Bourbon nose (wherever did he get that royal nose?) into his handsome beard that's streaked with three colours – red, grey, and white. And how often I've seen that beard shining with traces of slime from the slugs!

I asked Aimée carelessly whether she'd seen the two friends, Rabastens and Richelieu, again. She became excited, which surprised me:

'Ah! I forgot, I hadn't told you . . . You know we sleep over at the infant-school now because they're pulling down everything . . . Well, yesterday evening, I was working in my room round about ten o'clock and when I was closing the shutters before going to bed, I saw a tall shadow walking to and fro under my window, in all this cold! Guess who it was!'

'One of those two, of course.'

'Yes! But it was Armand. Would you ever have believed it of that shy chap?'

I said no, but actually I didn't find it at all hard to believe. That tall, dark creature with the sombre, serious eyes seemed to me much less of a nonentity than the hearty Marseillais. Nevertheless I saw that Mademoiselle Aimée's bird-like head was completely turned by this mild adventure. I asked her:

'What? Do you already find him as interesting as all that, that solemn crow?'

'No, of course not! I'm amused, that's all.'

That was that, and the lesson ended without further

confidences. It was only when we went out into the dark passage that I kissed her with all my might on her charming slim white neck and in the tendrils of her hair that smelt so nice. She's as amusing to kiss as a warm, pretty little animal and she returned my kisses tenderly. Oh, I'd have kept her with me all the time if only I could!

Tomorrow would be Sunday. No school. What a bore! It's the only place I find amusing.

That particular Sunday, I went to spend the afternoon where Claire lives – my sweet, gentle partner at my First Communion. She hasn't been coming to school for a year now. We walked down the Chemin des Matignons which runs into the road leading to the station. It's a lane that's leafy and dark with greenery in summer; in these winter months there aren't any leaves, of course, but you're still sufficiently hidden there to be able to spy on the people sitting on the benches along the road. We walked on the crackling snow. The frozen puddles creaked musically under the sun with the charming sound, that's like no other, of ice breaking up. Claire whispered about her mild flirtations with the boys at the dance on Sunday over at Trouillard's; rough, clumsy boys. I quivered with excitement as I listened to her.

'You know, Claudine, Montassuy was there too and he danced the polka with me, holding me tight against him. At that very minute, my brother, Eugène, who was dancing with Adèle Tricotot, let go of his partner, and jumped up in the air and banged his head against one of the hanging lamps. The lamp-glass turned upside down and that put out the lamp. While everyone was staring and saying "Ooh!" whatever d'you think happened? That fat Féfed turned off the other lamp and everything was as black as black . . . nothing but one candle right at the very far end of the little bar. My dear, all the time old mother Trouillard was fetching some matches, you heard nothing but screams and laughs and the sound of kisses. My brother was holding Adèle Tricotot just beside me and she kept on sighing like anything and saying "Let go of me, Eugène" in a muffled voice as if she'd got her skirts over her head. And that fat Féfed and his partner had fallen over on the floor. They were laughing and laughing, so much that they simply couldn't get up again!'

'What about you and Montassuy?'

Claire turned red with belated modesty.

'Ah, that's just what I was going to tell you . . . The first minute, he was so surprised to see the lamps go out that he only kept on holding my hand. Then he put his arm round my waist again and said very quietly: "Don't be frightened." I didn't say a word and I could feel him bending over me and kissing my cheeks. Ever so gently, feeling his way, and it was actually so dark that he made a mistake (Claire, you little hypocrite!) and kissed my mouth. I enjoyed it so much – it made me feel simply marvellous . . . In fact I was so excited that I nearly fell over and he had to hold me up by hugging me tighter still. Oh! he's nice, I love him!'

'Well, what happened after that, you slut?'

'After that, old mother Trouillard lit the lamps again, grumbling like anything. She swore that if such a thing ever happened again, she'd bring a complaint and they'd have the dances stopped.'

'The fact is, it really was going a bit far! . . . Ssh . . . be quiet . . . Who's that coming?'

We were sitting behind the briar-hedge, quite near the road that ran a couple of yards below us. There was a bench on the edge of the ditch so it was a marvellous hide-out for listening without being seen.

'It's those two masters!'

Yes, it was Rabastens and the gloomy Armand Duplessis who were walking along and talking. What an unhoped-for bit of luck! The coxcomb, Antonin, wanted to sit down on that bench because of the pale sunshine that had warmed him a little. We were about to hear their conversation and we shuddered with joy in our field, right above their heads.

'Ah!' said the southerner with satisfaction, 'one's quite *warrm* here. Don't you agree?'

Armand muttered some vague remark. The man from Marseilles started up again. He was going to do all the talking, I was certain!

'You know, *I* like this part of the world. Those two

24

schoolmistress ladies are extremely pleasant. I admit Mademoiselle Sergent is ugly! But that little Mademoiselle Aimée is a smart girl! I feel decidedly pleased with myself when she looks at me.'

The sham Richelieu sat up straight; his tongue was loosened:

'Yes, she's attractive, and so charming! She's always smiling and she chatters away like a hedge-sparrow.'

But he promptly regretted his expansiveness and added in a different voice:

'She's a very charming young lady. You're certainly going to turn her head, Don Juan!'

I nearly burst out laughing. Rabastens as Don Juan! I had a vision of him with his round head and plump cheeks adorned with a plumed hat . . . Up there, straining towards the road, the two of us laughed at each other with our eyes, without moving a muscle of our faces.

'But, goodness me,' went on the heartbreaker of the elementary school, 'she's not the only pretty girl round here. Anyone would think you hadn't noticed them! The other day, in the classroom, Mademoiselle Claudine came in and sang quite charmingly (I may say that I know what I'm talking about, eh?) and she's not a girl you'd overlook, with that hair flowing down her back and all round her and those very naughty brown eyes! My dear chap, I believe that girl knows more about things she oughtn't to know than she does about geography!'

I gave a little start of astonishment and we might easily have been discovered for Claire let off a laugh like a gas-escape which might have been overheard. Rabastens fidgeted on his bench beside the absorbed Duplessis and whispered something in his ear, laughing in a ribald way. The other smiled; they got up; they went away. The two of us up there were in ecstasies. We danced a war-dance of joy, as much to warm ourselves as to congratulate ourselves on this delicious piece of spying.

On my way home, I was already ruminating on various alluring tricks to excite that hulking ultra-inflammable Antonin still more. It would be something to pass the time during recreation when it rained. And I who believed he was in process of plotting the seduction of Mademoiselle Lanthenay! I was delighted that he wasn't trying to make up to her, for what little Aimée struck me as being so amorous that even a Rabastens might have succeeded – who knows? It's true that Richelieu was even more smitten with her than I had supposed.

At seven o'clock in the morning, I arrived at school. It was my turn to light the fire, worse luck! That meant breaking up firewood in the shed and ruining one's hands; carrying logs, blowing on the flames and getting stinging smoke in one's eyes . . . Good gracious, the first new building was already rising high and the boys' school, identical with it, had got most of its roof on! Our poor old half-demolished school looked like a tiny hovel by these two buildings that had so quickly sprouted out of the ground. The lanky Anaïs joined me and we went off to break up firewood together.

'D'you know, Claudine, there's a second assistant-mistress arriving today, and we're all going to be forced out of house and home. They're going to give us classes in the Infants' School.'

'What a brilliant idea! We shall catch fleas and lice. It's simply filthy over there.'

'Yes, but we'll be nearer the boys' classroom, old thing.'

(Anaïs really is shameless! However, she's perfectly right.)

'That's true. Now, you twopenny-halfpenny fire, are you going to catch or not? I've been bursting my lungs for the last ten minutes. Ah, I bet Monsieur Rabastens blazes up a lot quicker than you do!'

Little by little, the fire made up its mind to burn. The pupils arrived; Mademoiselle Sergent was late. (Why? It was the first time.) She came down at last, answered our 'Good morning' with a preoccupied air, then sat down at her desk saying: 'To your places' without looking at us and obviously without giving us a thought. I copied down my problems while I asked myself what thoughts were troubling her and I noticed, with uneasy surprise, that from time to time she darted quick looks at me – looks that were at once furious and vaguely gratified. Whatever could be up? I was not comfortable in my mind.

Not at all. I began to search my conscience . . . I couldn't think of anything except that she'd watched us going off for our English lesson, Mademoiselle Lanthenay and me, with a barely-concealed, almost rueful anger. Aha! so we were not to be left in peace, my little Aimée and I? Yet we were doing nothing wrong! Our last English lesson had been so delightful! We hadn't even opened the dictionary, or the *Selection of Phrases in Common Use*, or the exercise-book . . .

I meditated, inwardly raging as I copied down my problems in wildly untidy writing. Anaïs was surreptitiously eyeing me, obviously guessing something was up. I looked again at that terrible Redhead with the jealous eyes as I picked up my pen which I'd dropped on the floor by a lucky piece of clumsiness. But . . . but she'd been crying . . . I couldn't possibly be mistaken! Then why those angry, yet almost pleased glances? This was becoming unbearable; it was absolutely essential to question Aimée as soon as possible. I didn't give another thought to the problem to be transcribed:

> . . . *A workman is planting stakes to make a fence. He plants them at such a distance from each other that the bucket of tar, in which he dips their lower ends to a depth of 30 centimetres, is empty at the end of 3 hours. Given that the quantity of tar which remains on the stake equals 10 cubic centimetres, that the bucket is a cylinder whose radius at the base is 0.15 metres and whose height is 0.75 metres and is three-quarters full, that the workman dips 40 stakes an hour and takes 8 minutes' rest during that time, what is the number of stakes and what is the area of the property which is in the form of a perfect square? State also what would be the number of stakes necessary if they were planted 10 centimetres further apart. State also the cost of this operation in both cases, if the stakes cost 3 francs a hundred and if the workman is paid 50 centimes an hour . . .*

Must one also say if the workman is happily married? Oh, what unwholesome imagination, what depraved brain incubates those revolting problems with which they torture us? I detest them! And the workmen who band together to complicate the amount of work of which they are capable, who divide themselves into two squads, one of which uses one-third more strength than the other, while the other, by way of compensation, works two hours longer! And the number of needles a seamstress uses in twenty-five years when she uses needles at 50 centimes a packet for eleven years, and needles at 75 centimes for the rest of the time but if the ones at 75 centimes are ... etc., etc. ... And the locomotives that diabolically complicate their speeds, their times of departure, and the state of health of their drivers! Odious suppositions, improbable hypotheses that have made me refractory to arithmetic for the rest of my life!

'Anaïs, come up to the blackboard.'

The lanky bean-pole stood and made a secret grimace, like a cat about to be sick, in my direction. Nobody likes 'coming up to the blackboard' under the black, watchful eye of Mademoiselle Sergent.

'*Work out* the problem.'

Anaïs 'worked it out' and explained it. I took advantage of this to study the Headmistress at my leisure: her eyes glittered, her red hair blazed ... If only I could have seen Aimée Lanthenay before class! The problem was finished at last, thank goodness. Anaïs breathed again and returned to her place.

'Claudine, come to the blackboard. Write down the fractions $^{3325}/_{5712}$, $^{806}/_{925}$, $^{14}/_{56}$, $^{302}/_{1052}$ (Lord preserve me from fractions divisible by 7 and 11, also from those divisible by 5, by 9 and by 4 and 6, and by 1.127) and find their highest common factor.'

That was what I had been dreading. I began dismally and I made some idiotic blunders because my mind wasn't on what I was doing. How swiftly they were reprimanded by a sharp movement of the hand or a frown, those small lapses I permitted myself! At last I got through it and returned to my place, followed by a 'No witticisms here please!' because I'd replied to her observation 'You're forgetting to wipe out the numbers' with:

'Numbers must always be wiped out – they deserve to be.'

After me, Marie Belhomme went up to the blackboard and

produced howler after howler with the utmost good faith. As usual, she was voluble and completely self-confident when wildly out of her depth; flushed and undecided when she remembered the previous lesson.

The door of the small classroom opened and Mademoiselle Lanthenay entered. I stared at her avidly. Oh, those poor golden eyes had been crying and their lids were swollen! Those dear eyes shot one scared look at me and were then hurriedly averted. I was left in utter consternation; heavens, whatever could *She* have been doing to her? I turned red with rage, so much so that Anaïs noticed and gave a low, sneering laugh. The sorrowful Aimée asked Mademoiselle Sergent for a book and the latter gave it to her with marked alacrity, her cheeks turning a deeper crimson as she did so. What could all that mean? When I thought that the English lesson did not take place till tomorrow, I was more tormented by anxiety than ever. But what was the good? There was absolutely nothing I could do. Mademoiselle Lanthenay returned to her own classroom.

*

'Girls!' announced the wicked Redhead. 'Get out your school-books and your exercise-books. We are going to be forced to take refuge for the time being in the Infants' School.'

Promptly all the girls began to bustle about with as much frenzied energy as if their stockings were on fire. People shoved each other and pinched each other, benches were pushed askew, books clattered to the floor and we scooped them up in heaps into our big aprons. That gawk Anaïs watched me pile up my load, carrying her own luggage in her arms; then she deftly tweaked the corner of my apron and the whole lot collapsed.

She preserved her expression of complete detachment and earnestly contemplated three builders who were throwing tiles at each other in the playground. I was scolded for my clumsiness and, two minutes later, that pest Anaïs tried the same experiment on Marie Belhomme. Marie screamed so loud that she got some pages of Ancient History to copy out. At last our chattering, trampling horde crossed the playground and went into the Infants' School. I wrinkled my nose: it was dirty. Hastily cleaned up for us, it still smelt of ill-kept children. Let's hope the 'time being' isn't going to last too long!

Anaïs put down her books and promptly verified the fact that the windows looked out on the Headmaster's garden. As for me, I'd no time to waste in contemplating the assistant-masters; I was too anxious about the troubles I foreboded.

We returned to the old classroom with as much noise as a herd of escaped bullocks and we transported the tables. They were so old and so heavy that we bumped and banged them about as much as possible in the hope that one of them at least would completely come to bits and collapse in worm-eaten fragments. Vain hope! They all arrived whole. This was not our fault.

We didn't do much work that morning, which was one good thing. At eleven, when we went home, I prowled about trying to catch a glimpse of Mademoiselle Lanthenay, but without success. Had *She* put her under lock and key then? I went off to lunch so seething with suppressed rage that even Papa noticed it and asked me if I had a temperature . . . Then I returned to school very early, at quarter past twelve, and hung about, bored, among the few children who were there; country girls who were lunching at school off hard-boiled eggs, bacon, bread-and-treacle, and fruit. And I waited vainly, torturing myself with anxiety!

Antonin Rabastens came in (at least this made a diversion) and bowed to me with all the grace of a dancing bear.

'A thousand pardons, Mademoiselle. By the way, haven't the lady *teacherrs* come down yet?'

'No, Sir, I'm waiting for them. I hope they won't be long for "absence is the greatest of all ills!"' I had already expatiated half a dozen times on this aphorism of La Fontaine's in French essays which had been highly commended.

I spoke with a sweet seriousness. The handsome Marseillais listened, with an uneasy look on his kindly face. (He'll begin to think I'm a bit crazy, too.) He changed the subject.

'Mademoiselle, I've been told that you read a great deal. Does your father possess a large library?'

'Yes, Sir, two thousand, three hundred and seven volumes precisely.'

'No doubt you know a great many interesting things. And I realized at once, the other day – when you sang so charmingly – that you had ideas far beyond your age.'

(Heavens, what an idiot! Why couldn't he take himself off? Ah! I was forgetting he was a little in love with me. I decided to be more amiable.)

'But you yourself, Sir, I've been told you have a beautiful baritone voice. We hear you singing in your room sometimes when the builders aren't making a din.'

He turned red as a poppy with pleasure and protested with enraptured modesty. He wriggled as he exclaimed:

'Oh, Mademoiselle! . . . As it happens, you'll soon be able to judge for yourself, for Mademoiselle Sergent has asked me to give singing-lessons to the older girls who are studying for their certificate. On Thursdays and Sundays. We're going to begin next week.'

What luck! If I had not been so preoccupied, it would have been thrilling to tell the news to the others who knew nothing about it as yet. How Anaïs would drench herself in eau-de-Cologne and bite her lips next Thursday! How she would pull in her leather belt and coo as she sang!

'What? But I know nothing whatever about it! Mademoiselle Sergent hasn't said a word to us.'

'Oh! Perhaps I shouldn't have mentioned it? Would you be good enough to pretend you don't know?'

He implored me with ingratiating movements of his torso and I shook my head to fling back my curls which weren't in the least in my way. This hint of a secret between us threw him into ecstasies. It was obviously going to serve as a pretext for glances full of understanding – exceedingly commonplace understanding on his part. He went off, carrying himself proudly, with a farewell that already had a new touch of familiarity.

'Good-bye, Mademoiselle Claudine.'

'Good-bye, Sir.'

At half past twelve, the rest of the class arrived and there was still no sign of Aimée. I refused to play, pretending that I had a headache, and, inwardly, I chafed.

Oh! Oh! Whatever did I see? The two of them had come down, Aimée and her redoubtable chief; they had come down and were crossing the playground. And the Redhead had taken Mademoiselle Lanthenay's arm – an unheard-of proceeding! Mademoiselle Sergent was talking very softly to her assistant who, still a little scared, was raising her eyes towards the other who was much taller than herself. Those eyes already looked reassured and pretty again. The spectacle of this idyll turned my anxiety to chagrin. Before they had quite reached the door, I rushed outside and hurled myself into the midst of a wild game of 'Wolf', yelling 'I'm playing!' as if I were yelling 'Fire!' And, until the bell rang for class, I galloped till I was out of breath, now chasing, now being chased, doing all I could to stop myself from thinking.

During the game, I caught sight of the head of Rabastens. He was watching over the wall and enjoying the sight of these big girls running about and showing – some, like Marie Belhomme, unconsciously and others, like the gawky Anaïs, very consciously indeed – calves that were pretty or ludicrous. The amiable Antonin honoured me with a gracious smile, an excessively gracious one. I did not think it necessary to return it, on account of my companions, but I arched my chest and tossed my curls. It was essential to keep this young man entertained. (In any case, he seems to me a born blunderer and destined to put his foot in it on every conceivable occasion.) Anaïs, who had noticed him too, took to kicking up her skirts as she ran so as to exhibit legs which, however, were far from attractive, also to laughing and uttering bird-like cries. She would have acted flirtatiously in the presence of a plough-ox!

We went indoors and opened our exercise-books, still panting from our exertions. But, after a quarter of an hour, Mademoiselle Sergent's mother appeared and announced to her daughter, in a barbaric dialect, that two new girls had arrived. The class bubbled over with excitement: two 'new ones' to tease! And Mademoiselle left the room, very politely asking Mademoiselle Lanthenay to look after the class. Aimée arrived and I sought her eyes so as to smile at her with all my anxious tenderness. But she gave me back a far from confident look and my heart swelled absurdly as I bent over my knitting . . . I've never dropped so many stitches! I dropped so many that I had to go and ask Mademoiselle Aimée for help. While she was trying to remedy my mistakes, I whispered to her: 'Good afternoon, my sweet darling little Mademoiselle . . . Heavens, whatever's the matter! I'm worn to shreds with not being able to speak to you.' She looked round her uneasily and answered, very low:

'I can't tell you anything now. Tomorrow, at our lesson.'

'I'll never be able to wait till tomorrow! Suppose I pretend Papa wants to use his library tomorrow and ask if you can give me my lesson this evening?'

'No . . . All right, yes, ask her. But go back to your place at once – the big ones are staring at us.'

I said 'Thank you' out loud to her and went and sat down again. She was right. That gawk Anaïs was watching us closely, trying to guess what had been going on these last two or three days.

Mademoiselle Sergent returned at last, accompanied by two insignificant young things whose arrival caused a little stir on the benches.

She installed these newcomers in their places. The minutes dragged slowly by.

When, at last, it struck four, I went straight off to find Mademoiselle Sergent and I asked her, in one breathless burst:

'Mademoiselle, it would be awfully kind of you if you'd let Mademoiselle Lanthenay give me my lesson tonight instead of tomorrow night, Papa's got someone coming to talk business in the library so we won't be able to stay there.'

Ouf! I had brought out my sentence without pausing for breath. Mademoiselle frowned, studied my face for a moment, then made up her mind:

'Very well. Go and tell Mademoiselle Lanthenay.'

I rushed off and did so. She put on her hat and coat and I bore her off, quivering with anxiety to know all.

'Ah, how glad I am to have you to myself for a little. Tell me quick, whatever's gone wrong?'

She hesitated, beating about the bush.

33

'Not here. Wait. It's difficult to tell you all about it in the street. We'll be at your home in a minute.'

In the meantime, I squeezed her arm in mine but her smile was not the charming one of all the other times. As soon as the door of the library shut behind us, I took her in my arms and kissed her. I felt as if she had been kept imprisoned far away from me for a month, that poor little Aimée with those shadows under her eyes and those pale cheeks! Had she suffered very much, then? Yet the looks she gave me struck me as embarrassed rather than anything else, and she seemed feverish rather than sad. Moreover, she returned my kisses very hurriedly – and I don't at all like being kissed in double quick time!

'Come on, tell me . . . tell me everything right from the beginning.'

'But it's not a very long story . . . In fact, nothing much happened at all. It was Mademoiselle Sergent . . . well, she wanted . . . I mean, she preferred . . . she thought these English lessons were preventing me from correcting the exercise-books and making me go to bed too late . . .'

'Look here, for goodness' sake, don't waste time. And tell me the truth. She doesn't want you to come any more?'

I was trembling with anguish; I gripped my hands between my knees to make them keep still. Aimée fidgeted with the cover of the Grammar and began to tear off a strip where it was gummed. As she did so, she raised her eyes towards me. They had grown scared again.

'Yes, that's it. But she didn't say it the way you said it, Claudine. Listen to me a moment . . .'

I did not listen to a word; I felt as if I were dissolving with misery. I was sitting on a little stool on the floor, and, clasping my arms round her slim waist, I beseeched her:

'Darling, don't go away . . . If you only knew, I'd be too utterly wretched! Oh, find some excuse, make up something, come back, don't leave me! It's sheer bliss for me, just being with you! Doesn't it give *you* any pleasure at all? Am I just like Anaïs or Marie Belhomme to you? Darling, do, *do* come back and go on giving me English lessons! I love you so much . . . I didn't tell you . . . but now you can't help seeing I do! . . .

34

Come back, I implore you. She can't beat you for it, that red-haired beast!'

I was burning with fever and my nerves were becoming more and more frayed at feeling that Aimée's were not vibrating in sympathy. She stroked my head as it lay on her lap and only interrupted now and then with a quavering 'my little Claudine!' At last her eyes brimmed over and she began to cry as she said:

'I'm going to tell you everything. It's too wretched – you make me too unhappy! Well, last Saturday, I couldn't help noticing *She* was being much nicer to me than usual. I thought she was getting used to me and would leave the two of us in peace so I was awfully happy and relaxed. And then, towards the end of the evening, when we were correcting exercise-books at the same table, I suddenly looked up and saw she was crying. And she was looking at me in such a peculiar way that I was absolutely dumfounded. Then, all at once, she got up from her chair and went off to bed. The next day, after being awfully nice to me all day, when I was alone with her in the evening and was just going to say good night, she suddenly asked me: "You're very fond of Claudine, aren't you? And, no doubt, she returns your fondness?" And, before I had time to answer, she fell into a chair beside me and sobbed. And then she took my hands and said all sorts of things that simply took my breath away . . .'

'What things?'

'Well . . . she said to me: "My dear little thing, don't you realize you're breaking my heart with your indifference? Oh, my darling girl, how could you possibly not have noticed my great affection for you? My little Aimée, I'm jealous of the tenderness you show to that brainless Claudine who's quite definitely a little unhinged . . . If you'd only just not hate me, oh! if you'd only love me a little, I'd be a more tender friend than you could ever imagine . . ." And she looked into the very depths of my soul with eyes like red-hot pokers.'

'Didn't you answer her at all?'

'Of course not! I hadn't time to! Another thing she said was: "Do you think they're very useful to her or very kind to me, those English lessons you give her? It tears my heart every

35

time I see the two of you go off together! Don't go there – don't ever go there again! Claudine won't give it another thought in a week's time and I can give you more affection than she's capable of feeling!" Claudine, I assure you, I no longer had any idea what I was doing. She was mesmerizing me with those crazy eyes of hers and, suddenly, the room began to go round, and my head swam; and for two or three seconds, not more, I couldn't see anything at all. I could only hear her saying over and over again, and sounding terrified, "My God! . . . My poor little girl! I've frightened her . . . she's so pale, my little Aimée, my darling!" And, immediately after that, she helped me to undress, in the most kind, affectionate way, and I slept as if I'd spent the entire day walking . . . Claudine, my poor pet, you realize there was simply nothing I could do about it!'

I was stunned. So she had passionate friendships, that volcanic Redhead! At heart, I was not tremendously surprised; it was bound to end that way. Meanwhile, I sat there, utterly overwhelmed; faced with Aimée, this frail little creature bewitched by that fury, I did not know what to say. She dried her eyes. It seemed to me that her distress was over with her tears.

'But you . . . don't love her at all?'

She answered, without looking at me:

'No, of course not. But, really, she does seem to be awfully fond of me and I never suspected it.'

Her answer froze me completely. After all, I'm not completely out of my mind yet and I understand what people are trying to say to me. I let go her hands which I was holding and I stood up. Something had been broken. Since she was unwilling to admit frankly that she was no longer with me against the other, since she was hiding her deepest thoughts, I thought all was over. My hands were ice-cold and my cheeks were burning. After a painful silence, I was the first to speak:

'Dear Aimée of the lovely eyes, I implore you to come just once more to finish up the month. Do you think she will agree?'

'Oh, yes! I'll ask her.'

She said it promptly and spontaneously, already sure of

getting anything she wanted out of Mademoiselle Sergent now. How fast she was receding from me and how fast the other had triumphed! Cowardly little Lanthenay! She loved comfort like a warmth-starved cat and knew very well that her chief's friendship would be more profitable to her than mine! But I did not mean to tell her so or she would not come back for the last lesson and I still cherished a vague hope . . . The hour was over and I escorted Aimée to the door. In the passage, I embraced her fiercely, with a touch of despair. Once I was alone, I was surprised not to find myself feeling quite as sad as I believed myself to be. I had expected a tremendous, absurd explosion but, no, what I felt was more like a chill that froze me . . .

At supper, I broke in upon Papa's musings.

'Papa, you know those English lessons of mine?'

'Yes, I know. You're quite right to take them . . .'

'Please listen. I'm not going to take any more.'

'Ah, they tire you, do they?'

'Yes, they get on my nerves.'

'Then you're quite right.'

And his thoughts flew back to his slugs – if they had ever left them.

The night was shot through with stupid dreams. Mademoiselle Sergent, as a fury, with snakes in her red hair, was trying to embrace Aimée Lanthenay who ran away, screaming. I tried to go to her rescue but Antonin Rabastens held me back. He was dressed all in pastel pink and he pulled me back by the arm, saying: 'Listen, do listen! Here's a lyrical ballad that I sing and I'm really enraptured with it.' Then he warbled in his baritone:

> *'Beloved friends, when I am dead,*
> *Plant a sad* pillow *on my grrave . . .'*

He sang it to the tune of: 'Ah, how my French blood thrills with pride, to see her soldiers marching by!' An absurd night and one that did not rest me in the least.

*

I arrived late for school and contemplated Mademoiselle Sergent, secretly surprised to think that this audacious Redhead had had such success. She darted malicious, almost mocking looks at me, but I was so tired and dispirited that I had no heart left to answer her back.

When class was over, I saw Mademoiselle Aimée lining up the little ones in file (it was as if I had dreamt the whole of yesterday evening). I said good morning to her in passing; she looked tired, too. Mademoiselle Sergent was not there. I stopped and said:

'Are you feeling all right this morning?'

'Yes, of course, thank you. You look very dark under the eyes, Claudine.'

'Maybe. Any fresh news? The scene didn't start up again? Is she still as amiable to you as ever?'

She blushed and looked embarrassed.

'Oh, yes. Nothing more's happened and she's being very nice. I . . . think you don't know her properly . . . she's not in the least like what you imagine . . .'

Slightly nauseated, I let her go stammering on. When she had got her sentence well and truly entangled, I interrupted her:

'Perhaps you're the one who's right. You'll come on Wednesday for the last time?'

'Oh, indeed I will. I've asked her. It's all fixed. Definitely.'

How quickly things change! Since that scene yesterday evening, we had already begun to speak differently to each other. Today I did not dare to show a trace of the vociferous misery I had let her see last night. At all costs, I must make her laugh a little.

'How are your love-affairs? Is the handsome Richelieu going on all right?'

'Who do you mean? Armand Duplessis? Oh, yes, he's doing splendidly. Sometimes he stays two hours in the shadows under my window. But yesterday night, I let him know that I'd noticed him, and he went striding away at a great rate, on those long legs of his – they're just like the legs of a compass. And when Monsieur Rabastens wanted to bring him along the day before yesterday, he refused to come.'

'You know, Armand is seriously keen on you. I know what

38

I'm talking about. I overheard a conversation between those two masters last Sunday. Quite by chance, by the roadside. And . . . I'll only tell you this much! . . . Armand has got it badly. Only try and tame him – he's a wild bird.'

She was all animation now and wanted all the details, but I ran off.

Let me try and think about the singing-lessons we are to have from the seductive Antonin Rabastens. They're to begin on Thursday. I shall put on my blue skirt, with the pleated blouse that shows off my figure, and my apron. Not the big black apron I wear on weekdays with the close-fitting bib (though it's quite becoming), but the pretty little pale blue embroidered one I wear at home on Sundays. And that's all. I'm not going to take too much trouble for his friendship or my dear, kind little schoolmates will notice.

Aimée, Aimée! It really is a pity that she's flown away so soon, that charming little bird who might have consoled me for all those geese! Now, I feel quite certain that last lesson will serve no purpose at all. With a small nature like hers, frail and egotistical, a nature that likes its pleasures but knows how to look after its interests, it is useless to struggle against Mademoiselle Sergent. I only hope that this great disappointment will not sadden me for long.

Today, at recreation, I played madly to shake myself up and to get warm. Anaïs and I, grasping Marie Belhomme firmly by her 'midwife's hands', made her run till she was breathless and panting for mercy. Afterwards, under penalty of being locked up in the lavatories, I forced her to recite Théramène's speech on the death of Hippolyte in a loud, intelligible voice.

She declaimed Racine's alexandrines in a martyred voice and then escaped, flinging up her arms. The sisters Jaubert struck me as impressed. Good! If they don't like the classics, they'll be presented with modern verse on the next occasion.

The next occasion was not long delayed. Hardly had we got back into the classroom than we were clamped down to exercises in round and cursive handwriting in view of the approaching exams. For most of us had appalling writing.

'Claudine, you will dictate the examples while I go and find places for the younger ones' class.'

She went off to the 'Second Class' who, dislodged in their turn, were about to be installed goodness knows where. This promised as a good half-hour to ourselves.

I began:

'Children, today I am going to dictate to you something highly entertaining.'

Chorus of 'Ah!'

'Yes, some gay songs taken from *Wandering Palaces*.'

'That sounds awfully nice, even from the title,' observed Marie Belhomme with conviction.

'You're absolutely right. Are you ready? I'll begin.

> '*On the identical slow curve*
> *Whose slowness is implacable*
> *Ecstatically there vacillates and sinks*
> *The complex present of slow curves*'

I paused. The lanky Anaïs didn't laugh because she didn't understand. (Neither did I.) And Marie Belhomme, with her usual good faith, exclaimed:

'But you know quite well we've already done geometry this morning! And besides all that sounded too difficult. I haven't written down half what you said.'

The twins rolled four defiant eyes. I went on, imperturbably:

> '*The selfsame autumn sees those curves homologous,*
> *Parallel to your grief on the long autumn evenings,*
> *Flattening the slow curve of things and your brief*
>   *birdlike hoppings.*'

They followed laboriously, without making any further efforts to understand. I felt a delicious satisfaction at hearing Marie Belhomme complain once more and stop me:

'Wait a bit, wait a bit . . . you're going much too fast . . . The slow curve of what?'

I repeated: '*The slow curve of things and your brief birdlike hoppings*. . . Now copy that out for me, first in round script, then in cursive . . .'

These supplementary writing-lessons, designed to satisfy the examiners at the end of July, were my joy. I dictated the most extravagant things and I had immense pleasure in hearing these daughters of grocers, cobblers and policemen meekly reciting and writing down parodies of the Romantic School or of Francis Jammes' murmuring lullabies. I collected al these for the benefit of my dear little companions from the reviews and magazines my father received. And he certainly received plenty! All the periodicals from the *Revue des deux mondes* to the *Mercure de France* accumulated in our house. Papa confided to me the duty of cutting their pages: I allocated to myself the duty of reading them. For someone had to read them! Papa merely gave them a superficial, absent-minded glance, since the *Mercure de France* deals very seldom indeed with malacology. As for myself, I found them highly instructive, if not always comprehensible, and I used to warn Papa when the subscriptions were running out, 'You must renew yours, Papa, or you'll lose the good opinion of the postman.'

That gawk Anaïs, who is lacking in knowledge of literature – it's not her fault – muttered sceptically:

'These things you dictate to us at writing-lessons, I'm sure you deliberately make them up.'

'What a thing to say! These are lines dedicated to our ally, the Tsar Nicholas, so there!'

She could not call my bluff but her eyes remained incredulous.

Re-enter Mademoiselle Sergent who took one look at what we had written.

'Claudine!' she expostulated. 'Aren't you ashamed of dictating such absurdities to them? You'd do better to learn some arithmetic theorems by heart, that would be more useful to everyone!'

But there was no conviction behind her scolding, for in her secret heart, she's rather amused by these hoaxes. All the same, I listened without a smile and my resentment returned at feeling her so near me, this woman who had forced the affections of that unreliable little Aimée . . . Heavens! It was

41

half past three and in half an hour she would be coming to my home for the last time.

Mademoiselle Sergent rose from her seat and said:

'Shut your exercise-books. The big ones who are taking their Certificate, stay behind, I have something to say to you.'

The others went off, deliberately dawdling over putting on their hoods and shawls. They were annoyed at not being able to stay and listen to the announcement, obviously bristling with interest, that was about to be made to us. The red-haired Headmistress addressed us and, in spite of myself, I had to admire, as always, her clear-cut voice and the decision and precision of her phrases.

'Girls, I imagine you have no illusions about your apparent inability to grasp even the rudiments of music. I make an exception of Claudine, who plays the piano and reads fluently at sight. I might well let her give you lessons, but you are too lacking in discipline to obey one of your classmates. As from tomorrow, you will come on Sundays and Thursdays at nine o'clock to practise tonic sol-fa and sight-reading under the direction of Monsieur Rabastens, the assistant-headmaster, as neither Mademoiselle Lanthenay nor myself is in a position to give you lessons. Monsieur Rabastens will be assisted by Mademoiselle Claudine. Try not to behave too disgracefully. And be here at nine o'clock tomorrow.'

I added a muttered: 'Dis-miss!' that was caught by her redoubtable ear. She frowned, only to smile afterwards, in spite of herself. Her little speech had been delivered in such a peremptory tone that it practically called for a military salute – and she had realized it. But, to tell the truth, it looked as if I could no longer annoy her. This was discouraging. She must be very sure indeed of her triumph to display such magnanimity!

She went away and everyone began excitedly talking at once. Marie Belhomme simply could not get over it.

'Really, I say, making us have lessons with a young man! It's a bit thick! Still, it'll be amusing all the same. Don't you think so, Claudine?'

'Yes. One's got to have *some* slight distraction.'

'Won't you be simply terrified, giving us singing-lessons with one of the masters?'

'It doesn't mean a thing to me. I don't care twopence either way.'

I didn't listen much. I was waiting, with inward trepidation, wondering why Mademoiselle Aimée Lanthenay did not come at once. Anaïs was in raptures. Her face wore a sneering grin; she was clutching her ribs, as if she were convulsed with laughter, and jostling Marie Belhomme who groaned without knowing how to defend herself. 'Ha, ha!' mocked Anaïs, 'you'll make a conquest of the handsome Antonin Rabastens. He won't be able to resist them long – those long, slim hands of yours, those midwife's hands! And your dainty waist and your eloquent eyes! Aha! my dear – this romantic story's going to end in a marriage!' She grew wildly excited and began to dance about in front of Marie whom she had harassed into a corner and who was hiding her unlucky hands and protesting at the unseemly remarks.

Still Aimée did come! My nerves were so much on edge that I could not keep still and went and prowled as far as the door of the staircase leading to the 'temporary' (still!) rooms of the mistress. Ah! I had been right to come and look! Up there on the landing, Mademoiselle Lanthenay was all ready to set off. Mademoiselle Sergent was holding her by the waist and talking to her very low, with an air of tender insistence. Then she gave Aimée, whose veil was pulled down, a long kiss. Aimée let herself be kissed and yielded graciously; she even stopped and turned back as she went down the stairs. I escaped without their having noticed me but, once again, I felt very unhappy. Wicked, wicked little thing to have broken away from me so quickly to bestow her caresses and her golden eyes on the woman who had been our common enemy! . . . I no longer knew what to think . . She joined me in the classroom where I had remained rooted to the spot in a brown study.

'Are you coming, Claudine?'

'Yes, Mademoiselle. I'm ready.'

Out in the street, I no longer dared to question her – what would she reply? I preferred to wait till we got home and merely to make conventional conversation on the way. I observed that it was cold, foretold that we should have more

43

snow and that the singing-lessons on Sundays and Thursdays would probably be amusing . . . But I spoke without conviction, and she too realized that all this chatter meant nothing at all.

When we were settled under the lamp in the library, I opened my exercise-books and I looked at her. She was prettier than she had been the other evening; a little paler, and there were shadows round her eyes that made them look larger.

'Are you tired? You look as if you were.'

She was embarrassed by all my questions. Whyever should she be? She turned quite pink again and looked everywhere but at me. I was certain she felt vaguely guilty about me. I went on remorselessly:

'Tell me, is she still being so frightfully friendly towards you, the loathsome Redhead? Have the rages and the kisses of the other night started up again?'

'No, of course not . . . She's being very kind to me . . . I assure you she takes tremendous care of me . . .'

'She hasn't "mesmerized" you again?'

'Oh no, there's no question of that . . . I think I exaggerated a little the other evening because my nerves were rather on edge.'

As she said it, her face became very confused. I didn't care – I wanted to know the truth. I went up close to her and took her hands – her tiny little hands.

'Oh darling, do tell me what else! Don't you want to say anything more to your poor Claudine who was so wretched the day before yesterday?'

But anyone would have said that she had managed to restrain herself and had suddenly decided to say nothing. By degrees she assumed a calm little expression, artificially natural, and looked at me with those clear, untruthful cat's eyes of hers.

'No. Look, Claudine, I assure you that she leaves me completely in peace and that she's even gone out of her way to be very kind. You and I made her out to be much nastier than she is, you know . . .'

What was that cold voice and those eyes that were

44

shuttered in spite of being open to their widest extent? It was her classroom voice and that I couldn't stand. I thrust back my desire to cry, so as not to make a fool of myself. So it was all over between us then? And if I tormented her with questions, shouldn't we part at loggerheads? . . . I took up my English Grammar; there was nothing else to do. She opened my exercise-book with marked alacrity.

That was the first – and the only – time I took a serious lesson with her. With a heart swelling and ready to burst, I translated whole pages of:

'*You have some pens but he had not a horse.*'

'*We should have your cousin's apples if he had plenty of pen-knives.*'

'*Have you any ink in your ink-pot? No, but I have a table in my bedroom, etc., etc.*'

Towards the end of the lesson, that extraordinary Aimée asked me point-blank:

'My little Claudine, you aren't angry with me?'

I was not altogether lying when I answered:

'No. I'm not *angry* with you.'

It was almost true. I did not feel angry, only unhappy and exhausted. I escorted her to the door and I kissed her, but she turned her head so much away as she held out her cheek that my lips almost touched her ear. The heartless little thing! I watched her go off under the lamp-post with a vague desire to run after her. But what would have been the good?

I slept pretty badly and my eyes proved it. There were shadows under them that reached to the middle of my cheeks. Luckily, that rather becomes me. I noticed this in the looking-glass as I was fiercely brushing my hair (quite golden this morning) before setting off for the singing-lesson.

I arrived half an hour too early and I couldn't help laughing when I found two out of my four classmates already installed in the school! We inspected each other closely and Anaïs gave an approving whistle at my blue dress and my charming apron. She had trotted out for the occasion the apron she wears on Thursdays and Sundays. It's red, embroidered in white and makes her look paler than ever. Her hair was done in a 'helmet' with the puff in front pushed well forward, almost overhanging her forehead, and she'd squeezed herself till she could hardly breathe into a new belt. Charitably, she observed out loud that I looked ill but I replied that it suited me to look tired. Marie Belhomme came running in, harum-scarum and scatter-brained as usual. She too had adorned herself, in spite of being in mourning. Her big frilly collar of ruched crêpe made her look like a bewildered black Pierrot. With her long, velvety eyes and her lost, innocent expression, she was quite charming. The two Jauberts arrived together, as always, ready to behave irreproachably and never to raise their eyes and to speak ill of all the rest of us after the lesson. We warmed ourselves, clustered round the stove, as we teased the handsome Antonin in advance. Attention! Here he was . . . . A noise of voices and laughter sounded nearer and nearer, then Mademoiselle Sergent opened the door, followed by the irresistible assistant-master.

Rabastens was a splendid sight! He wore a fur cap and a dark blue suit under his overcoat. He removed his cap and coat on entering, after a 'Young ladies!' accompanied by a low bow. He had decorated his green jacket with a rust-red chrysanthemum in the best of taste, and his grey-green tie, patterned with interlacing white circles, was highly impressive. He had obviously knotted it with studious care in front of the mirror. In a flash, we were all demurely lined up, our hands surreptitiously pulling down our blouses to smooth out the faintest trace of unalluring creases. Marie Belhomme was already enjoying herself so whole-heartedly that she gave a loud giggle and then stopped, frightened at her own audacity. Mademoiselle Sergent knitted her terrible eyebrows and was obviously annoyed. She had given me a look as she came in. I thought: 'I bet her little friend already tells her every single thing!' I kept obstinately assuring myself that Aimée was not worth so much misery but I was not in the least convinced by my own arguments.

'Young ladies,' said Rabastens in his guttural voice. 'Would one of you be good enough to lend me her book?'

The lanky Anaïs hurriedly offered her a copy of Marmontel's piano pieces so as to get herself noticed and was rewarded with an exaggeratedly affable 'Thank you'. That hulking fellow must practise his manners in front of that long mirror of his wardrobe. It is true that he doesn't possess a wardrobe with a long mirror.

'Mademoiselle Claudine,' he said to me with a fascinating ogle (fascinating for him, I mean), 'I am charmed and extremely honoured to become your colleague. For you give singing-lessons to these young ladies, do you not?'

'Yes, but they are not in the least obedient to one of their own classmates,' Mademoiselle Sergent cut in sharply. She was becoming impatient with all this chit-chat. 'With your assistance, Monsieur, she will obtain better results. Otherwise they will fail in their Certificate, for they do not seem to have grasped even the rudiments of music.'

Well done! *That* would teach the gentleman to spin out meaningless phrases! My companions listened with unconcealed astonishment; no one had ever displayed such gallantry towards them before. What reduced them to stupefaction were the compliments lavished on me by the fulsome Antonin.

Mademoiselle Sergent took the 'Marmontel' and indicated the gulf his new pupils refused to cross, some from inattentiveness, some from sheer inability to understand. The one exception was Anaïs, whose memory allowed her to learn all the sol-fa exercises by heart without having to beat time and without distorting them. How true it was that they 'had not grasped even the rudiments of music', those little duffers! And, as they made it a kind of point of honour not to obey me, they were certainly going to be marked 'zero' in the forthcoming exam. This prospect enraged Mademoiselle Sergent, who could not sing in tune and so could not act as a singing-teacher, any more than could Mademoiselle Lanthenay, who had never properly recovered from a long-ago attack of laryngitis.

'Make them sing one by one to begin with,' I said to the southerner (he was beaming and preening himself like a peacock at being in our midst). 'They all make mistakes in time, every single one of them, but not the same mistakes. And, up to now, I haven't been able to stop them.'

'Let's see, Mademoiselle . . .?'

'Marie Belhomme.'

47

'Mademoiselle Marie Belhomme, would you do this exercise for me in tonic sol-fa?'

It was a little polka in G, totally innocent of any nasty traps, but poor Marie, who couldn't be less musical, has never been able to sol-fa it correctly. Under this direct attack, she was seized with tremors; her face turned crimson and her eyes swam.

'I'll bet one silent bar, then you'll begin on the first beat: *Ray, te, te, lah, soh, fah, fah* . . . Not awfully difficult, is it?'

'Yes, Sir,' answered Marie who had quite lost her head from shyness.

'Good. I'll begin . . . One, two, one . . .'

'*Ray, te, te, lah, soh, fah, fah*,' twittered Marie in a voice like a hen with a sore throat.

She had not missed the opportunity of beginning on the second beat! I stopped her.

'No, do listen! One, two, *Ray, te, te* . . . have you got it? Monsieur Rabastens is beating one empty bar. Start again.'

'One, two, one . . .'

'*Ray, te, te* . . .' she began again fervently, making the same mistake! To think that, for three whole months, she's been singing that polka out of time! Rabastens intervened, patient and discreet.

'Allow me, Mademoiselle Belhomme. Would you please beat time along with me?'

He took her wrist and guided her hand.

'You'll understand better this way: one, two, one . . . But, come on! Sing!'

She did not begin at all, this time. Scarlet as a result of this unexpected gesture, she had completely lost countenance. I was immensely amused. But the handsome baritone, highly flattered at the poor little thing's distress (she was as fluttered as a linnet), made a point of insisting. That gawk Anaïs had her cheeks puffed out with suppressed laughter.

'Mademoiselle Anaïs, may I ask you to sing this exercise, to show Mademoiselle how it should be done?'

That one needed no pressing! She cooed her little piece 'with expression', lingering on the high notes and being none too correct in her time. Still, she knew it by heart and her rather absurd way of singing a sol-fa exercise as if it were a sentimental song pleased the southerner who congratulated her. She tried to blush, couldn't manage to, and was obliged to confine herself to lowering her eyes, biting her lips and drooping her head.

I said to Rabstens:

'Sir, would you make us go through some of the two-part exercises? I've done everything I could but they still don't even begin to know them.'

I was in a serious mood that morning: firstly, because I didn't feel much like laughing; secondly, because, if I played the fool too much during this first lesson, Mademoiselle Sergent would stop the others. Moreover, I was thinking of Aimée. Wasn't she going to come downstairs this morning? Only a week ago, she'd never have dared lie in bed so late!

With my mind on all this, I gave out the parts; the firsts to Anaïs, reinforced by Marie Belhomme; the seconds to the two new boarders. As for myself, I would come to the rescue of whichever turned out to be the weaker. Rabastens supported the seconds.

Then we executed the little duet, I standing by the handsome Antonin who trolled out 'Ah! Ahs!' full of expression in his baritone as he leant over in my direction. We must have made an extraordinarily funny group. That incorrigible southerner was so preoccupied in displaying his charms that he made mistake after mistake, without anyone noticing it, of course. The stylish chrysanthemum he wore in his buttonhole fell out and dropped on the floor. When he had sung his piece, he picked it up and threw it on the table, saying, as if he were appealing for personal compliments: 'Well, I think that didn't go too badly, do you?'

Mademoiselle Sergent dampened his enthusiasm by replying:

'Yes, but let them sing by themselves without you or Claudine. Then you'll see.'

(I could have sworn, from his discomfited looks, that he had forgotten what he was here for. He's going to be a first-class teacher, that Rabastens! So much the better! When the Headmistress doesn't come to the lessons, we'll be able to do exactly what we like with him.)

49

'Yes, I'm sure, Mademoiselle. But if these young ladies will take a little trouble, I'm sure they'll soon come to know enough to satisfy the examiners. The standard in music is very low indeed, as you must be the first to realize.'

Well, well, so he was getting his own back now, was he? He couldn't have found a better way of bringing home to the Redhead that she was incapable of singing a scale. She understood the spite behind the remark and averted her sombre eyes. Antonin went up a little in my esteem, but he had antagonized Mademoiselle Sergent who said sharply:

'I wonder if you would be good enough to make these children practise some more? I should rather like them to sing one by one so as to acquire a little self-possession and confidence.'

It was the turn of the twins who possessed non-existent, uncertain voices without much sense of rhythm, but those two plodders always get by, they work with such exemplary diligence! I can't stand those Jauberts, so virtuous and so modest. And I could just see them working at home, going over each exercise fifty times, before coming to the Thursday lessons, the irreproachable sneaks.

To end up with, Rabastens 'gave himself the pleasure', as he said, of hearing me sing. He asked me to read the most boring things at sight, ghastly sentimental songs and airs adorned with gargling runs and trills whose out-of-date *coloratura* seemed to him the last word in art. From vanity, because Mademoiselle Sergent was there, and Anaïs too, I sang my best. And the unspeakable Antonin went into ecstasies; he got himself completely tied up in tortuous compliments, in labyrinthine sentences from which I deliberately did not try to extricate him. I was enjoying myself too much listening to him with my eyes riveted on his with earnest attention. I don't know how he would have got to the end of a sentence crammed full of parentheses if Mademoiselle Sergent had not come up to us and asked:

'Have you given these girls some pieces to study for homework during the week?'

'No,' he had given them nothing at all. He could not get it

50

into his head that he had not been summoned here to sing duets with me!

But whatever had become of little Aimée? I simply had to know. So I deftly overturned an inkpot, taking care to get plenty of ink on my fingers. Then I let out an 'Oh!' of desolation, spreading out all my fingers like spiders. Madame Sergent took the time to remark that this was typical of me and sent me off to wash my hands under the pump.

Once outside, I wiped my fingers with the blackboard sponge to take off the worst of it, then I searched about, peering into every corner. Nothing in the house. I went outside again and walked as far as the little wall that separated us from the Headmaster's garden. Still nothing. But no! There were people talking on the other side. Who? I leant over the wall to look down into the garden which is a yard or two lower than our playground and there, under the leafless hazels, in the pallid sunshine, so faint you could hardly feel it, I saw the sombre Richelieu talking to Mademoiselle Aimée Lanthenay. Two or three days ago I'd have stood on my head and waved my feet in astonishment at this spectacle, but my recent betrayal had slightly inured me to shocks.

That shy, unsociable Duplessis! At the moment, he had found his tongue and no longer kept his eyes lowered. He had burnt his boats then?

'Tell me, Mademoiselle, didn't you suspect? Oh, do say you did!'

Aimée, her face quite pink, was quivering with joy. Her eyes were more golden than ever and they kept alertly watching and listening all about her as she spoke. She gave a charming laugh to indicate that she hadn't suspected anything at all, the liar!

'Come, you must have suspected when I used to spend my evenings under your windows. But I love you with all my might . . . not just to flirt for a term and then go off on my holidays and forget you. Will you listen to me seriously, as I am speaking to you now?'

'Is it as serious as all that?'

'Yes, I assure you it is. Will you authorize me to come and talk to you tonight in the presence of Mademoiselle?'

Oh bother! I heard the door of the classroom opening: they were coming to see what had become of me. In two bounds I was far from the wall and almost beside the pump. I flung myself on my knees on the ground and when the Headmistress, accompanied by Rabastens, came up to me, she found me energetically rubbing the ink on my hands with sand, 'because water won't take it off'.

This was a great success.

'Leave off doing that,' said Mademoiselle Sergent, 'you can take it off at home with pumice-stone.'

The handsome Antonin addressed a 'Good-bye' to me that was both gay and melancholy. I had stood up and I gave him my most undulating toss of the head which makes my curls ripple softly all down my cheeks. Behind his back, I laughed: the great hobbledehoy, he thought he had completed my conquest! I returned to the classroom to fetch my hood and I walked home brooding over the conversation I had overhead behind the little wall.

What a pity I hadn't been able to hear the end of their amorous dialogue! Aimée would have consented, without being pressed, to accept the attentions of this inflammable but honest Richelieu and he was capable of asking her to marry him. What is it that makes people so infatuated with this little woman who, strictly speaking, isn't even pretty? She's fresh, it's true, and she has magnificent eyes; but, after all, there are plenty of beautiful eyes in really pretty faces, yet all the men stare at her! The builders stop mixing mortar when she passes by, winking at each other and clicking their tongues. (Yesterday, I heard one of them say to his mate as he pointed her out: 'Strewth, I wouldn't half like to be a flea in her bed!') The boys in the streets put on swank for her and the old gentlemen who frequent the Café de la Perle and take their Vermouths there every evening discuss with interest 'that little girl who teaches at the school, who makes your mouth water like a fruit tart that isn't sugared enough'. Builders, retired businessmen, headmistress, schoolmaster, why do they all fall for her? As for myself, I'm not quite so interested in her since I've discovered what a traitress she is. And I feel quite empty; empty of my tenderness; empty of my fierce misery of that first evening.

They've been pulling it down fast and now they've nearly pulled it down altogether, poor old school! When they were demolishing the ground floor, we watched, with great curiosity, the discovery of some double walls. We had always thought those walls thick and solid; now they turned out to be as hollow as cupboards with a kind of black passage between them where there was nothing but dust and an appalling, ancient, repulsive stench. I took much pleasure in frightening Marie Belhomme by telling her that these hiding-places had been built in the old days for the walling-up of women who were unfaithful to their husbands and that I'd seen white bones lying among the rubble. She looked at me with wide, scared eyes and asked: 'Is it really true?' Then she hurried to the walls to 'see the bones'. The next minute, she was back at my side.

'I didn't see a thing. It's just another of your fibs you're telling me!'

'May I lose the use of my tongue this instant if those hiding-places in the walls weren't hollowed out for a criminal end! And, besides, you're a nice one to tell me I'm fibbing, considering you've got a chrysanthemum hidden in your Marmontel – the one Monsieur Antonin Rabastens was wearing in his buttonhole!'

I shouted this at the top of my voice because I had just caught sight of Mademoiselle Sergent coming into the playground, with Dutertre in her wake. Oh! we *see* him often enough, to do him justice! And what noble devotion to duty that doctor must have to be incessantly leaving his clinic to come and ascertain whether the state of our school is satisfactory! That school is dispersing, bit by bit at the moment; the first class to the Infants' School, the second over there to the Town Hall. No doubt he fears that our education may be suffering from these successive displacements, the worthy District Superintendent!

They had heard, the two of them, what I had just said – naturally, I'd done it on purpose! – and Dutertre seized the opportunity to come over to us. Marie wanted to sink into the ground. She moaned and hid her face in her hands. But he was decent enough to be all smiles as he approached. He slapped the silly noodle on the shoulder and she trembled with alarm:

'Little one, what's that devilish Claudine saying to you? Do you preserve the flowers our handsome assistant wears? Mademoiselle Sergent, your pupils' hearts are thoroughly awakened, you know! Marie, do you want me to tell your mother so as to make her realize that her daughter's no longer a child?'

Poor Marie Belhomme! Quite incapable of answering one word, she stared at Dutertre, she stared at me, she stared at the Headmistress, with eyes like a startled fawn and was on the verge of tears . . . Mademoiselle Sergent, who was not entirely delighted at the opportunity the District Inspector had found of gossiping with us, watched him with jealous and admiring eyes. She did not dare carry him off. (I knew him well enough to guess he might easily refuse to go.) As for me, I was rejoicing in Marie's confusion, in Mademoiselle Sergent's impatient displeasure (so her little Aimée wasn't enough for her any more, then?) and also at the sight of our good doctor's obvious pleasure at staying beside us. Apparently my eyes must have expressed my mingled feelings of rage and satisfaction for he laughed, showing his pointed teeth.

'Claudine, what's making your eyes sparkle like that? Is it devilment?'

I answered 'Yes' with my head, merely tossing my hair without speaking, an irreverence that drew Mademoiselle Sergent's bushy eyebrows together in a frown . . . I didn't care. She couldn't have everything, that nasty Redhead; her District Superintendent and her little assistant. No, definitely not . . . More offhandedly than ever, Dutertre came close to me and slipped his arm round my shoulders. The lanky Anaïs watched us with curiosity, screwing up her eyes.

'Are you feeling well?'

'Yes, Doctor, thank you very much.'

'Be serious.' (As if *he* were being serious!) 'Why have you always got those dark shadows under your eyes?'

'Because the good Lord made them like that.'

'You oughtn't to read so much. I bet you read in bed?'

'A little, not much. Mustn't one?'

'We-ell . . . All right, you can read. What *do* you read? Come on, tell me.'

He was getting excited and he gripped my shoulders with a brusque gesture. But I'm not so stupid as I was the other day and I didn't blush – at least, not yet. The Headmistress had decided to go and scold the little ones who were playing with the pump and drenching themselves. How she must be boiling inwardly! My heart danced at the thought!

'Yesterday, I finished *Aphrodite*. Tonight I shall begin *La Femme et le pantin*.'

'Indeed? You *are* going the pace! Pierre Loüys? The deuce! Not surprising that you . . . I should very much like to know how much you understand of all that. Everything?'

(I don't think I'm a coward, but I shouldn't have liked to continue this conversation alone with him in a wood or on a sofa; his eyes glittered so! Besides, he obviously imagined I was about to confide smutty secrets to him . . .)

'No, I don't understand it all, unfortunately. But quite a lot of things, all the same. Then I've also read, last week, *Susanne* by Léon Daudet. And I'm just finishing *L'Année de Clarisse*. It's one of Paul Adam's and I simply adore it!'

'Yes, yes. And do you get to sleep afterwards? . . . But you'll tire yourself, if you go on like that. Take a little care of yourself, it would be a pity to wear yourself out, you know.'

What was he really thinking? He looked at me from so close to, with such a visible desire to caress me – to kiss me – that, suddenly, a shameful burning flush covered my face like rouge and I lost my self-assurance. Perhaps *he* was frightened too – of losing his self-possession – for he let me go, breathing hard. He left me after giving my hair a stroke right down from my head to the tip of my longest curls, as if he were stroking the back of a cat. Mademoiselle Sergent came up to us again, her hands shaking with jealousy, and the two of them went off together. I saw them talking very fast to each other: she seemed to be anxiously imploring him while he lightly shrugged his shoulders and laughed.

They ran into Mademoiselle Aimée and Dutertre stopped, lured by her seductive eyes, and joked with her familiarly. She looked flushed, and a little embarrassed, but pleased. This time Mademoiselle Sergent displayed no jealousy; on the contrary . . . Whereas my heart always jumps a trifle when that little creature appears. Ah! How badly that's all turned out!

I buried myself so deep in my thoughts that I didn't notice that gawk Anaïs executing a war-dance round me.

'Will you leave me in peace, you filthy monster! I don't feel like playing today.'

'Oh yes, I know! You've got the District Superintendent on your mind . . . My goodness me, you don't know which one to listen to these days – Rabastens, Dutertre, who else? Have you made your choice? And what about Mademoiselle Lanthenay?'

She whirled round me, her eyes diabolical in a face that was motionless but secretly furious. For the sake of getting some peace, I flung myself on her and pounded her arms with my fists: she yelled at once, like a coward, and made her escape. I pursued her and hemmed her in in the corner by the pump where I poured some water on her head, not much, just the dregs of the communal drinking-cup. She lost her temper completely.

'You know, that's idiotic. That's not the thing to do. I happen to have a cold. You're making me cough!'

'Cough away! Doctor Dutertre will give you a free consultation . . . and throw in a little something extra!'

The arrival of the lovelorn Duplessis interrupted our quarrel. He was transfigured, since two days ago, that Armand! His radiant eyes proclaimed that Aimée had granted him her hand, along with her heart and her faith, all tied up in one parcel! But when he observed his sweet fiancée joking and laughing over there between Dutertre and the Headmistress, with the Superintendent teasing her and Mademoiselle Sergent encouraging her, his eyes clouded. Aha! So I wasn't the only one who was jealous! I really believe he would have turned round and gone away if the Redhead herself hadn't called out to him. He ran up to them with great strides and bowed low to Dutertre who shook his hand familiarly, as if congratulating him. The pale Armand blushed, became radiant once more and looked at his little fiancée with tender pride. Poor Richelieu, I feel distressed about him! I don't know why, but I've an idea that this Aimée, who half-pretends to be unconscious and who commits herself so hastily, will bring him no happiness. Anaïs was so busy watching the group, determined not to miss a single gesture, that she forgot all about abusing me.

'I say,' she whispered to me very low, 'what are they doing all together like that? Whatever's up?'

I blurted out:

'What's up is that Monsieur Armand – the compass – Richelieu – has gone and asked for Mademoiselle Lanthenay's hand and she's bestowed it on him and they're engaged! And, at this particular moment, Dutertre is congratulating them. *That's* what's up!'

'Ah . . . Is that really true? You mean, he's asked for her hand, *to get married*?'

I couldn't help laughing; she had let the word out so naturally, with a guilelessness that was quite unlike her! But I did not let her vegetate in her innocent surprise.

'Run – run and fetch something – it doesn't matter what – from the classroom and listen to what they say. If I go, they'll be suspicious at once!'

She dashed off. As she passed the group, she adroitly lost her wooden sabot (we all wore sabots in the winter) and kept her ears stretched as she put it on again, taking as long as possible. Then she vanished and reappeared, ostentatiously carrying her mittens which she slipped on her hands as she returned to me.

'What did you overhear?'

'Monsieur Dutertre was saying to Armand Duplessis: "I am not going to wish you good luck, Monsieur. That would be superfluous when you're marrying such a girl as this." And Mademoiselle Aimée Lanthenay lowered her eyes – like this. But, honestly, I'd never have believed it was all fixed up – as definite as all that!'

I was astonished too, but for a different reason! Aimée was going to get married and this no longer produced any effect on Mademoiselle Sergent? There must certainly be something behind all this that I knew nothing about! Why should she have gone to such lengths to conquer Aimée, why make those tearful scenes, only to hand her over now, with no further regrets, to this Armand Duplessis whom she hardly knew? The devil take them both! Now, once again, I'd got to wear myself to a frazzle to discover what was at the bottom of all this. After all, it may well be that she's only jealous of women.

To clear my mind, I organized a big game of 'he' with my classmates and the 'country bumpkins' of the second division who were becoming sufficiently grown-up to be allowed to play with us. I drew two lines about three yards apart, stationed myself in the middle as 'he' and the game began, punctuated by shrill cries and by a certain number of falls for which I was responsible.

The bell rang and we went in for the deadly boring needlework lesson. I took up my tapestry with disgust. After ten minutes, Mademoiselle Sergent left us, on the pretext of having to give out some material to the 'little class' which, homeless once again, was temporarily (of course!) installed in an empty room near us in the Infants' School. I was quite ready to bet that, in point of fact, the Redhead was going to spend more time on her little Aimée than on handing out supplies.

After I'd done about twenty stitches in my tapestry, I was seized with a sudden access of stupidity which prevented me from knowing whether I should change the shade to fill in an oak-leaf or whether I should keep the same wool with which I had just finished a willow leaf. So I went out, work in hand, to ask advice from the omniscient Headmistress. I crossed the corridor and went into the little classroom. The fifty small girls shut up in there were squealing, pulling each other's hair, laughing, dancing about and drawing funny men on the blackboard. And not a sign of Mademoiselle Sergent, not a sign of Mademoiselle Lanthenay! This was becoming very queer! I went out again and pushed open the door of the staircase: no one on the stairs! Suppose I went up? Yes, but whatever could I say if I were found there? Pooh! I would say that I was coming to look for Mademoiselle Sergent because I'd heard her old peasant of a mother calling her.

Ssh! I went upstairs in my gym shoes, very quietly, leaving my sabots below. Nothing at the top of the stairs. But the door of one room stood slightly ajar and, promptly, my one thought was to look through the opening. Mademoiselle Sergent, sitting in her big armchair, luckily had her back to me. She was holding her assistant on her lap, like a baby. Aimée was sighing softly and fervently kissing the Redhead who was clasping her tight. Well done! No one could say this Headmistress bullied her subordinates! I could not see their faces because the back of the chair was too high, but I didn't need to see them. My heart pounded in my ears and, suddenly, I dashed down the staircase in my silent rubber shoes.

Three seconds later, I was back in my place next to the lanky Anaïs who was busy reading the *Supplément* and looking at the picture with much delectation. So that she shouldn't notice I was upset, I asked to look too, as if I were really interested! There was a seductive story by Catulle Mendès which I should have enjoyed, but my mind was not much on what I was reading; it was still far too full of what I had spied on up there! I had got more than I asked for and I certainly had not believed their caresses were as ardent as that . . .

Anaïs showed me a drawing by Gil Baëer of a slim young man, without a moustache, who looked like a woman in disguise. Carried away by reading the *Carnet de Lyonette* and some amorous pieces by Armand Sylvestre, she said, with troubled eyes: 'I've got a cousin who looks like that. His name's Raoul. He's at college and I go and see him in the holidays every summer.' This revelation explained her relatively virtuous behaviour recently; she hardly ever wrote to boys nowadays. The sisters Jaubert were putting up a great show of being scandalized on account of this naughty magazine while Marie Belhomme overturned her ink-pot to come and have a look. When she had looked at the pictures and read a little, she fled, flinging up her long hands and crying: 'It's disgusting! I don't want to read the rest before recreation!' She had hardly sat down again and begun to mop up her spilt ink than Mademoiselle Sergent returned, grave but with rapt, sparkling eyes. I stared at that Redhead as if I were not sure she was the same person I had seen kissing upstairs.

'Marie, you will write me a composition on the subject of clumsiness and bring it to me at five o'clock this afternoon. Girls, tomorrow a new assistant-mistress, Mademoiselle Griset, will be arriving. You won't have anything to do with her; she will only be taking the lower class.'

I was on the point of asking: 'And Mademoiselle Aimée – is she leaving then?' But the answer came of its own accord.

'Mademoiselle Lanthenay is wasting her intelligence in the second class. Henceforward, she will give you history lessons, also drawing and needlework, in here, under my supervision.'

I looked at her and smiled, nodding my head as if to congratulate her on this decidedly satisfactory arrangement. This roused her temper at once and she said, frowning: 'Claudine, how much have you done to your tapestry? All that? You certainly haven't exhausted yourself!'

I put on my most idiotic expression as I replied:

'But, Mademoiselle, I went to the second class just now to ask if I was to use Number 2 green for the oak-leaf and there wasn't anyone there. I called up the staircase to you but there wasn't anyone there either.'

I spoke slowly and loudly, so that all the noses bent over the knitting and the sewing were raised inquisitively. Everyone was listening avidly; the bigger girls were wondering what the Headmistress could be doing so far away, abandoning the pupils to their own devices. Mademoiselle Sergent turned a darker crimson still and answered hastily: 'I had gone to see where it would be possible to put the new assistant. The school building is nearly finished – they're drying it out with big fires – and no doubt we shall soon be able to move into it.'

I made a gesture of protest and apology which meant:

'Oh! It's not for me to know where you were . . . you could only be where your duty called you.' But I felt a savage satisfaction at the thought that I could have replied: 'No, zealous teacher, you couldn't care less about the new assistant. It's the other one, Mademoiselle Lanthenay, who takes up all your thoughts, and you were up in your room with her, kissing her full on the mouth.'

While I was hatching rebellious thoughts, the Redhead regained her self-control. Exceedingly calm now, she addressed the class in a precise voice . . .

'Take your exercise-books. The ones marked: *French Composition*. Explain and comment on the following thought: "Time does not respect what has been done without him." You have one hour and a half.'

Oh, anguish and despair! What ineptitudes have got to be trotted out again now? I don't care a button whether time respects what is done without inviting him or not! Always subjects like that, or worse! Yes, worse – because it's almost New Year's Eve and we shan't escape the usual little set-piece about New Year gifts: venerable custom of giving and receiving (*mem*: i before e except after c) same; joy of children, tender emotion of parents; sweets, toys, etc.; – not forgetting the touching note on the little poor children who don't get any presents and whom we must help on this day so that they have their share of joy! Horror, horror!

While I inwardly raged, the others were already scribbling their 'roughs'. That gawk Anaïs was waiting for me to begin so that she could model her opening on mine and Marie Belhomme had already filled a page with ineptitudes – sentences that contradicted one another and reflections quite beside the point. After yawning for quarter of an hour, I made up my mind and wrote straight into my 'Fair-Copy' book without doing a rough, much to the indignation of the others.

At four o'clock, as we came out of school, I realized, without regret, that it was my turn to sweep up with Anaïs. Naturally this chore revolts me but today I didn't care. Actually, I would rather do it than not. As I was going off to fetch the watering-can, I ran at last into Mademoiselle Aimée. Her cheeks were flushed and her eyes shining.

'Good afternoon, Mademoiselle. When's the wedding?'

'What! But . . . these children always know everything! But it's not decided yet . . . at least, the date isn't. It'll be in the long vacation, probably . . . Tell me, you don't think he's ugly, Monsieur Duplessis?'

'Ugly – Richelieu ugly? No, of course not. He's much better than the other one, ever so much better! Do you love him?'

'But, naturally I do, since I'm taking him for my husband!'

'As if that were a reason! Don't give me silly answers like that – do you think you're talking to Marie Belhomme? You don't love him in the least – you think he's nice and you want to get married to see what it's like. And out of vanity, too, to annoy your friends at the Training College who'll stay old maids. That's all there is to it! Don't play too many tricks on him, that's the best I can wish him, because he certainly deserves to be loved better than you'll ever love him.'

It came out slap! And I promptly turned on my heels and ran off to fetch water to sprinkle the floor. She stayed there rooted to the spot, abashed. At last she went off to supervise the sweeping of the junior classroom or to tell her dear Mademoiselle Sergent what I had just said. Let her go! I didn't want to bother any more about those two crazy women, one of whom wasn't crazy at all. I was so excited that I sprinkled recklessly; I even sprinkled Anaïs's feet and the geography maps, then I swept till my arms ached. It was a relief to tire myself out like that.

Singing-lesson. Enter Antonin Rabastens wearing a sky-blue tie. 'Hail, fair sun!' as the Provençal girls used to say to Roumestan. Goodness, Mademoiselle Aimée Lanthenay was there too, followed by a little creature even smaller than herself, who moved with unusual suppleness and seemed to be about thirteen. She had a rather flat face, green eyes, a fresh complexion and silky, dark hair. This little girl suddenly stopped in the doorway, overcome with shyness. Mademoiselle Aimée turned towards her, laughing: 'Now then, come along, don't be frightened: Luce, do you hear?'

So it was her sister! I had completely forgotten this detail. She had talked to me about this sister, who would probably be coming to school, in the days when we were friends . . . It struck me as so funny, her bringing along this little sister, that I pinched Anaïs, who clucked, and I tickled Marie Belhomme, who miaowed, and I executed a silent two-step behind Mademoiselle Sergent's back. Rabastens found these pranks charming and little sister Luce stared at me with her slit-like eyes. Mademoiselle Aimée began to laugh (she laughs at everything these days, she's so happy!) and said to me:

'Now *please* Claudine, don't frighten her out of her wits as a start. She's shy enough by nature as it is.'

'Mademoiselle, I will protect her like my own personal virtue. How old is she?'

'She was fifteen last month.'

'Fifteen? Well, after that, I'll never trust anyone again! I thought she was a good thirteen.'

The little thing, who had turned quite red, looked down at her feet – they were pretty, too. She nestled against her sister and clutched her arm for reassurance. Aha! I'd give her courage!

'Come along, little girl, come over here to me. Don't be afraid. This gentleman, who displays such intoxicating ties in our honour, is our good singing-master. You'll only see him on Thursdays and Sundays, unfortunately. Those big girls there are some of your classmates – you'll soon get to know them. As for me, I'm the model pupil, the rarest of all birds. I never get scolded ('strue, isn't it, Mademoiselle?) and I'm always good, like I am today. I'll be a second mother to you!'

Mademoiselle Sergent was amused though she tried not to show it; Rabastens was admiring, and the eyes of the new girl expressed doubts of my sanity. But I let her alone; I'd had all the fun I wanted with that Luce. She stayed close to her sister who called her 'little silly' and I had lost interest in her. I asked right out, making no bones about it:

'Where are you going to put this child to sleep, as nothing's finished yet?'

'With me,' replied Aimée.

I pinched my lips, I looked the Headmistress straight in the face and I said, very distinctly:

'Frightful bore for you, that!'

Rabastens laughed behind his hand (did he know some-thing?) and emitted the opinion that perhaps we might begin to sing. Yes, we might; and we actually did sing. The little new girl dissociated herself completely and remained obstinately mute.

'You don't know this music well, Mademoiselle Lanthenay

Junior?' inquired the exquisite Antonin, smiling like a commercial traveller.

'I know it a little, Sir,' answered little Luce in a faint, lilting voice that must have been pleasant to hear when it was not strangled with terror.

'Very well, then?'

Very well, then, nothing. Why couldn't he leave the child in peace, that dandy of the Canebière?

At that very moment, Rabastens whispered to me: 'Anyway, if these young ladies are tired, I think the singing-lessons are a waste of time!'

I glanced all round me, startled at his audacity in speaking to me under his breath. But he was right; my companions were occupied with the new girl, coaxing her and speaking gently to her and she was answering happily, quite reassured by finding herself kindly received. As to that cat Lanthenay and her beloved tyrant, huddled together in the embrasure of the window that looked on to the garden, they had completely forgotten us. Mademoiselle Sergent had put her arm round Aimée's waist; they were talking very low – or not talking at all, which came to the same thing. Antonin, whose gaze had followed mine, could not stop himself from laughing.

'They get on tremendously well together!'

'They certainly do. It's touching, this friendship, isn't it, Sir?'

The big simpleton did not know how to hide his feelings and blurted out, very low:

'Touching? I'd call it embarrassing for the others! Sunday night, I went to take back the music books and those ladies were here in the classroom, with no light on. I came in – after all it's a public place, this classroom – and, in the dusk, I caught sight of Mademoiselle Sergent and Mademoiselle Aimée, close together kissing like hot cakes. Do you imagine they moved aparrt? Not a bit of it! Mademoiselle Sergent just turned round and lannguidly asked: "Who's there?" Well, I'm hardly what you'd call shy, but all the same, I just stood there, looking at them like a dumb ox.'

(Let him talk as much as he liked, our candid assistant-master; I had nothing to learn from *him*! But I was forgetting the most important thing.)

'What about your colleague, Sir? I imagine he's awfully happy now he's engaged to Mademoiselle Lanthenay?'

'Yes, poorr boy. But, to my mind, it's nothing to be so happy about.'

'Oh? Why ever not?'

'Hmm. The Headmistress does anything she likes with Mademoiselle Aimée – not very pleasant for a future husband. I'd be annoyed if my wife were dominated like that by someone other than myself.'

I privately agreed with him. But the others had finished interviewing the newcomer and it was prudent for us to stop talking. Back to singing then, but no . . . it was no good. Who should dare to enter at that moment but Armand, disturbing the tender whispering of the two women? He stood enraptured beside Aimée who flirted with him, fluttering her eyelids with their curling lashes, while Mademoiselle Sergent watched them with the tender eyes of a mother-in-law who has married off her daughter. My classmates resumed their conversations and carried them on till the clock struck the hour. Rabastens was right. What queerr, sorry, what queer singing-lessons!

This morning, on coming to school, I saw a pale young girl standing in the entrance. She had dull hair, grey eyes and a skin with no bloom on it, and she was hugging a woollen shawl over her shoulders with the heart-rending air of a thin, cold, frightened cat. Anaïs pointed her out to me with a thrust of her chin, making a grimace of displeasure. I shook my head pityingly and said to her, very low: '*There's* someone who's going to be unhappy here, you can see that at a glance. The two others get on too well together not to make her life a misery.'

Little by little, the other pupils arrived. Before going inside, I observed that the two school buildings were being finished at a prodigious pace; apparently Dutertre had promised a large bonus to the contractor if everything was ready on the date he had fixed. He must do a good deal of underhand jobbery, that creature!

Drawing lesson, under the direction of Mademoiselle Aimée Lanthenay. 'Reproduction in line of any everyday object.' This time it was a cut-glass decanter, placed on Mademoiselle's desk, that we had to draw. These drawing lessons were invariably gay, since they furnished a thousand pretexts for getting up: one discovered 'impossibilities'; one made blots of Indian ink wherever they were least desirable. Promptly, the usual storm of complaints broke out. I opened the attack:

'Mademoiselle Aimée, I *can't* draw the decanter from where I am – the stove-pipe hides it!'

Mademoiselle Aimée, deeply occupied in tickling the red hair on the nape of the Headmistress's neck (the latter was writing a letter), turned towards me.

'Bend your head forward. You can see it then, I think.'

'Mademoiselle,' took up Anaïs, 'I *can't* see the model *at all*, because Claudine's head gets in the way!'

'Oh, how irritating you are! Turn your table round a little, then you can both see.'

It was Marie Belhomme's turn now. She moaned:

'Mademoiselle, I haven't any more charcoal. And the sheet of paper you've given me has got a tear in the middle and so I *can't* draw the decanter.'

'Oh!' grated Mademoiselle Sergent, exasperated. 'Have you finished bothering us, all of you? Here's a sheet of paper, here's some charcoal and now, don't let me hear one more word from any of you or I'll make you draw an entire dinner-service!'

There was a terrified silence. You could have heard a fly breathe . . . for five whole minutes. At the sixth minute, a faint buzzing began again; someone dropped a sabot; Marie Belhomme coughed; I got up to go and measure the height and breadth of the decanter with outstretched arm. The lanky Anaïs did the same, as soon as I had finished, and took advantage of the fact that one had to shut one eye to crumple her face into frightful grimaces that made Marie laugh. I finished sketching the decanter in charcoal and I got up to go and fetch the Indian ink from the cupboard behind the desk where the two mistresses sat. They had forgotten us; they were talking to each other in low voices and laughing. Now and then Mademoiselle Aimée drew back with a shocked little grimace which became her very prettily. In fact, they were now so little inhibited by our presence that it wasn't worth restraining ourselves either. Very well, now was our chance!

I shout out an inviting 'Psst!' that brought all the heads up, and, indicating the loving Sergent–Lanthenay couple to the class, I stretched out my hands in benediction over their two heads, from behind. Marie Belhomme burst out laughing with delight, the Jauberts lowered reproving noses, and, without having been seen by the interested parties, I buried myself once more in the cupboard, took out the Indian ink and brought it back to my place.

In passing, I looked at Anaïs's drawing. Her decanter resembled herself; it was too tall and had too long and thin a neck. I wanted to warn her of this but she didn't hear me; she was too absorbed in preparing some 'goonygoonya' in her lap to send to the new arrival in a pencil-box, the great pest! (Goonygoonya is charcoal pounded into Indian ink so as to make an almost dry mortar that stains unwary fingers deeply, likewise frocks and exercise-books.) That poor little Luce was going to blacken her hands and dirty her drawing, when she opened the box, and would get scolded. To avenge her, I snatched Anaïs's drawing and drew, in ink, a belt, with a buckle, encircling the waist of the decanter. Underneath, I wrote: *Portrait of the Lanky Anaïs*. She raised her head at the very moment I finished writing and pushed her box of goonygoonya over to Luce with a gracious smile. The little thing turned red and thanked her. Anaïs bent once more over her drawing and let out a resounding 'Oh!' of indignation which recalled our cooing teachers to reality.

'What's all this? Anaïs, you've gone mad, I presume?'

'Mademoiselle, look what Claudine's done to my drawing!'

Swelling with rage, she took it up to the desk and laid it down. Mademoiselle Sergent cast a stern eye over it, then, suddenly, burst out laughing. Rage and despair on the part of Anaïs who would have wept with spleen if tears didn't come so hard to her. Resuming her gravity, the Headmistress declared: 'This kind of joke isn't going to help you to get satisfactory marks in your exam, Claudine. But you've made quite an accurate criticism of Anaïs's drawing for it was indeed too tall and too narrow.' The great weedy thing returned to her place, frustrated and embittered. I told her:

'That'll teach you to send goonygoonya to that child who hasn't done a thing to you!'

'Oho! So you want the little one to make up for your lack of success with her elder sister – that's why you defend her with so much ardour!'

Wham!

That was a tremendous slap which resounded on her cheek. I'd aimed it with all my might, adding a 'Mind your own business' for good measure. The class, completely out of hand, buzzed like a beehive; Mademoiselle Sergent descended from her desk for so serious an affair. It was so long since I had hit one of my companions that people were beginning to believe I had become rational. (In the old days, I had the annoying habit of settling my quarrels on my own, with kicks and blows, without thinking it necessary to tell tales like the others.) My last battle dated back more than a year.

Anaïs was crying over the table.

'Mademoiselle Claudine,' said the Headmistress severely, 'I insist on your controlling yourself. If you are going to start hitting your companions again, I see myself being forced to refuse to admit you any longer to the school.'

But her words fell flat: my blood was up. I smiled at her so insolently that she promptly lost her temper.

'Claudine, lower your eyes!'

I did not lower a thing.

'Claudine, leave the room!'

'With pleasure, Mademoiselle!'

I left the room but, outside, I realized that I was bareheaded. I went back at once to collect my hat. The class was dismayed and silent. I noticed that Aimée had gone up close to Mademoiselle Sergent and was talking to her in a rapid, very low voice. I had not reached the doorway before the Headmistress called me back:

'Claudine, come here. Go and sit down in your place. I do not want to expel you, since you'll be leaving the class after the Certificate ... And, after all, you are not a mediocre pupil, though you are often a bad pupil, and I have no wish to deprive myself of you except as a last resort. Put your hat back in its place.' What that must have cost her! She was still so shaken that her heartbeats made the pages of the exercise-book she was holding flutter. I said: 'Thank you, Mademoiselle,' very modestly. Then, seated once more in my place beside the tall Anaïs, who was silent and a little frightened by the scene she had provoked, I thought with astonishment about the possible reasons which could have decided this vindictive Redhead to recall me. Had she been afraid of the effect it might produce in the principal town of the district? Had she thought I should chatter at the top of my voice, that I should tell everything I knew (at least), all the irregularity in this school, the pawing of the big girls by the District Superintendent and his prolonged visits to our teachers? What about the way those two ladies frequently abandoned their classes in order to exchange endearments behind closed doors? What about Mademoiselle Sergent's decidedly broad taste in reading (*Journal amusant*, unsavoury Zolas and worse still) and the handsome, gallant assistant-master with the sentimental baritone who flirted with the girls who were taking their Certificate? Wasn't there a whole heap of suspicious things the parents did not know about because the big ones who found the School amusing never told them and the little ones hadn't got their eyes open? Had she dreaded a semi-scandal which would gravely endanger her reputation and the future of the handsome School which was being built at considerable expense? I believe so. And moreover, now that my temper had cooled, like her own, I preferred to remain in this hole where I had more fun than anywhere else. Feeling quite good again, I looked at Anaïs's mottled cheek and whispered to her gaily:

'Well, old thing? That keeping you warm?'

She had been so terrified of my expulsion, since I could have accused her of being the cause of it, that she bore me no resentment.

'I should just think it is keeping me warm! You've got a jolly heavy hand, you know! You must be crazy to fly into a rage like that.'

'Come on, let's forget it. I think I must have had a rather violent nervous twitch in my right arm.'

Somehow or other, she managed to rub out the 'belt' of her decanter and I finished off mine. Mademoiselle Aimée corrected our drawings with feverish, shaky fingers.

This morning I found the playground empty – or very nearly. On the staircase of the Infants' School, a great deal of talking was going on; voices were calling to each other and shrieking: 'Do be careful!' – 'Gosh, it's heavy!' I rushed up.

'What's everyone doing?'

'You can see for yourself,' said Anaïs. 'We're helping their ladyships to move out of here and go into the new building.'

'Quick, give me something to carry!'

'There's plenty of stuff up there – go and find some.'

I went upstairs into the Headmistress's room, the room where I had spied at the door. I was inside it at last! Her old peasant mother, her starched cap all askew, entrusted me and Marie Belhomme with carrying down a big hamper containing all her daughter's toilet things. She does herself well, the Redhead! Her dressing-table was furnished with every conceivable object: large and small cut-glass bottles, nail-buffers, scent-sprays, tweezers and powder-puffs. There was also a huge washbasin and jug. All those weren't at all the typical toilet accessories of country schoolmistresses. To be sure of this, one had only to look at Mademoiselle Aimée's toilet things, as well as those belonging to that pale, silent Griset, which we transported afterwards – a basin, a water-jug of very modest dimensions, a little round mirror, a toothbrush, some soap, and that was all. Nevertheless, that little Aimée was very smartly dressed, especially these last few weeks, all bedizened and scented. How did she manage it? Five minutes later, I noticed that the bottom of her water-jug was dusty. Good; *that* problem was solved.

The new building, which contained three classrooms and a dormitory on the first floor, together with the assistant-mistresses' little rooms, was still too chilly for my taste, and smelt disagreeably of plaster. Between the two, they were erecting the main municipal building which would comprise the Town Hall on the ground floor and various private apartments on the first and would link up the two wings already completed.

As I was coming downstairs again, I had the marvellous idea of climbing the scaffolding, as the builders were still at lunch. In a moment I had skimmed up a ladder and was wandering about among the 'scaffolds' and thoroughly enjoying myself. Bother! There were the workmen coming back! I hid behind a piece of masonry, waiting for a chance to climb down again, but they were already on the ladder. Well, those two wouldn't give me away, even if they did see me. I knew both of them well by sight.

They lit their pipes and began to chat.

'You can bet your boots, I wouldn't lose any sleep over *that* one.'

'Which one d'you mean?'

'That there new teacher what came yesterday.'

'Coo, she don't half look miserable – not a bit like them other two.'

'Don't you talk to me about them other two, they fair make me sick. I'm fed up with them, anyone'd think they was husband and wife. Every blooming day, I see them from here and every blooming day it's the same thing. They starts kissing like anything, then they shuts the window and you can't see nothing more. Don't you so much as mention 'em again! Oh, I grant you the little one's a nice juicy piece, but I'm through, I tell you. And that other master who's going to marry her! That chap must have his eyes stuck together with mud to do such a bloody silly thing!'

I was enjoying myself hugely, but, as the bell was ringing for school, I only had just time to climb down on the inside (there were ladders all over the place), and I arrived, white with plaster and mortar. I was lucky to get off with a sharp: 'Where have you sprung from? If you get yourself so dirty, you won't be allowed to help with moving the furniture again.' I was jubilant at having heard the builders talk about those two women with so much good sense.

Reading out loud. *Selected passages.* Both! To distract myself, I unfolded on my lap a copy of the *Echo de Paris*, brought in case of boring lessons: I was enjoying Lucien Muhlfeld's thrilling *Mauvais Désir*, when Mademoiselle Sergent called upon me: 'Claudine, read on from there.' I hadn't the faintest idea where we had got to, but I hurriedly stood up, determined to 'do something desperate' rather than let my paper be pinched. At the very moment I was thinking of upsetting an ink-pot, tearing a page out of my book or shouting 'Long live Anarchy!', someone knocked at the door ... Mademoiselle Lanthenay rose, opened the door and stood aside, and Dutertre appeared.

Had that doctor buried all his patients then, that he had so much spare time? Mademoiselle Sergent ran to meet him; he shook hands with her, glancing meanwhile at little Aimée, who had turned bright pink and was laughing in an embarrassed way. But why? She wasn't as shy as all that! All those people were beginning to wear me out by forcing me to be incessantly trying to find out what they were thinking or doing ...

Dutertre had obviously seen me, since I was standing up, but he contented himself with smiling at me from a distance and remained close to those two females. All three of them were chatting together in an undertone: I sat down demurely and watched. Suddenly, Mademoiselle Sergent – who had not left off lovingly contemplating the handsome District Superintendent – raised her voice and said: 'You can go and see for yourself now, Monsieur; I'll go on with the children's lesson and Mademoiselle Lanthenay will show you the way. You'll easily identify the crack I was telling you about. It runs from top to bottom of the new wall, on the left of the bed. It's decidedly worrying in a new house and I can't sleep with an easy mind.' Mademoiselle Aimée did not answer and made a slight gesture of objecting. Then she changed her mind and disappeared, ahead of Dutertre who held out his hand to the Headmistress and shook hers vigorously, as if to thank her.

I certainly did not regret not having been expelled, but, however used I was to their astonishing behaviour and their peculiar morals, this dumbfounded me. I asked myself what she hoped to gain by sending this chaser of skirts and this young girl off together to her room to examine a crack which, I was ready to swear, was non-existent.

'There's a *cracked* story for you!' I whispered this observation into the ear of the gawky Anaïs. She gripped her knees together and chewed india-rubber frantically to show her delight in these dubious happenings. Fired by her example, I pulled a packet of cigarette-papers out of my pocket (I *only* eat the kind called *Nil*) and chewed enthusiastically.

'I say, old thing,' said Anaïs, 'I've discovered something gorgeous to eat.'

'What? Old newspapers?'

'No – the lead in these pencils that are red one end and blue the other – you know the kind. The blue end is slightly better. I've already pinched five from the stationery cupboard. It's delicious!'

'Give me a bit to try . . . No, not up to much. I'll stick to my *Nil*.'

'Idiot, you don't know what's good!'

While we were talking in whispers, Mademoiselle Sergent was making little Luce read aloud. But she was too preoccupied to listen to her. I had an idea! What excuse could I invent to get that child put beside me in class? I would try and make her tell me all she knew about her sister Aimée. She would probably talk all right . . . all the more as she followed me, whenever I went through the classroom, with startled, curious eyes that had a hint of a smile in them. They were green eyes – a strange green that turned brown in shadow – and edged with long, black lashes.

What a long time they were staying over there! Wasn't she going to come and hear our geography, that shameless creature?

'I say, Anaïs, it's two o'clock.'

'Well, what of it? Nothing to moan about! Wouldn't be half bad if we got off having to be heard the lesson. Done your map of France, old thing?'

'So, so . . . Haven't finished the canals. I say, it wouldn't do for the Regional Inspector to turn up today. He'd find everything in a fine old mess. You look . . . Mademoiselle Sergent

73

isn't paying any attention to us . . . she's got her nose glued to the window!'

Anaïs was suddenly convulsed with laughter.

'What can they be doing? I can see Monsieur Dutertre from here, measuring the width of the crack.'

'Do you think it's wide, the crack?' asked Marie Belhomme innocently. She was shading in her mountain chains by rolling an unevenly sharpened drawing-pencil over her map.

Such guilelessness made me give a spurt of laughter. Had it been too loud? No, Anaïs reassured me.

'Go on, you needn't worry. Mademoiselle's so absorbed, we could dance in the classroom without getting ourselves punished.'

'Dance? Want to have a bet with me that I will?' I said, getting up quietly.

'Oh! I bet you two glass alleys that you won't dance without catching a verb to write out!'

Delicately, I removed my sabots and placed myself in the middle of the classroom between the two rows of tables. Everyone raised their heads: obviously the promised feat had excited lively interest. Now for it! I threw back my hair which was getting in my way, I picked up my skirt between two fingers and I began a 'red-hot polka' which roused no less general admiration for being silent. Marie Belhomme was exultant and could not restrain a yelp of delight, deuce take her! Mademoiselle Sergent started and turned round, but I had already hurled myself back on my bench like lightning and I heard the Headmistress inform the little idiot, in a distant, bored voice:

'Marie Belhomme, you will copy me out the verb *to laugh* in medium round hand. It is really very tiresome that big girls of fifteen cannot behave themselves properly unless one has one's eye on them.'

Poor Marie had a good mind to cry. Still, one shouldn't be as silly as that! And I promptly claimed the two marbles from Anaïs who handed them over with somewhat ill grace.

What could those two crack-observers be up to? Mademoiselle Sergent was still looking out of the window. It struck half past two; they could not be much longer now. At least she must be made aware that we had noticed the unwonted absence of her little favourite. I coughed, but without success. I coughed again and asked in a virtuous voice, the voice of the Jauberts:

'Mademoiselle, we have some maps for Mademoiselle to look over. Is there a geography lesson today?'

The Redhead turned round sharply and shot a glance at the clock. Then she frowned with annoyance and impatience.

'Mademoiselle Aimée will be back in a moment. You know quite well that I sent her over to the new school. You can go over your lesson while you are waiting – you can never know it thoroughly enough.'

Good! It was quite possible we shouldn't have to recite our homework today. There was much joy and a buzz of activity as soon as we knew we had nothing to do. Then the comedy of 'going over the lesson' began. At each table, a girl took up her book while her neighbour closed hers and was supposed to repeat the lesson or to answer the questions her companion asked her. Out of twelve girls, the Jaubert twins were the only ones who really went over their work. The rest asked each other fantastic questions, preserving earnest, diligent expressions and serious lips that seemed to be reciting under their breath. The gawky Anaïs had opened her atlas and was interrogating me:

'What is a lock?'

I answered, as if I were repeating something by heart:

'Tst! Don't go and bore me with your old canals: look at Mademoiselle's expression, it's more amusing."

'What do you think of the conduct of Mademoiselle Aimée Lanthenay?'

'I think she's frequenting shady haunts with the District Superintendent, overseer of cracks.'

'What is known as a "crack"?'

'A fissure, sometimes called in French a *lézarde* or a female lizard. This lizard should normally be found in a wall but it is sometimes met with elsewhere, even in places completely sheltered from the sun.'

'What is known as a "fiancée"?'

'A hypocritical little slut who plays tricks on an assistant-master who's in love with her.'

'What would you do in the place of the said assistant-master?'

'I'd give the District Superintendent a good hard kick on the backside and I'd give the little pet who takes him off to observe cracks a couple of smart slaps.'

'What would be the result of that?'

'The arrival of another assistant-master and another assistant-mistress.'

The lanky Anaïs hoisted up her atlas from time to time to giggle behind it. But I had had enough. I wanted to go outside, to try and see *them* coming back. The only thing was to employ vulgar means.

'Mmmselle? . . .'

No reply.

'Mmmselle, beg pard'n, c'n I leave the room?'

'Yes, go, and don't be long.'

She said it carelessly and listlessly: obviously her whole mind was over there in the room where the new wall might be cracked. I went out hurriedly, ran over to the lavatories (they were 'temporary' too!) and stayed close to a door, pierced with a lozenge-shaped hole, ready to take refuge in the loathsome little kiosk if anyone came. At the very moment I was about to return despairingly to the classroom – for, alas, the customary time had elapsed – I saw Dutertre emerging (all alone) from the new school, putting on his gloves with a satisfied air. He was not coming back here but going straight off to the town. Aimée was not with him, but I didn't care; I had seen enough already. I turned to go back to the classroom but suddenly drew back, frightened. Twenty paces away – behind a new wall six foot high which sheltered the boys' little 'convenience' (exactly like ours and equally temporary) – there had appeared the head of Armand. Poor Duplessis, pale and ravaged, was staring in the direction of our new school. I saw him for five seconds, then he disappeared, running at full speed along the path that led to the woods. I was not laughing any more. What was going to be the end of all this? I went indoors, quickly, without further lingering.

The class was still seething. Marie Belhomme had drawn a set of squares on the table and was gravely playing a pleasant game of noughts and crosses with the newly-arrived little Lanthenay – poor little Luce! – who must find this a fantastic school. And Mademoiselle Sergent was still looking out of the window.

Anaïs, who was in process of colouring the portraits of the most hideous men in the *History of France* with crayons, welcomed me with a 'Come on, what did you see?'

'No more joking, old thing! Armand Duplessis was spying on them over the wall by the lavatories. Dutertre has gone back to the town and Richelieu's dashed off, running like a madman!'

'Go on! I bet you're telling lies!'

'I assure you I'm not. This is no time for lying. I saw it, on my honour, I did! My heart's in a positive flutter!'

The hope of the drama that might ensue kept us silent for a moment. Anaïs asked:

'Are you going to tell the others?'

'Good heavens, no. Those dunderheads would spread it all over the place. Only Marie Belhomme. I say, Marie!'

I told all to Marie whose eyes grew rounder than ever and who prophesied: 'It'll all end badly!'

The door opened and we all turned our heads in a single movement. It was Mademoiselle Aimée, a little out of breath and her colour high. Mademoiselle Sergent ran up to her and checked, only just in time, the hug she was on the point of giving her. The Headmistress had come to life again; she drew the little slut over to the window and questioned her avidly. (And what about our geography lesson?)

The prodigal child showed no excessive emotion as she gave brief answers which did not appear to satisfy the curiosity of her worthy superior. To a more anxious question she replied 'No,' shaking her head with a mischievous sigh. At that, the Redhead heaved a sigh of relief. We three, at the front table, looked on, rigid with attention. I felt some alarm for that immoral little thing. I would definitely have warned her to be aware of Armand but the other, her tyrant, would promptly have alleged that I had gone and denounced her

77

behaviour to Richelieu, by means of anonymous letters, perhaps. So I refrained.

They were beginning to irritate me with their whisperings! So I decided to make an end of them. I emitted a low 'hush!' to attract my classmates' attention and we began to buzz. At first the buzz was no more than a continuous bee-like hum; then it rose and swelled until it forced an entrance into the ears of our infatuated teachers, who exchanged an uneasy glance. But Mademoiselle Sergent boldly took the offensive:

'Silence! If I hear any buzzing, I shall keep the class in until six o'clock! Do you suppose we can give you regular lessons as long as the new school remains unfinished? You are old enough to know that you ought to work on your own when one of us is prevented from acting as your teacher. Give me an atlas. Any girl who does not know her lesson without one mistake will do one extra homework for a week!'

Whatever you may say, she's got character, that ugly, passionate, jealous woman; everyone was silent the moment she raised her voice. The lesson was recited at top speed and no one felt any inclination to be frivolous for we could feel a threatening breeze blowing, laden with impots and detentions. While this was going on, I thought that nothing would console me if I were not present at the meeting of Armand and Aimée; I would rather have got myself expelled (much as that would have cost me) than not see what would happen.

At five minutes past four, when the daily 'Shut your books and get into line' sounded in our ears, I went off, sorely against my will. Well, the exciting, unhoped-for tragedy wasn't billed for today! I would arrive early at school tomorrow so as to miss nothing of what might happen.

The next morning, having arrived long before the official time, I had time to kill. So I began a desultory conversation with the shy, melancholy Mademoiselle Griset who was as pale and nervous as ever.

'Do you like it here, Mademoiselle?'

She looked all round her before answering:

'Oh, not very much. I don't know anyone. I feel a little dull.'

'But isn't your colleague nice to you . . . and Mademoiselle Sergent too?'

'I . . . I don't know. No, really, I don't know if they're nice; they never pay any attention to me.'

'How extraordinary!'

'Yes . . . at meals they talk to me a little, but once the exercise-books are corrected they go off and I'm left all alone with Mademoiselle Sergent's mother who clears the table and then shuts herself up in the kitchen.'

'And where do they go off to, the two of *them*?'

'Why, to their room.'

Did she mean to their *room* or their *rooms*? Poor little wretch! She certainly earned her seventy-five francs a month!

'Would you like me to lend you some books, Mademoiselle, if you're bored in the evenings?'

(What joy! Her faced turned almost pink with it!)

'Oh, I should love that . . . Oh, how very kind of you . . . you don't think it would annoy the Headmistress?'

'Mademoiselle Sergent? If you think she'd even know, you've still got illusions about the interest that Redhead takes in you!'

She smiled, almost confidently, and asked me if I would lend her *Roman d'un jeune homme pauvre* which she was just longing to read! Certainly, she should have it tomorrow, her romantic novelette. I felt sorry for her, poor abandoned creature! I might easily have raised her to the rank of ally, but how could one rely on this pathetic, anaemic, far too timid girl?

The favourite's sister, little Luce Lanthenay, came up with noiseless steps, at once pleased and scared to be talking to me.

'Good morning, little monkey: say "Good morning, Your Highness" to me. Say it at once. Did you sleep well?'

I stroked her hair roughly. This did not seem to displease her and she smiled at me with her green eyes that were exactly like those of Fanchette, my beautiful cat.

'Yes, Your Highness, I slept well.'

'Where do you sleep?'

'Up there.'

'With your sister Aimée, of course?'

79

'No, she has a bed in Mademoiselle Sergent's room.'

'A bed? Have you seen it?'

'No . . . I mean, yes . . . it's a divan. Apparently it can be opened up into a bed. She told me so.'

'She told you so? Fathead! Dim donkey! Nameless object! Scum of the human race!'

She was terror-stricken for I had punctuated my abuse with lashes with a book-strap (oh, not very hard lashes!) and, when she vanished up the stairs, I shouted this crowning insult after her: 'Twirp of a female! You deserve to be like your sister!'

A divan that opened up! It would be easier for me to open up this wall! Upon my word, kids like that don't notice anything! Yet she looks vicious enough, that child, with those eyes that slant up at the corners . . .

The gawky Anaïs arrived while I was still painting and asked what was the matter with me.

'Nothing at all. I've merely beaten little Luce to teach her a thing or two.'

'Is there any news?'

'None at all. No one's come down yet. D'you want to play marbles?'

'What game? Haven't got nine alleys to play "Square".'

'But I've got the two I won off you. Come on, we'll have a chase.'

We had a very lively chase: the marbles received knocks hard enough to splinter them. While I was taking a long aim for a difficult shot, Anaïs exclaimed 'Ssh! Look there!'

It was Rabastens who was coming into the playground. Moreover the handsomest of Antonins was already got up to kill and radiant – far too radiant. His face lit up at the sight of me and he came straight up to us.

'Young ladies! . . . How the excitement of the game makes you glow with lovely colour, Mademoiselle Claudine!'

The lout could hardly be more absurd! But, all the same, just to annoy Anaïs, I looked at him complacently and thrust out my chest and fluttered my eyelashes.

'What brings you over to us so early, Sir? Those ladies, our mistresses, are still up in their rooms.'

'The fact is, I don't quite know what I *have* come to say,

except that Mademoiselle Aimée's fiancé didn't dine with us last night. Some people declare that they met him, looking ill; anyhow he still hasn't returned. I think he's in a bad way and I should like to warn Mademoiselle Lanthenay of the disturrbing state of her fiancé's health.'

'The disturbing state of her fiancé's health . . .' He expresses himself well, that Marseillais! He ought to set himself as 'announcer of deaths and serious accidents'. So the crisis was approaching! But though yesterday I myself had been thinking of putting Aimée on her guard, now I no longer wanted him to go and warn her. So much the worse for her! I felt malicious and greedy for excitement this morning and I deliberately set out to keep Antonin at my side. Nothing could be simpler: it was enough to open my eyes innocently wide and to droop my head so that my hair fell loose all about my face. He swallowed the bait at once.

'Sir, do please tell me if it's true that you write charming verses? I've heard people in the town say so.'

It was a lie, of course. But I'd have invented anything to stop him from going upstairs to the schoolmistresses. He blushed and stammered, overcome with delight and surprise:

'Who could have told you? . . . But no . . . no . . . I certainly don't deserve . . . It's extraordinary, I didn't think I'd ever mentioned it to a soul!'

'You see how fame has betrayed your modesty! (I should begin to talk like him in a minute.) Would it be indiscreet to ask you . . .'

'I entreat you, Mademoiselle . . . you see me utterly confused . . . All I could offer you to read would be some humble poems, amorous . . . but chaste! (He spluttered.) I should never, naturally have dared to allow myself . . .'

'Sir, isn't the bell ringing for the boys to come in to class over on your side?'

If only he'd go away, if *only* he'd go away! In a moment Aimée would come down, he would warn her, she would be on her guard and we shouldn't see a thing!

'Yes . . . but it isn't time yet. It's those fiendish urchins hanging on to the chain . . . you can't leave them a second!

And my colleague still hasn't come. Ah, it's harrd work being all on one's own to keep an eye on everything!'

No one can say he isn't frank! This method of 'keeping an eye on everything' which consists in coming and saying sweet nothings to the big girls can't exhaust him unduly.

'You see, Mademoiselle, I shall have to go and be severe. But Mademoiselle Lanthenay . . .'

'Oh, you can always tell her at eleven o'clock, if her fiancé's still absent . . . which would surprise me! Perhaps he'll be coming back any minute now?'

Oh, for goodness' sake go and be severe, you great blundering oaf! You've bowed enough and smiled enough; be off with you, vanish! At long last, he did.

The lanky Anaïs, rather vexed at the master's lack of attention to her, disclosed to me that he was in love with me. I shrugged my shoulders. 'Come on, let's finish our game. It's more fun than talking insane nonsense.'

The game ended while the others were arriving and the teachers were coming down at the last moment. Those two never let each other out of sight! That little horror of an Aimée was lavishing girlish wiles on the Redhead.

We went into class and Mademoiselle Sergent left us in the hands of her favourite who asked us the results of the problems set the day before.

'Anaïs, to the blackboard. Read out the terms of the problem.'

It was a fairly complicated problem but the lanky Anaïs, who is gifted for arithmetic, moved with remarkable ease among mail-coaches, watch-hands, and proportional shares. Then – horror! – it was my turn.

'Claudine, to the blackboard. Extract the square root of two million, seventy-three thousand, six hundred and twenty.'

I professed an intolerable loathing for those little things you have to extract. And, as Mademoiselle Sergent wasn't there, I suddenly decided to play a trick on my ex-friend; she had only herself to blame, the fickle wretch! I hoisted the standard of rebellion. Standing in front of the blackboard, I shook my head and said gently: 'No.'

'What do you mean, no?'

'No, I don't want to extract roots today. It doesn't appeal to me.'

'Claudine, have you gone mad?'

'I don't know, Mademoiselle. But I feel that I shall fall ill if I extract this root or any other like it.'

'Do you want a punishment, Claudine?'

'I want anything in the world, except roots. It isn't because I'm disobedient, it's because I can't extract roots. I'm awfully sorry, I assure you.'

The class jumped for joy; Mademoiselle Aimée lost patience and raged.

'Once and for all, will you obey me? I shall report you to Mademoiselle Sergent and then we shall see.'

'I repeat, I'm simply in despair.'

Internally, I shrieked at her: 'Nasty little bitch, I'm not going to show *you* any consideration. On the contrary, I'll do everything I can to annoy you.'

She descended the two stairs from the desk and advanced on me, in the vague hope of intimidating me. With great difficulty, I stopped myself from laughing and preserved my expression of respectful regret . . . That tiny little thing! Upon my word, she only came up to my chin! The class was enjoying itself hugely; Anaïs was eating a pencil, both the wood and the lead, in great mouthfuls.

'Mademoiselle Claudine, are you going to obey, yes or no?'

With exaggerated mildness, I began again; she was quite close to me, so I lowered my voice a trifle:

'Once again, Mademoiselle, make me do anything you like . . . give me fractions to reduce to the same denomination, similar triangles to construct . . . *cracks to verify* . . . anything, anything, at all. But not that, oh *not* square roots.'

The rest of the class, with the exception of Anaïs, had not taken it in, for I had slipped in my impertinence quickly, without stressing it. The other girls were merely amused by my resistance but Mademoiselle Lanthenay had received a shock. Turning scarlet, she lost her head and said shrilly:

'That's . . . that's too much! I shall go and call Mademoiselle Sergent . . . Oh, it's really too much!'

She made a bee-line for the door. I ran after her and caught her up in the corridor while the class laughed uproariously, shrieked with joy and climbed up on the benches and stood on them. I held Aimée back by her arm while she tried with all her feeble strength to throw my hands off. She did not say a word; she did not look at me and she kept her teeth clenched.

'Now will you listen to me when I speak to you! We've got beyond the stage of making small-talk, you and I. I swear to you that if you report me to Mademoiselle Sergent, I shall go straight and tell your fiancé the story of the crack. *Now* do you still mean to go up to the Headmistress's room?'

She had stopped dead, still without saying a word; her eyes were obstinately lowered and her mouth compressed.

'Come on, say something! Are you coming back to the classroom with me? If you don't come back at once, I shan't go back either; I shall go and warn your Richelieu. Hurry up and choose.'

At last, she opened her lips and whispered, without looking at me: 'I won't say anything. Let me go, I won't say anything.'

'You really mean it? You realize that if you tell the Redhead about it, she won't be able to keep it to herself for five minutes and I shall soon know. You really mean it? It's a . . . promise?'

'I won't say anything, let me go. I'll come straight back to the classroom.'

I let go her arm and we went back without a word. The noise of the hive stopped abruptly. My victim, at the desk, laconically ordered us to make a fair copy of the problems. Anaïs asked me under her breath, 'Did she go up and tell?'

'No, I made my humble excuses. You see, I didn't want to push a joke like that too far.'

Mademoiselle Sergent did not return. Her little assistant retained her shut face and her hard eyes till the end of the class. At half past ten, we were already thinking about going home. I took some cinders from the stove to stuff them in my sabots, an excellent means of warming them – officially forbidden, that goes without saying. But Mademoiselle Lanthenay's mind was far from cinders and sabots! She was sullenly ruminating her anger and her golden eyes were two cold topazes. I didn't care. In fact, I was even delighted.

Whatever was that? We pricked up our ears. Shouts; a
man's voice cursing, mingled with another voice trying to
drown it . . . were some of the builders having a fight? I did
not think so; I sensed something else. Little Aimée was
standing up, very pale; she too felt that something else was
coming. Suddenly Mademoiselle Sergent flung herself into the
classroom; the crimson had fled from her cheeks.

'Girls, go home at cone. It isn't time, but that doesn't matter
. . . Off with you, off with you – don't get into line. Do you
understand, get out!'

'Whatever's the matter?' shrieked Mademoiselle Lanthenay.

'Nothing, nothing . . . but get them to go and don't *you* stir
from here. Better lock the door . . . Haven't you gone yet, you
little idiots!'

Obviously, circumspection had gone to the winds! Rather
than leave the school at such a moment, I would have let
myself be flayed alive! I went out in the general scurry of my
bewildered classmates. Outside, the vociferating voice could
be clearly heard . . . Good heavens! It was Armand, more livid
than a drowned man, his eyes hollow and wild. He was
stained green all over with moss, and there were twigs in his
hair – he had obviously slept in the woods . . . Mad with rage
after that night spent in brooding over his misery, he wanted
to rush into the classroom, yelling and brandishing his fists:
Rabastens was holding him back with both arms and rolling
his eyes in terror. What a fuss! What a scene!

Marie Belhomme fled, frightened out of her wits, the
Second Division behind her; Luce vanished – I had just time
to catch her malicious little smile; the Jauberts had run to the
playground-door without turning their heads. I could not see
Anaïs but I could have sworn she was huddled in some corner
and not losing any of the spectacle.

The first word I heard distinctly, was 'Trollops!' Armand
had dragged his panting colleague right into the classroom
where our mute mistresses stood clasping each other tight. He
shouted: 'Whores! I'm not going to go without telling you
what you are, even if I do lose my job for it! Filthy little bitch!
Ah, so you let yourself be fumbled for money by that swine of
a District Inspector! You're worse than a street walker but

85

that one there is even worse than you, that damned redhead who's making you like herself. Two bitches, two bitches, you're two bitches, this house is . . .' I did not hear what. Rabastens, who must have double muscles like Tartarin de Tarascon, succeeded in dragging away the unfortunate man who was choking with insults. Mademoiselle Griset, losing her head, pushed the little girls, who were coming out of the small classroom, back into it again and I escaped, my heart rather shaken. But I was glad that Duplessis had exploded without further delay for Aimée could not now accuse me of having warned him.

When we returned in the afternoon, the one and only person we found there was Mademoiselle Griset who repeated the same phrase to each new arrival. 'Mademoiselle Sergent is ill and Mademoiselle Lanthenay is going home to her family; you're not to come back to school for a week.'

Fine, so off we went. But, honestly, this is no ordinary school!

DURING THE WEEK of unexpected holidays which this commotion procured for us, I went down with measles. This compelled me to spend three weeks in bed, then another fortnight convalescing. And they kept me in quarantine still another fortnight on the pretext of 'school safety'. If I hadn't had books and Fanchette, however should I have got through it! That doesn't sound very kind to Papa, yet he looked after me as if I were a rare slug. Convinced that one must give a little invalid everything she asks for, he brought me *marrons glacés* to make my temperature go down! Fanchette spent a whole week on my bed, washing herself from ears to tail, playing with my feet through the blanket and nestling in the hollow of my shoulder as soon as I stopped smelling of fever. I returned to school, a little thinner and paler, and immensely curious to see that extraordinary 'teaching staff' again. I'd had so little news during my illness! No one came to see me, not even Anaïs or Marie Belhomme, for fear of possible infection.

Half past seven was striking when I entered the playground on a morning in late February that was as mild as spring. At once I was surrounded and everyone made a fuss of me. The two Jauberts conscientiously asked me whether I was completely cured before coming near me. I was a little stunned by all this noise. At last they let me breathe and I hastily asked the lanky Anaïs the latest news.

'I'll tell you all. Armand Duplessis has left, to begin with.'

'Sacked or sent somewhere else, poor old Richelieu?'

'Only sent somewhere else. Dutertre got busy finding him another post.'

'Dutertre?'

'Naturally! If Richelieu had talked, that would have stopped the District Superintendent from ever becoming a Deputy. Dutertre has been solemnly saying all over town that the unfortunate young man had had a very dangerous attack of brain-fever and that they'd called him in, as school doctor, just in time.'

'Ah! So they called him in just in time? Providence had planted the remedy next door to the ill . . . And Mademoiselle Aimée? Sent away too?'

'Certainly not! Oh, *she*'s in no danger! By the end of a week, he didn't appear any more. And she was giggling with Mademoiselle Sergent just as usual.'

It was too much! That odd little creature who had neither heart nor brain, who lived without memory and without remorse, would begin all over again. She would humbug an assistant-master and romp with the District Superintendent until there was another crisis and she would live quite contentedly with that jealous, violent woman who was going to pieces as a result of these adventures. I hardly heard Anaïs telling me that Rabastens was still there and was constantly inquiring after me. I'd forgotten him, that pathetic lout Antonin!

The bell rang but it was the new school that we trooped into now. And the central building that linked the two wings was almost finished.

Mademoiselle Sergent installed herself at the desk that was all new and shining. Farewell the old rickety, scarred, uncomfortable tables; now we sat down at handsome sloping ones, provided with benches with backs to them and desks with hinged lids. We were only two to a bench now; instead of the lanky Anaïs, I now had as my neighbour . . . little Luce Lanthenay. Luckily the tables were extremely close together and Anaïs was near me, at a table parallel to mine, so that we could gossip together as comfortably as before. They had put Marie Belhomme beside her for Mademoiselle Sergent had intentionally placed two 'lively' ones (Anaïs and me), next to two 'torpid' ones (Luce and Marie) so that we should shake them up a little. We certainly would shake them up! At least I would, for I could feel all the rebelliousness that had been suppressed during my illness boiling up in me. I took in my new surroundings and arranged my books and exercise-books, while Luce sat down and watched me with a sidelong, timid glance. But I didn't deign to speak to her yet: I merely exchanged remarks about the new school with Anaïs who was avidly nibbling some unknown substance that looked to me like green buds.

'Whatever are you eating – old crab-apples?'

'Lime buds, old thing. Nothing so good. Now's just the moment, when it's getting on for March.'

'Give us a bit? . . . Really, it's awfully good. It's sticky like the gum on fruit-trees. I'll get some off the limes in the playground. And what other hitherto unknown delicacies are you stuffing yourself with nowadays?'

'Oh, nothing startling. I can't even eat coloured pencils any more. This year's lot are gritty. Beastly – absolute rubbish. However, to make up for that, the blotting-paper's excellent. There's also something good to chew, but not to swallow . . . the samples of handkerchief linen that the Bon Marché and the Louvre send out.'

'Ugh! That doesn't appeal to me in the least . . . I say, young Luce, are you going to try and be good and obedient sitting here beside me? Otherwise, I promise you slaps and pinches. So beware!'

'Yes, Mademoiselle,' answered the little thing, looking none too reassured, with her lashes downcast on her cheeks.

'You can say *tu* to me. Look at me, so as I can see your eyes? That's right. Now, you know that I'm mad, I'm sure you've been told that. Well, if anyone annoys me, I become furious and I bite and scratch, especially since my illness. Give me your hand: there, that's what I do.'

I dug my nails into her hand; she did not squeal, only tightened her lips.

'You didn't yell, good. I'll put you through questioning at recreation.'

*

In the Second classroom, whose door had been left open, I had just witnessed the entrance of Mademoiselle Aimée. Fresh, curled, and rosy, she wore her coaxing, mischievous expression and her eyes were more velvety and golden than ever. Little trollop! She flashed a radiant smile at Mademoiselle Sergent who forgot herself for a moment in contemplating her, then came out of her ecstasy and addressed us sharply:

'Your exercise-books. History essay: *The war of 1870*. Claudine,' she added more gently, 'can you do this essay in spite of not having followed the classes these last two months?'

'I'm going to try, Mademoiselle: I'll do the essay with less detailed development, that's all.'

I did, in fact, dash off a little essay. It was excessively short and, when I got towards the end, I lingered over it and applied myself to it, spinning out the last fifteen lines so as to be able to spy and ferret out what was going on about me. The Headmistress, the same as ever, preserved her expression of concentrated passion and jealous daring. Her Aimée, who was carelessly dictating problems in the other classroom, wandered closer and closer while she read aloud. All the same, last winter, she did not have that confident, coquettish walk – the walk of a spoilt pussy-cat! Now she was the adored, cherished little animal that is developing into a tyrant, for I caught glances from Mademoiselle Sergent that implored her to find some pretext to bring her over to her, glances to which the scatterbrained creature replied with capricious shakes of her head and amused eyes that said No. The Redhead, who had definitely become her slave, could bear it no longer and went across to her, asking very loud: 'Mademoiselle Lanthenay, you haven't got the Attendance Register in your room, have you?' Good, she had gone; they were chattering in whispers. I took advantage of this solitude in which we were left to put little Luce through a severe inquisition.

'Ah, ah, let that exercise-book alone, will you and answer my questions. Is there a dormitory upstairs?'

'Oh yes. We sleep there now, the boarders and me.'

'All right. You're a dolt.'

'Why?'

'That's none of your business. Do you still have singing-lessons on Thursdays and Sundays?'

'Oh, we tried to have one without you, Mademoiselle . . . Claudine, I mean, but it didn't go a bit well. Monsieur Rabastens doesn't know how to teach us.'

'Good. Has the cuddler been here while I was ill?'

'Who's that?'

'Dutertre.'

'I can't remember . . . Oh yes, he did come once, but not into the classrooms. And he only stayed a few minutes talking to my sister and Mademoiselle Sergent in the playground.'

'Is she nice to you, the Redhead?'

Her slanting eyes darkened.

'No . . . she tells me I've no intelligence . . . that I'm lazy . . . that my sister must have taken all the intelligence in the family as she's taken all the beauty . . . Anyway, it's always the same story wherever I've been with Aimée: people only pay attention to her and *I'm* pushed into the background . . .'

Luce was on the verge of tears in her fury against this sister who was more 'fetching' as they say here and who thrust her aside and eclipsed her. For all that, I didn't think her any better than Aimée: only shyer and more timid because she was used to remaining lonely and silent.

'Poor kid! You've left friends over there, where you used to be?'

'No, I didn't have any friends. The girls were too rough and used to laugh at me.'

'Too rough? Then it upsets you when I beat you or push you about?'

She laughed, without raising her eyes:

'No, because I realize that you . . . that you don't do it cruelly, out of beastliness . . . well, that it's a kind of joke and you don't really mean it. It's like when you call me "dolt", I know it's only for fun. In fact, I quite like feeling a bit frightened, when there isn't the least danger.'

Tralala! They're both alike, these two little Lanthenays; cowardly, naturally perverse, egotistical and so devoid of all moral sense that it's amusing to watch them. All the same, this one detested her sister and I thought I could drag any number

91

of revelations about Aimée out of her by cramming her with sweets and also by beating her.

'Have you finished your essay?'

'Yes, I've finished . . . but I didn't know the stuff a bit . . . I'm sure I'll get rotten marks . . .'

'Give me your exercise-book.'

I read her essay, which was very so-so; then I dictated some things she'd forgotten and remodelled her sentences a little. She was in a welter of joy and astonishment and observed me slyly, with surprised, enchanted eyes.

'There, you see, it's better like that . . . Tell me, do the boarders in the boys' school have their dormitory opposite yours?'

Her eyes lit up with mischief.

'Yes, and at night they go to bed the same time as we do, on purpose. And, you know, the windows have no shutters so the boys try and see us in our chemises. We lift up the corners of the curtains to look at *them* and it's no good Mademoiselle Griset keeping watch on us till the light's put out. We always find a way of pulling a curtain right up, all of a sudden, and that makes the boys come back every night to spy.'

'Well, well! You have a gay time undressing up there!'

'We certainly do!'

She was becoming lively and more familiar. Mademoiselle Sergent and Mademoiselle Lanthenay were still together in the Second classroom. Aimée showed the Redhead a letter and the two of them burst out laughing, but they kept their laughter very low.

'Do you know where your sister's ex-Armand has gone to bury his sorrows, young Luce?'

'No, I don't. Aimée never talks to me about her private affairs.'

'I thought as much. Has she got her room upstairs too?'

'Yes, the nicest and most comfortable of the assistant-mistresses' rooms – much prettier and warmer than Mademoiselle Griset's. Mademoiselle's had curtains with pink flowers put in it and linoleum on the floor, my dear, and a goatskin rug. And they've enamelled the bed white. Aimée even wanted to make me believe that she'd bought all these lovely things out of her savings. I told her straight: "I'll ask Mamma if it's true." Then she said: "If you mention it to Mamma, I'll have you sent back home on the excuse that you're not working." So, as you can imagine, there was nothing for me to do but keep my mouth shut.'

'Ssh. Mademoiselle's coming back.'

And, indeed, Mademoiselle was approaching, abandoning her tender, laughing expression for her school-mistress's face.

'Have you finished, girls? I am going to dictate you a problem in geometry.'

Dolorous protests arose, demanding another five minutes' grace. But Mademoiselle Sergent was not moved by these supplications, which were repeated three times a day, and began calmly to dictate the problem. Heaven confound similar triangles!

I was careful to bring sweets to school often with the object of seducing young Luce completely. She took them, hardly saying thank you, filled her little hands with them and hid them in an old mother-of-pearl rosary-case. For ten sous' worth of too-hot English peppermints, she would have sold her big sister and one of her brothers into the bargain. She opened her mouth, breathed in the air as to feel the cold of the peppermint and exclaimed: 'My tongue's freezing, my tongue's freezing,' her eyes rapturous. Anaïs shamelessly begged sweets off me, stuffed her cheeks with them, then hastily asked again, with an irresistible grimace of affected disgust:

'Quick, quick . . . give me some more to take the taste away – those had gone bad.'

As if by chance, while we were playing 'He', Rabastens came into the playground, bearing some exercise-books or other as an excuse. He feigned an amiable surprise at seeing me again and profited by the occasion to thrust a love-song under my nose. He proceeded to read its amorous words in a cooing voice. Poor noodle of an Antonin, you're no longer any use to me now – and you never were *much* use! The very most you're good for is to keep me amused for a little while and to excite the jealousy of my schoolfriends. If only you'd go away . . .

'Monsieur, you'll find those ladies in the end classroom. I think I saw them coming downstairs . . . weren't they, Anaïs?'

Thinking I was sending him away on account of the malignant glances of my companions, he threw me an eloquent look and departed. I shrugged my shoulders at the 'Hmm-Hms' I heard from the lanky Anaïs and from Marie Belhomme and we went on with an exciting game of 'turn-the-knife' in which the beginner, Luce, made mistake after mistake. She's young, poor thing, she doesn't know! The bell rang for class.

It was a sewing-lesson, a test for the examination. That is to say they made us do the samples of sewing, demanded in the exam, in one hour. We were handed out small squares of linen and Mademoiselle Sergent wrote up on the blackboard, in her clear writing, full of strokes like hammers:

Buttonhole – Ten centimetres of whipping. Initial G in marking-stitch. Ten centimetres of hem in running-stitch.

I groaned at this announcement because I could just manage the buttonhole and the whipping but the running-stitch hem and the initial in marking-stitch were things I didn't 'execute to perfection', as Mademoiselle Aimée noted with regret. Luckily I had recourse to a simple and ingenious device. I gave little Luce, who sews divinely, some sweets and she worked a marvellous G for me. 'We must help one another.' (Very appropriately, we had commented on this charitable aphorism only the day before.)

Marie Belhomme had confected a letter G that looked like a squatting monkey and, in her usual cheerful, crazy way, was roaring with laughter at her own work. The boarders, with their heads bent and their elbows held in were talking imperceptibly as they sewed. From time to time they exchanged meaning looks with Luce in the direction of the boys' school. I suspected that, at night, they spied some amusing spectacles from the vantage-point of their peaceful white dormitory.

Mademoiselle Lanthenay and Mademoiselle Sergent had exchanged desks; it was Aimée who invigilated our sewing-lesson while the Headmistress was making the girls in the Second Class read aloud. The favourite was occupied in inscribing the title of an Attendance Register in a beautiful round hand when her Redhead called out to her from the distance:

'Mademoiselle Lanthenay!'

'What do you want?' cried Aimée. Thoughtlessly, she used the familiar *tu*.

There was a stupefied silence. We all looked at each other: Anaïs began to clutch her ribs so as to be able to laugh longer; the two Jauberts bent their heads over their sewing; the boarders slyly dug each other with their elbows; Marie Belhomme burst out in a stifled laugh that sounded like a sneeze, and, at the sight of Aimée's face of consternation, I exclaimed out loud:

'Ah! She's so awfully kind!'

Little Luce was hardly laughing at all. It was obvious that she must have heard them address each other in that intimate way before. But she was staring at her sister with mocking eyes.

Mademoiselle Aimée turned on me furiously:

'Anyone may happen to make a mistake at times, Mademoiselle Claudine! And I apologize to Mademoiselle Sergent for my slip of the tongue!'

But the latter, having recovered from the shock, was quite aware that we should not swallow the explanation. She shrugged her shoulders as a sign of giving up in face of the irremediable blunder. This made a gay finale to the boring sewing-lesson. I'd badly needed this sprightly distraction.

When school was over at four o'clock, I did not go straight home. Instead, I astutely forgot an exercise-book and came back. I knew that, during the time for sweeping, the boarders took turns to carry water up to their dormitory. I did not know that dormitory yet; I wanted to visit it and Luce had told me: 'Today, *I'm doing the water*.' Treading like a cat, I climbed upstairs, carrying a full pail in case of awkward encounters. The dormitory had white walls and a white ceiling and was furnished with eight white beds. Luce showed me hers but I hadn't the faintest interest in her bed! I went straight to the windows which did, indeed, let one see into the boys' dormitory. Two or three big boys of fourteen or fifteen were prowling about it and looking in our direction: as soon as they saw us, they laughed and gesticulated and pointed to their beds. A lot of scamps! All the same, how tempting they are! Luce, shocked or pretending to be, hurriedly shut the window. But I'm pretty sure that, at bedtime, she displays less prudishness. The ninth bed, at the end of the dormitory, was placed under a kind of canopy that shrouded it in white curtains.

'That,' explained Luce, 'that's the mistress on duty's bed. The assistant-mistresses are supposed to take it in turn, week by week, to sleep in our dormitory.'

'Ah! So it's sometimes your sister Aimée, sometimes Mademoiselle Griset?'

'Well, of course . . . that's how it ought to be . . . but up to now, it's always Mademoiselle Griset . . . I don't know why.'

'Ah, so you don't know why? Hypocrite!'

I gave her a bang on the shoulder; she complained, but without conviction. Poor Mademoiselle Griset!

Luce went on enlightening me:

'At night, Claudine, you simply can't imagine what fun we have when we to go bed. We laugh, we run about in our chemises, we have pillow-fights. Some of the girls hide behind the curtains to get undressed because they say it embarrasses them. The oldest one, Rose Raquenot, washes so little that her underclothes are grey by the end of the three days she wears them. Yesterday, they hid my nightdress so I had to stay in the wash-room, absolutely naked. Luckily Mademoiselle Griset came along! Then we make fun of one of them who's so plump she had to powder herself all over with starch so as not to chafe herself. Oh, and I'd forgotten Poisson who wears a nightcap that makes her look like an old woman and who won't undress till we've left the wash-room. Oh, believe me, we have heaps of fun!'

The wash-room was scantily furnished with a big zinc-covered table on which stood a row of eight basins, eight tablets of soap, pairs of towels and eight sponges. All these objects were exactly alike: the linen was marked in indelible ink. It was all very neatly kept.

I inquired:

'Do you have baths?'

'Yes . . . and that's something else that's frightfully funny! In the new wash-house they heat up a huge wine-vat full of water . . . as big as a room. We all get undressed and we cram ourselves into it to soap ourselves.'

'Quite naked?'

'Of course – how'd we manage to soap ourselves otherwise? Rose Raquenot didn't want to strip, of course, because she's too thin. If you could only see her,' added Luce, lowering her voice. 'She's got practically nothing on her bones, and it's absolutely flat on her chest, like a boy! But Jousse is just the reverse. She's like a wet-nurse, *they* are as big as that! And the one who wears an old woman's nightcap – you know, Poisson – she's got hair all over her like a bear, and she's got blue thighs.'

'What do you mean, blue?'

'Yes, really blue. Like when it's freezing and your skin's blue with cold.'

'It must be most engaging!'

'Oh, no, it certainly isn't. If I were a boy, I wouldn't be a bit keen on having a bath with her!'

'But mightn't it have more effect on *her*, having a bath with a boy?'

We giggled. But I started at the sound of the voice and the footsteps of Mademoiselle Sergent in the corridor. So as not to be caught, I hid myself under the canopy reserved for the unique occupation of Mademoiselle Griset. Then, when the danger had passed, I escaped and dashed downstairs, calling out 'Good-bye' under my breath.

Next morning, how good my dear countryside looked! How gaily my pretty Montigny was sunning itself in this warm, precocious spring! Last Sunday and Thursday, I'd already ranged through the delicious woods, full of violets, with my co-First Communicant, my gentle Claire. She told me all about her flirtations . . . ever since the weather had turned mild her 'follower' arranged for them to meet in the evening at the corner of the Fir Plantation. Who knows if she won't end up by going too far! But it's not *that* which attracts her. Provided someone pours out choice words she doesn't quite understand, provided someone kisses her and goes down on

97

his knees, and everything happens *like it does in books* . . . well, she's perfectly satisfied.

In the classroom, I found little Luce collapsed over a table, sobbing fit to choke herself. I raised her head by main force and saw that her eyes were swollen as big as eggs, she'd dabbed them so much.

'Oh! Really! You look far from beautiful like that! What's the matter, little thing? What are you *blubbing* about?'

'She . . . she . . . b-beat me!'

'Do you mean, your sister?'

'Yee-es!'

'What had you done to her?'

She dried her eyes a little and began to tell her story.

'You see, I hadn't understood my problems, so I hadn't done them. That put her in a temper, so she said I was a dolt, that it wasn't worth while our parents' paying my fees, that she was disgusted with me, and so on and so on . . . So I answered back: "Oh, you bore me stiff." Then she beat me, she slapped my face. She's a beastly, horrible scold. I loathe her.'

There was a fresh deluge.

'My poor Luce, you're a goose. You shouldn't have let yourself be beaten, you should have thrown her ex-Armand in her teeth . . .'

The sudden scare in the little thing's eyes made me turn round: I caught sight of Mademoiselle Sergent listening to us from the doorway. Help! What was she going to say?

'My compliments, Mademoiselle Claudine. You are giving this child some pretty advice.'

'And you a pretty example!'

Luce was terrified by my reply. As for me, I didn't care in the least. The Headmistress's fiery eyes were glittering with rage and emotion! But this time, too subtle to lose her temper openly, she shook her head and merely observed:

'It's lucky the month of July is not far off, Mademoiselle Claudine. You realize, don't you, that it's becoming more and more impossible for me to keep you here?'

'Apparently. But, you know, it's due to our misunderstanding each other. Our relationship got off on the wrong foot.'

'Go off to recreation, Luce,' she said, without answering me.

The little thing did not wait to be told twice. She left the room at a run, blowing her nose. Mademoiselle Sergent went on:

'It's entirely your own fault, I assure you. You showed yourself full of ill-will towards me when I first arrived and you have repelled all my advances. For I made you plenty of them, though it was not my place to do so. All the same, you seemed to me intelligent – and pretty enough to interest me . . . who have neither sister nor child.'

Hanged if I'd ever thought of it . . . I couldn't have been more clearly told that I would have been 'her little Aimée' if I'd been willing. Well, well! No, that meant nothing to me, even in retrospect. Nevertheless, it would have been me of whom Mademoiselle Lanthenay would have been jealous at this very moment . . . What a comedy!

'That's true, Mademoiselle. But, as fate would have it, it would have turned out badly all the same, on account of Mademoiselle Aimée Lanthenay. You put so much fervour into acquiring her . . . friendship – and into destroying any she might have for me!'

She averted her eyes.

'I did not seek, as you pretend I did, to destroy . . . Mademoiselle Aimée could have gone on giving you her English lessons without my preventing her . . .'

'For goodness' sake don't say that! I'm not quite an idiot and there are only the two of us here! For a long time I was furious about it, devastated even, for I'm very nearly as jealous as you are . . . Why did you take her? I've been so unhappy, yes, there, you can be pleased, I've been so unhappy! But I realize now that she didn't care for me – who *does* she care for? I've realized too that she's not really worth much: that was enough for me. I've thought that I'd do quite enough foolish things without committing the folly of wanting to take her away from you. There! Now the only thing I want is that she shouldn't become too much the little queen of this school and that she shouldn't over-torment that little sister of hers who's fundamentally no better – and no

99

worse – than she is, I assure you . . . I never tell tales at home – never – about anything I may see here. I shan't come back again after the holidays and I shall sit for the Certificate because Papa's got it into his head that he's keen on it and because Anaïs would be only too delighted if I didn't pass the exam . . . You might leave me in peace till then – I don't torment you at all nowadays . . .'

I could have gone on talking for a long time, I think, but she was no longer listening to me. I was not going to contend with her for her little darling, that was all that she had been interested to hear. Her gaze had become introspective: she was pursuing an idea of her own. She roused herself, suddenly becoming the Headmistress again, after this conversation on an equal footing, and said to me:

'Hurry out to the playground, Claudine. It's after eight, you must get into line.'

'What were you chattering so long about in there with Mademoiselle?' demanded the lanky Anaïs. 'Does that mean you're matey with her, now?'

'Two girls together, my dear!'

In the classroom, little Luce squeezed up to me, threw me affectionate looks and clasped my hands. But her caresses irritated me; I only like hitting her and teasing her and protecting her when the others upset her.

Mademoiselle Aimée came into the classroom like a whirlwind, exclaiming in a loud whisper: 'The Inspector! The Inspector!' There was an uproar. Anything is an excuse for disorder here; under cover of arranging our books with impeccable neatness, we opened all our desks and chattered hurriedly behind the lids. The lanky Anaïs sent all the completely distracted Marie Belhomme's exercise-books flying and prudently thrust a *Gil blas illustré*, that she had concealed between two pages of her *History of France*, into her pocket. I myself hid Rudyard Kipling's marvellously-told stories of animals (there's a man who really knows about them!) – though they were hardly very reprehensible reading. We buzzed, we stood up, we gathered up papers, we took out the sweets hidden in our desks, for this venerable Blanchot, the Inspector, has eyes that squint but that poke into everything.

Mademoiselle Lanthenay, in her classroom, was hustling the little girls, tidying her desk, shouting and flapping about. And now, from the Third room, there appeared the wretched Griset, in great dismay, demanding help and protection. 'Mademoiselle Sergent, will the Inspector ask to see the little ones' exercise-books? They're dreadfully dirty . . . the smallest ones can only do pothooks . . .' The malicious Aimée laughed in her face; the Headmistress replied with a shrug: 'You'll show him whatever he asks to see, but if you think he'll bother with your urchins' copy books!' And the pathetic, dazed creature returned to her classroom where her little beasts were making an appalling din, for she hadn't a ha'porth of authority.

We were ready, or as near as maybe. Mademoiselle Sergent exclaimed: 'Quick, get out your selected pieces. Anaïs, spit it out at once, that slate-pencil you have in your mouth! On my word of honour, I'll turn you out in front of Monsieur Blanchot if you go on eating those revolting things! Claudine, couldn't you stop pinching Luce Lanthenay for one single instant! Marie Belhomme, take those off at once, those three scarves you have on your head and round your neck. And also take that stupid expression of your face. You're worse than the little ones in the Third Class and not one of you is worth the rope to hang you with!'

She simply had to discharge her nervous irritation. The Inspector's visits always upset her and because Blanchot was on good terms with the Deputy who detested his possible successor Dutertre, who was Mademoiselle Sergent's protégé, like poison. (Heavens, how complicated life is!) At last everything was more or less in order; the lanky Anaïs stood up, looking quite alarmingly tall, her mouth still dirty from the grey pencil she had been nibbling, and began *The Dress* by that maudlin poet Manuel:

In the wretched garret where daylight scarce could pierce
Wife and husband argued in a quarrel fierce . . .

Only just in time! A tall shadow passed across the panes giving on to the corridor; the entire class shuddered and rose

101

to its feet – out of respect – at the moment when the door opened to admit old Blanchot. He had a solemn face framed in large pepper-and-salt whiskers and a formidable Franche-Comté accent. He pontificated, he chewed his words enthusiastically like Anaïs chewing india-rubber, he was always dressed with a stiff, old-fashioned correctness; what an old bore! Now we were in for a whole hour of him! He would be sure to ask us idiotic questions and prove to us that we ought all to 'embrace the career of teaching'. I'd rather do even that than embrace *him*!

'Your ladies! . . . Sit down, my children.'

'His children' sat down, modest and mild. I wished to goodness I could get away. Mademoiselle Sergent danced attendance on him with an expression at once respectful and malevolent, while her assistant, the virtuous Lanthenay, shut herself up in her own classroom.

Monsieur Blanchot placed his silver-headed cane in a corner and promptly began to exasperate the Headmistress (well done!) by drawing her over to the window to talk about Certificate syllabuses, zeal, assiduity and all that sort of thing! She listened, she replied: 'Yes, Inspector.' Her eyes had retreated under her brows; she was obviously longing to hit him. He had finished boring her; now it was our turn.

'What was the girl reading when I came in?'

Anaïs, the 'girl' in question, hid the pink blotting-paper she was chewing and broke off the narrative, obviously a scandalous one, she was pouring into the ears of Marie Belhomme. The latter, shocked and crimson but attentive, rolled her birdlike eyes with a modest dismay. Smutty Anaïs! What could those stories possibly be?

'Come, my child, tell me what you are reading.'

'*The Dress*, Sir.'

'Kindly continue.'

She began again, with an air of mock intimidation, while Blanchot examined us with his dirty-green eyes. He was severe on any hint of coquetry and he frowned when he saw a black velvet ribbon on a white neck or curly tendrils escaping over forehead and temples. He always scolded *me* every time he visited us about my hair, which was always loose and curly, and also about the big white pleated collars I wore on my dark dresses. Although these had the simplicity I like, they were attractive enough for him to find my clothes appallingly reprehensible. The lanky Anaïs had finished *The Dress* and he was making her logically analyse (oh, my goodness!) five or six lines of it. Then he asked her:

'My child, why have you tied that black velvet about your neck?'

Now we were in for it! What did I tell you? Anaïs, flummoxed, answered idiotically that it was 'to keep her warm'. Cowardly fat-head!

'To keep you warm, you say? Don't you think a scarf would have served that purpose better?'

A scarf! Why not a woollen muffler, you doddering old bore? I couldn't help laughing and this drew his attention to myself.

'And you, my child, why is your hair not properly done and hanging all loose instead of being twisted up on your head and secured with hairpins?'

'Sir, that gives me migraines.'

'But you could at least plait it, I presume?'

'Yes I could, but Papa doesn't like me to.'

I can't tell you how he irritated me! After a disapproving little smack of his lips, he went and sat down and tormented Marie Belhomme about the War of Secession, one of the Jauberts about the coastline of Spain and the other about right-angled triangles. Then he sent me to the blackboard and ordered me to draw a circle. I obeyed. It was a circle . . . if you chose to call it one.

'Inside it, inscribe a rose-window with five lights. Assume that it is lit from the left and indicate with heavy strokes the shadows the petals receive.'

That didn't bother me at all. If he'd wanted to make me calculate figures, I'd have been in a hopeless mess but I knew all about rose-windows and shadows. I got through it quite well, much to the annoyance of the Jauberts who were sneakily hoping to see me scolded.

'That's . . . good. Yes, that's not bad at all. You're sitting for the Certificate Examination this year?'

'Yes, Sir, in July.'

'Then, no doubt, you wish to enter the Training College afterwards?'

'No, Sir. I shall go back home.'

'Indeed? As a matter of fact, in my opinion, you have not the slightest vocation for teaching. Very regrettable.'

He said that exactly as if he were saying: 'In my opinion, you are an infanticide.' Poor man, let him keep his illusions! But I could only wish he had been able to see the Armand Duplessis drama or the way we were left on our own for hours while our two mistresses were upstairs, billing and cooing . . .

'Be so good as to show me your Second Class, Mademoiselle.'

Mademoiselle Sergent took him off to the Second classroom where she remained with him to protect her little darling against inspectorial severity. I profited by his absence to sketch a caricature of old Blanchot and his huge whiskers on the blackboard. This sent the girls into ecstasies. I added donkey's ears, then I quickly rubbed it out and went back to my place. Little Luce slipped her arm coaxingly under mine and tried to kiss me. I pushed her away with a light slap and she pretended that I was 'simply horrid'!

'Simply horrid? I'll teach you to take liberties like that with me! Try and muzzle your feelings and tell me if it's still always Mademoiselle Griset who sleeps in the dormitory.'

'No, Aimée's slept there twice two days running.'

'That makes four times. You're a duffer; not even a duffer, a total nitwit! Do the boarders keep quieter when it's your chaste sister who's sleeping under the canopy?'

'Not a bit. And one night even, when one of the girls was ill, we got up and opened a window . . . I even called out to my sister to give us some matches because we couldn't find any, and she didn't budge. She didn't breathe any more than if there were no one in the bed at all! Does that mean that she's a very heavy sleeper?'

'Heavy sleeper! Heavy sleeper! What a goose you are! Good Lord, why have you allowed beings so utterly deprived of intelligence to exist on this earth? They make me weep tears of blood!'

'What have I done now?'

'Nothing! Oh, nothing at all! Only here come some thumps on your back to improve your heart and your wits and teach you not to believe in the virtuous Aimée's alibis.'

Luce squirmed over the table in mock despair, ravished at being bullied and pummelled. But I had suddenly remembered something.

'Anaïs, whatever were you telling Marie Belhomme that raised such blushes that the nation's over the Bastille pale beside them?'

'What Bastille?'

'Never mind. Tell me quick.'

'Come a bit closer.'

Her vicious face was sparkling; it must have been something very sordid.

'All right, then. Didn't you know? Last New Year's Eve, the Mayor had his mistress at his house – the fair Julotte – and, besides, his secretary had brought a woman from Paris. Well, at dessert, they made them both undress . . . take off even their chemises, and they did the same. And they set to and danced a quadrille like that, old dear!'

'Not bad! Who told you that?'

'It was Papa who told Mamma. I was in bed, only they always leave my bedroom door open because I pretend I'm frightened and so I hear everything.'

'Your home life must be far from dull. Does your father often tell stories like that?'

'No, not always such good ones. But sometimes I roll about in my bed with laughing.'

She told me some pretty dirty bits of gossip about our neighbourhood: her father works at the Town Hall and knows every scrap of scandal in the district. I listened to her and the time passed.

Mademoiselle Sergent returned: we had only just time to open our books at random, but she came straight up to me without looking at what we were doing.

'Claudine, could you make your classmates sing in front of Monsieur Blanchot? They know that pretty two-part song now – *Dans ce doux asile.*'

'*I'm* perfectly willing. Only it makes the Inspector so sick to see me with my hair loose that he won't listen!'

'Don't say silly things, this isn't the day for them. Hurry up and make them sing. Monsieur Blanchot seems decidedly dissatisfied with the Second Class; I'm counting on the music to smooth him down.'

I had no difficulty in believing that he must be decidedly dissatisfied with the Second Class: Mademoiselle Aimée Lanthenay occupies herself with it whenever she has nothing else to do. She gorges her girls with written work so as to be able to chat peacefully with her dear Headmistress while they're scribbling. I was perfectly willing to make the girls sing, whatever it cost me!

Mademoiselle Sergent brought back the odious Blanchot: I ranged our class and the first division of the Second in a semi-circle and entrusted the firsts to Anaïs and the seconds to Marie Belhomme (unfortunate seconds!). I would sing both parts at once; that's to say I'd quickly change over when I felt one side weakening. Off we went! One empty bar: one, two, three.

> *Dans ce doux asile*
> *Les sages sont couronnés,*
> *Venez!*
> *Aux plaisirs tranquilles*
> *Ces lieux charmants sont destinés . . .*

What luck! That tough old pedagogue nodded his head to the rhythm of Rameau's music (out of time, as it happened), and appeared enchanted. It was the story of the composer Orpheus taming the wild beasts all over again.

'That was well sung. By whom is it? Gounod, I believe?' (Why does he pronounce it *Gounode?*)

'Yes, Sir.' (Don't let's annoy him.)

'I was sure it was. It is an extremely pretty piece.'

(Pretty piece yourself!)

On hearing this unexpected attribution of a melody of Rameau's to the author of *Faust*, Mademoiselle Sergent compressed her lips so as not to laugh. As to Blanchot, now serene once more, he uttered a few amiable remarks and went away, after having dictated to us – as a Parthian shot – this theme for a French composition:

'Explain and comment on this thought of Franklin's: Idleness is like rust, it wears a man out more than work.'

Off we go! Let us contrast the shining key, with its rounded contours which the hand polishes and turns in the lock twenty times a day, with the key eaten away with reddish rust. The good workman who labours joyously, having risen at dawn, whose brawny muscles, etc., etc . . . Let us set him against the idler, who lying languidly on oriental divans watches rare dishes, etc., etc. . . . succeed each other on his sumptuous table, etc., etc . . . dishes which vainly attempt to reawaken his appetite, etc., etc . . . Oh, that won't take long to hash out!

Nonsense, of course, that it isn't good to laze in an armchair! Nonsense, of course, that workers who labour all their life don't die young and exhausted! But naturally one mustn't say so. In the 'Examination Syllabus' things don't happen as they do in life.

Little Luce was lacking in ideas and whining in a low voice for me to provide her with some. I generously let her read what I had written; she wouldn't get much from me.

At last it was four o'clock. We went off home. The boarders went upstairs to eat the refreshments Mademoiselle Sergent's mother had prepared for them. I left with Anaïs and Marie Belhomme after having looked at my reflection in the window-panes to make sure that my hat wasn't crooked.

On the way, we shared a sugar-loaf and castigated Blanchot as if we were breaking it over his back. He bores me stiff, that old man, who wants us always to be dressed in sackcloth and wear our hair scraped back.

'All the same, I don't think he's awfully pleased with the Second Class,' remarked Marie Belhomme. 'If you hadn't wheedled him round with the music!'

'What d'you expect?' said Anaïs. 'Mademoiselle Lanthenay doesn't exactly over-exert herself with anxiety over the welfare of her class.'

'The things you say! Come, come, she can't do everything!

107

Mademoiselle Sergent has attached her to her person – she's the one who dresses her in the morning.'

'Oh, that's bunkum!' Anaïs and Marie exclaimed both at once.

'It isn't bunkum in the least! If ever you go into the dormitory and into the mistresses' rooms (it's awfully easy, you've only to take some water up with the boarders), run your hand over the bottom of Mademoiselle Aimée's basin. You needn't be afraid of getting wet, there's nothing but dust in it.'

'No, that's going a bit far, all the same!' declared Marie Belhomme.

The lanky Anaïs made no further comment and went away meditating; no doubt she would pass on all these charming details to the big boy with whom she was flirting that week. I knew very little about her escapades; she remained secretive and sly when I sounded her about them.

I was bored at school; a tiresome symptom and quite a new one. Yet I wasn't in love with anyone. (Indeed, perhaps that was the reason.) I was so apathetic that I did my schoolwork almost accurately, and I was quite unmoved as I watched our two mistresses caressing each other, billing and cooing and quarrelling for the pleasure of being more affectionate than ever when they made it up. Their words and gestures to each other were so uninhibited nowadays that Rabastens, in spite of his self-possession, was taken aback by them and spluttered excitably. Then Aimée's eyes would gleam with delight like those of a mischievous cat and Mademoiselle Sergent would laugh at seeing her laughing. Upon my word, they really were amazing! It's fantastic, how exacting the little thing has become! The other changes countenance at the faintest sigh from her, at a pucker of her velvety eyebrows.

Little Luce is acutely conscious of this tender intimacy: she watches every move, hot on the trail, and learns things for herself. Indeed she is learning a great deal for she seizes every opportunity of being alone with me, and brushes up against me coaxingly, her green eyes almost closed and her fresh little mouth half-open. But no, she doesn't tempt me. Why doesn't she transfer her attentions to the lanky Anaïs, who is also highly interested in the goings-on of the two love-birds who serve us as teachers in their spare moments and who is extremely surprised at them, for she is oddly ingenuous in some ways?

This morning I beat little Luce to a jelly because she wanted to kiss me in the shed where they keep the watering-cans. She didn't yell but began to cry until I comforted her by stroking her hair. I told her:

'Silly, you'll have plenty of time to work off your superfluous feelings later on, as you're going on to the Training College!'

'Yes, but *you're* not going on there!'

'No, thank goodness! But you won't have been there two days before two "Third Years" will have quarrelled over you, you disgusting little beast!'

She let herself be insulted with voluptuous pleasure and threw me grateful glances.

Is it because they've changed my old school that I'm so bored in this one? I no longer have the dusty 'nooks' where one could hide in the passages of that rambling old building where one never knew whether one was in the staff's quarters or in our own and where it was so natural to find oneself in a master's room that one hardly needed to apologize on returning to the classroom.

Is it because I'm getting older? Can I be feeling the weight of the sixteen years I've nearly attained? That really would be too idiotic for words.

Perhaps it's the spring? It's also too fine – almost indecently fine! On Thursdays and Sundays I go off all alone to meet my First Communion partner, my little Claire, who's heavily embarked on an absurd adventure with the Secretary at the Town Hall who doesn't want to marry her. From all accounts, there's an excellent reason that prevents him! It seems that, while he was still at college, he underwent an operation for some peculiar disease, one of those diseases whose 'seat' is never mentioned, and people say that, if he still wants girls, he can never again 'satisfy his desires'. I don't understand awfully well, in fact I don't really understand at all, but I'm sick and tired of passing on to Claire what I've vaguely learnt. She turns up the whites of her eyes, shakes her head, and replies, with an ecstatic expression: 'Oh, what does that matter, what does that matter? He's so handsome, he has such a lovely moustache and, besides, the things he says to me make me quite happy enough! And then, he kisses me on the neck, he talks to me about poetry – and sunsets – whatever more d'you expect me to want?' After all, if that satisfies her . . .

When I've had enough of her ravings, I tell her I'm going home to Papa so that she'll leave me on my own. But I don't go home. I stay in the woods and I hunt out a particularly delicious corner and lie down there. Hosts of little creatures scamper over the ground under my nose (they even behave extremely badly sometimes, but they're so tiny!) and there are so many good smells there – the smell of fresh plants warming in the sun . . . Oh, my dear woods!

I arrived late at school (I find it hard to go to sleep: my thoughts start dancing in my head the moment I turn out the lamp), to find Mademoiselle Sergent at the mistress's desk, looking dignified and scowling, and all the girls wearing suitable prim, ceremonious expressions. Whatever did all that mean? Ah, the gawky Anaïs was huddled over her desk, making such tremendous efforts to sob that her ears were blue with the exertion. I was going to have some fun! I slid in beside little Luce, who whispered in my ear: 'My dear, they've found all Anaïs's letters in a boy's desk and the master's just brought them over for the Headmistress to read!'

She was, indeed, reading them, but very low, only to herself. What bad luck. Heavens, what bad luck! I'd cheerfully have given three years of Antonin Rabasten's life to go through that correspondence. Oh! would no one inspire the Redhead to read us two or three well-chosen passages out loud? Alas, alas, Mademoiselle Sergent had come to the end . . . Without a word to Anaïs, who was still hunched over the table, she solemnly rose and walked over, with deliberate steps, to the stove beside me. She opened it, deposited the scandalous papers, folded in four, inside; then she struck a match, applied it to the letters, and closed the little door. As she stood up again, she said to the culprit:

'My compliments, Anaïs, you know more about these things than many grown-up people do. I shall keep you here until the exam, since your name is entered for it, but I shall tell your parents that I absolve myself from all responsibility for you. Copy out your problems, girls, and pay no more attention to this person who is not worth bothering about.'

Incapable of enduring the torture of having Anaïs's effusions burn, I had taken out the flat ruler I use for drawing while the Headmistress was majestically declaiming. I slipped the ruler under my table and, at the risk of getting caught, I used it to push the little handle that moved the damper. No one saw a thing: perhaps the flame, thus stifled of draught, would not burn everything up. I should know when class was over. I listened; the stove stopped roaring after a few seconds. Wouldn't it soon strike eleven? I could hardly keep my mind on what I was copying, on the 'two pieces of linen which, after being washed, shrank $\frac{1}{19}$ – in length and $\frac{1}{22}$ – in breadth; they could have shrunk considerably more without my being interested.

Mademoiselle Sergent left us and went off to Aimée's classroom, no doubt to tell her the good story and laugh over it with her. As soon as she had disappeared, Anaïs raised her head. We stared at her avidly: her cheeks were blotched and her eyes were swollen from having been violently rubbed, but she kept her eyes obstinately fixed on her exercise-book. Marie Belhomme leant over to her and said with vehement sympathy: 'I say, old thing, I bet you'll get a fearful wigging at home. Did you say lots of awful things in your letters?' Anaïs did not raise her eyes but said out loud so that we should all hear: 'I don't care a fig, the letters weren't mine.' The girls exchanged indignant looks: 'My dear, would you believe it! My dear, what a liar that girl is!'

At last, the hour struck. Never had break been so long in coming! I dawdled over tidying my desk so as to be the last one left behind. Outside, after having walked fifty yards or so, I pretended I'd forgotten my atlas and I left Anaïs in order to fly back to school: 'Wait for me, will you?'

I dashed silently into the empty classroom and opened the stove: I found a handful of half-burnt papers in it which I drew out with the most tender precautions. What luck! the top and bottom ones had gone but the thick wad in the middle was almost intact; it was definitely Anaïs's writing. I took the packet away in my satchel so as to read them at home at leisure, and I rejoined Anaïs, who was quite calm, and strolling about while she waited for me. We set off again together: she stared at me surreptitiously. Suddenly, she stopped dead and gave an agonized sigh . . . I saw her gaze anxiously fixed on my hands and then I noticed they were black from the burnt papers I had touched. I wasn't going to lie to her – certainly not. I took the offensive:

'Well, what's the matter?'

'So you went and searched in the stove, eh?'

'Certainly I did! No danger of my losing a chance like that of reading your letters!'

'Are they burnt?'

'No, luckily: here, look inside.'

I showed her the papers, keeping a firm hold on them. She darted positively murderous looks at me but did not dare pounce on my satchel, she was too sure I'd thrash her! I decided to comfort her a little; she made me feel almost sorry for her.

'Listen, I'm going to read what isn't burnt – because I just can't bear not to – and then I'll bring you the whole lot back this afternoon. So I'm not such a beast after all, am I?'

She was highly mistrustful.

'Word of honour! I'll give you them back at recreation before we go into class.'

She went off, helpless and uneasy, looking even longer and yellower than usual.

At home, I went through those letters at last. Immense disappointment! They weren't a bit what I'd imagined. A mixture of silly sentimentalities and practical directions: 'I always think of you when there's moonlight . . . Do make sure, on Thursday, to bring the corn-sack you took last time, to Vrimes' field; Mama would kick up a shindy if she saw grass-stains on my frock!' Then there were obscure allusions which must have reminded young Gangneau of various smutty episodes . . . In short, yes, a disappointment. I would give her back her letters which were far less amusing than her cold, whimsical, humorous self.

I gave them back to her; she could not believe her own eyes. She was so overjoyed at seeing them that she couldn't resist making fun of me for having read them. Once she'd run and thrown them down the lavatory, she resumed her shut, impenetrable face, without the faintest trace of humiliation. Happy disposition!

Bother, I've caught a cold! I stay in Papa's library, reading Michelet's absurd *History of France*, written in alexandrines. (Am I exaggerating a bit?) I'm not in the least bored, curled up in this big armchair, surrounded by books, with my beautiful Fanchette for company. She's the most intelligent cat in the world and she loves me disinterestedly in spite of the miseries I inflict on her, biting her in her pink ears and making her go through the most complicated training.

She loves me so much that she understands what I say and comes and rubs against my mouth when she hears the sound of my voice. She also loves books like an old scholar, this Fanchette, and worries me every night after dinner to remove two or three volumes of Papa's big Larousse from their shelf. The space they make leaves a little square room in which Fanchette settles down and washes herself; I shut the glass door on her and her imprisoned purr vibrates with a noise like an incessant, muffled drum. From time to time, I look at her; then she makes me a sign with her eyebrows which she raises like a human being. Lovely Fanchette, how intelligent and understanding you are! (Much more so than Luce Lanthenay, that inferior breed of cat!) You amused me from the moment you came into the world; you'd only got one eye open when you were already attempting warlike steps in your basket, though you were still incapable of standing up on your four matchsticks. Ever since, you've lived joyously, making me laugh with your belly-dances in honour of cockchafers and butterflies, your clumsy calls to the birds you're stalking, your way of quarrelling with me and giving me sharp taps that re-echo on my hands. Your behaviour is quite disgraceful: two or three times a year I catch you on the garden walls, wearing a crazy, ridiculous expression, with a swarm of tom-cats round you. I even know your favourite, you perverse Fanchette – he's a dirty-grey Tom, long and lean, with half his fur gone. He's got ears like a rabbit's and coarse, plebeian limbs. How can you make a *mésalliance* with this low-born animal, and make it so often? But, even at those demented seasons, as soon as you catch sight of me, your natural face returns for a moment; and you give me a friendly mew which says something like: 'You see what I'm up to. Don't despise me too much, nature has her urgent demands. But I'll soon come home again and I'll lick myself for ages to purify myself of this dissolute life.' O, beautiful Fanchette, your bad behaviour is so remarkably becoming to you!

When my cold was over, I observed that people at school were beginning to get very agitated about the approaching exams; we were now at the end of May and we 'went up' on the 5th of July! I was sorry not to be more moved, but the others made up for me, especially little Luce Lanthenay, who burst into floods of tears whenever she got a bad mark. As for Mademoiselle Sergent, she was busy with everything, but most of all, with the little thing with the beautiful eyes who kept her 'on a string'. She'd blossomed out, that Aimée, in an astonishing way! Her marvellous complexion, her velvety skin and her eyes, 'that you could strike medals out of', as Anaïs says, make her into a spiteful and triumphant little creature. She is so much prettier than she was last year! No one would pay any more attention now to the slight crumpling of her face, to the little crease on the left of her lip when she smiles; and, anyhow, she has such white, pointed teeth! The amorous Redhead swoons at the mere sight of her and our presence no longer restrains her from yielding to her furious desire to kiss her darling every two minutes.

On this warm afternoon, the class was murmuring a *Selected Passage* that we had to recite at three o'clock. I was almost dozing, oppressed by a nervous lassitude. I was incapable of any more effort, when all of a sudden I felt I wanted to scratch somebody, to give a violent stretch and to crush somebody's hands; the somebody turned out to be

Luce, my next-door neighbour. She found the nape of her neck being clutched and my nails digging into it. Luckily, she didn't say a word. I fell back into my irritated listlessness . . .

The door opened without anyone having even knocked: it was Dutertre, in a light tie, his hair flying, looking rejuvenated and pugnacious. Mademoiselle Sergent sprang to her feet, barely said good afternoon to him and gazed at him with passionate admiration, her tapestry fallen unheeded on the floor. (Does she love him more than Aimée? or Aimée more than him? Curious woman!) The class had stood up. Out of wickedness, I remained seated, with the result that, when Dutertre turned towards us, he noticed me at once.

'Good afternoon, Mademoiselle. Good afternoon, little ones. *You* seem in a state of collapse!'

'I'm floppy. I haven't a bone left in me.'

'Are you ill?'

'No, I don't think so. It's the weather – general slackness.'

'Come over here and let's have a look at you.'

Was all that going to start over again . . . those medical pretexts for prolonged examinations? The Headmistress launched looks of blazing indignation at me for the way I was sitting and for the way I was talking to her beloved District Superintendent. I decided to put myself out and obey. Besides, he adores these impertinent manners. I dragged myself lazily over to the window.

'One can't see here because of that green shadow from the trees. Come out into the corridor, there's some sunlight there. You look wretched, my child.'

Triple-distilled lie! I looked extremely well. I know myself: if it was because I had rings round my eyes that he thought I was ill, he was mistaken. It's a good sign when I have dark circles under my eyes, it means I'm in excellent health. Luckily it was three in the afternoon, otherwise I should have been none too confident about going out, even into the glass-paned corridor, with this individual whom I mistrust like fire.

When he had shut the door behind us, I rounded on him and said:

'Now, look here, I *don't* look ill. Why did you say I did?'

'No? What about those eyes with dark circles right down to your lips?'

'Well, it's the colour of my skin, that's all.'

He had seated himself on the bench and was holding me in front of him, standing against his knees.

'Shut up, you're talking nonsense. Why do you always look as if you were cross with me?'

'. . . ?'

'Oh yes, you know quite well what I mean. You know, you've got a nice, funny little phiz that sticks in one's head once one's seen it!'

I gave an idiotic laugh. If only heaven would send me some wit, some smart repartee, for I felt terribly destitute of them!

'Is it true you always go for walks all by yourself in the woods?'

'Yes, it's true. Why?'

'Because, you little hussy, perhaps you go to meet a lover? You're so well chaperoned!'

I shrugged my shoulders.

'You know all the people round here as well as I do. Do you see any of *them* as a possible lover for me?'

'True. But you might be vicious enough . . .'

He gripped my arms and flashed his eyes and teeth. How hot it was here! I would have been only too pleased if he would have let me go back to the classroom.

'If you're ill, why don't you come and consult me at my house?'

I answered too hurriedly, 'No! I won't go . . .' And I tried to free my arms, but he held me firmly and raised burning, mischievous eyes to mine. They were handsome eyes too, it's true.

'Oh, you little thing, you charming little thing, why are you frightened? You're so wrong to be frightened of me! Do you think I'm a cad? You've absolutely nothing to fear . . . nothing. Oh, little Claudine, you're so frightfully attractive with your warm brown eyes and your wild curls! You're made like an adorable little statue, I'll swear you are . . .'

He stood up suddenly, clasped me in his arms and kissed me; I hadn't time to escape, he was too strong and virile, and

116

my head was in a whirl . . . What a situation! I no longer knew what I was saying, my brain was going round and round . . . Yet I couldn't go back to the classroom, all red and shaken as I was, and I could hear him behind me . . . I was certain he was going to want to kiss me again . . . I opened the front door, rushed out into the playground and dashed up to the pump where I drank a mug of water. Ouf! . . . I must go back . . . But he must be ambushed in the passage. Ah! After all, who cares! I'd scream if he tried to do it again . . . It was because he'd kissed me on the corner of the mouth, which was the best he could do, that beast!

No, he wasn't in the corridor. What luck! I went back into the classroom and there I saw him, standing by the desk and calmly chatting to Mademoiselle Sergent. I sat down in my place; he looked at me searchingly and inquired:

'You didn't drink too much water, I hope? These kids, they swallow mugfuls of cold water, it's shockingly bad for the health.'

I was bolder with everyone there.

'No, I only drank a mouthful. That was quite enough, I shan't take any more.'

He laughed and looked pleased:

'You're a funny girl. But you're not a complete idiot.'

Mademoiselle Sergent did not understand, but the uneasiness that puckered her eyebrows gradually smoothed itself out. All that remained was her contempt for the deplorable manners I displayed towards her idol.

Personally, I was furious with him: he was stupid! The lanky Anaïs guessed that something was up and could not restrain herself from asking me: 'I say, did he examine you awfully close to, to make you so upset?' But I certainly wasn't going to tell *her*. 'Don't be an idiot! I tell you, I went out to the pump.' Little Luce, in her turn, rubbed herself against me like a fidgety cat and ventured to question me: 'Do tell me, Claudine darling, whatever made him take you off like that?'

'To begin with I'm not "Claudine darling" to *you*. And, besides, it's none of your business, you little rat. He had to consult me about the standardization of pensions. And that's that.'

117

'You never want to tell me anything. And I tell *you* all!'

'All what? A fat lot of use it is to me to know that your sister doesn't pay her board or yours either – and that Mademoiselle Olympe heaps her with presents – and that she wears silk petticoats – and that . . .'

'Ssh! Oh, *please*, stop! I'd be absolutely done for if they knew I'd told you all that!'

'Then, don't ask *me* anything. If you're good, I'll give you my lovely ebony ruler, the one with the brass edges.'

'Oh, you *are* sweet! I'd like to kiss you but that annoys you . . .'

'That'll do. I'll give it you tomorrow – if I feel like it!'

For my passion for 'desk-furniture' was becoming appeased, which was yet another very bad symptom. All my classmates (and I used to be just like them) were crazy about 'school equipment'. We ruined ourselves on exercise-books of cream-laid paper bound in shimmering tinfoil with a moiré pattern, on rosewood pencils, on lacquered penholders shiny enough to see one's face in, on olive-wood pencil-boxes, on rulers made of mahogany or of ebony, like mine, which had its four edges bound with brass and which made the boarders, who were too poor to afford one like it, green with envy. We had big satchels like lawyers' briefcases in more-or-less crushed more-or-less Morocco. And if the girls didn't have their school text-books sheathed in gaudy bindings for their New Year presents, and if I didn't either, it was simply and solely because they were not our own property. They belonged to the Town Council which generously provided us with them on condition we left them at the School when we left it never to return. Moreover, we loathed those bureaucratic books; we didn't feel they belonged to us and we played horrible tricks on them. Unforeseen and fantastic mishaps befell them: some of them had been known to catch fire at the stove, in winter; there were others over which inkpots took a particular delight in upsetting; in fact, they attracted disaster! And all the affronts put upon the dreary 'Council Books' were the subject of long lamentations from Mademoiselle Lanthenay and terrible lectures from Mademoiselle Sergent.

*

118

Lord, how idiotic women are! (Little girls, women, it's all one.) Would anyone believe that, ever since that inveterate wolf Dutertre's 'guilty attempts' on my person, I've felt what might be called a vague pride? It's very humiliating to me, that admission. But I know why; in my heart of hearts, I tell myself: 'If that man, who's known heaps of women, in Paris and all over the place, finds me attractive, it must be because I'm not remarkably ugly!' There! It was a pleasure to my vanity. I didn't really think I was repulsive, but I like to be sure I'm not. And besides, I was pleased at having a secret that the lanky Anaïs, Marie Belhomme, Luce Lanthenay and the others didn't suspect.

The class was well trained now. All the girls, even down to those in the Third Division knew that, during recreation, they must never enter a classroom in which the mistresses had shut themselves up. Naturally, our education hadn't been perfected in a day! One or other of us had gone at least fifty times into the classroom where the tender couple was hiding. But we found them so tenderly entwined, or so absorbed in their whisperings, or else Mademoiselle Sergent holding her little Aimée on her lap with such total lack of reserve that even the stupidest were nonplussed and fled as soon as the Redhead demanded: 'What do you want *now*?', terrified by the ferocious scowl of her bushy eyebrows. Like the others, I frequently burst in and sometimes even without meaning to: the first few times, when they saw it was me and they were too close together, they hastily got up or else one of them would pretend to pin up the other's loosened hair. But they ended up by not disturbing themselves on my account. So I no longer found it entertaining.

Rabastens doesn't come over any more: he has declared over and over again that he is 'too intimidated by this intimacy' and this expression seemed to him a kind of pun which delighted him. As for *them*, they no longer think of anything but themselves. They dog each other's footsteps and live in each other's shadow: their mutual adoration is so absolute that I no longer think of tormenting them. I almost envy their delicious oblivion of everything else in the world.

*

119

There! I was sure it would happen sooner or later! A letter from little Luce that I found when I got home, in a pocket of my satchel.

My Darling Claudine,
I love you very much. You always look as if you didn't know anything about it and that makes me die of misery. You are both nice and nasty to me, you don't want to take me seriously, you treat me as if I were a little dog: you can't imagine how that hurts me. But just think how happy we could be, the two of us; look at my sister Aimée with Mademoiselle, they're so happy that they don't think of anything else now. I implore you, if you're not annoyed by this letter, not to say anything to me tomorrow morning at school, I'd be too embarrassed at that moment. I'll know very well, just from the sort of way you talk to me during the day, whether you want to be my friend or not.

I kiss you with all my heart, my darling Claudine and I count on you, too, to burn this letter because I know you wouldn't want to show it so as to get me into trouble, that's not your way. I kiss you again very lovingly and I'm longing so impatiently for it to be tomorrow!
                                                        Your little Luce

Good heavens no, I *don't* want to! If that appealed to me, it would be with someone stronger and more intelligent than myself, someone who'd bully me a little, whom I'd obey, and not with a depraved little beast who has a certain charm, perhaps, scratching and mewing just to be stroked, but who's too inferior. I don't love people I can dominate. I tore up her letter straight away, charming and unmalicious as it was, and put the pieces in an envelope to return them to her.

The next morning I saw a worried little face pressed against the window, waiting for me. Poor Luce, her green eyes were pale with anxiety! What a pity, but all the same I couldn't, just for the sake of giving her pleasure . . .

I went inside; as luck would have it, she was all alone.

'Look, little Luce, here are the bits of your letter. I didn't keep it long, you see.'

120

She said nothing and took the envelope mechanically.

'Crazy girl. Besides, whatever were you doing up there . . . I mean up there on the first floor . . . behind the locked doors of Mademoiselle Sergent's room? That's where that leads you! *I* can't do anything for you.'

'Oh!' she said, prostrated.

'But yes, my poor child. It isn't from virtue, you can be sure. My virtue's still far too small, I don't trot it out and about yet. But you see, in my green youth I was consumed by a great love. I *adored* a man who died making me swear on his deathbed never to . . .'

She interrupted me, moaning:

'There, there, you're laughing at me again. I didn't want to write to you, you've no heart. Oh, how unhappy I am! Oh, how cruel you are!'

'And besides, you're deafening me! What a row! What d'you bet I give you a few kicks to bring you back to the straight and narrow path?'

'Oh, what do I care? Oh, I could almost laugh!'

'Take that, you little bad lot! And give me a receipt.'

She had just been dealt a heavy slap which had the effect of promptly silencing her. She looked at me stealthily with gentle eyes and began to cry, already comforted, as she rubbed her head. How she loves to be beaten; it's astounding.

'Here come Anaïs and lots of the others, try and look more or less respectable. They'll be coming in to class in a moment, the two turtle-doves are on their way down.'

Only a fortnight till the Certificate! June oppresses us. We bake, half asleep, in the classrooms; we're silent from listlessness; I'm too languid to keep my diary. And in this furnace heat, we still have to criticize the conduct of Louis XV, explain the role of the gastric juices in the process of digestion, sketch acanthus leaves, and divide the auditory apparatus into the inner ear, the middle ear, and the outer ear. There's no justice on the earth! Louis XV did what he wanted to do, it's nothing to do with *me*! Oh Lord, no! With *me* less than anyone!

It was so hot that it made one lose one's desire to make

oneself look attractive – or rather, the fashion palpably changed. Now we displayed our skin. I inaugurated dresses with open square necks, something on medieval lines, with sleeves that stopped at the elbow. My arms were still rather thin, but nice all the same, and, as to my neck, I back it against anyone's. The others imitated me; Anaïs did not wear short sleeves but she profited by mine to roll her own up to the shoulders; Marie Belhomme displayed unexpectedly plump arms above her bony hands and a fresh neck that would be fat later on. Oh Lord, what *wouldn't* one display in a temperature like this! With immense secrecy, I replaced my stockings with socks. By the end of three days, they all knew it and told each other about it and implored me under their breath to pull my skirt up.

'Let's see your socks . . . are you really wearing them?'

'Look!'

'Lucky devil! All the same, *I* wouldn't dare.'

'Why? Respect for the decencies?'

'No . . . but . . .'

'Shut up, I know why . . . You've got hair on your legs!'

'Oh, you liar of all liars! You can look . . . I haven't any more than you have. Only I'd be ashamed to feel my legs quite bare under my dress!'

Little Luce exhibited some skin shyly – skin that was marvellously white and soft. The gawky Anaïs envied this whiteness to such an extent that she pricked her arms with needles on sewing-days.

Farewell to repose! The approach of the examinations, the honour that our possible successes would reflect on this fine new school had at last dragged our teachers from their sweet solitude. They kept us, the six candidates, in close confinement; they pestered us with endless repetitions; they forced us to listen, to remember, even to understand, making us come in an hour before the others and leave an hour after them! Nearly all of us became pale, tired and stupid; some of us lost appetite and sleep as a result of work and anxiety. I myself remained looking almost fresh, because I didn't worry overmuch and I have a matt skin. Little Luce did too; like her

sister Aimée, she possesses one of those enviable, indestruct-
ible pink and white complexions . . .

We knew that Mademoiselle Sergent was going to take us
all together to the principal town of the Department and we
should stay with her at the same hotel. She would take charge
of all the expenses and we would settle our accounts on our
return. But for that cursed exam, we should have found this
little trip enchanting.

These last days have been deplorable. Mistresses and pupils
alike have been so atrociously nervy that they explode every
other minute. Aimée flung her exercise-book in the face of a
boarder who had made the same idiotic mistake for the third
time in an arithmetic problem, then promptly fled to her own
room. Little Luce was slapped by her sister and came and
threw herself in my arms for me to comfort her. I hit Anaïs
when she was teasing me at the wrong moment. One of the
Jauberts was seized, first with a frantic burst of sobbing, then
with a no less frantic attack of nerves, because, she screamed,
'she would never manage to pass! . . .' (wet towels, orange-
flower water, encouragements). Mademoiselle Sergent, also
exasperated, made poor Marie Belhomme, who regularly
forgets next day what she learnt the day before, spin round
like a top in front of the blackboard.

I can only rest properly at night in the top of the big walnut-
tree, on a long branch that the wind rocks . . . the wind, the
darkness, the leaves . . . Fanchette comes and joins me up
there; each time I hear strong claws climbing up, with such
sureness! She mews in astonishment: 'What on earth are you
doing up in this tree? *I'm* made to be up here, but you . . . it
always shocks me a little!' Then she wanders about the little
branches, all white in the blackness, and talks to the sleeping
birds, ingenuously, in the hope they'll come and obligingly let
themselves be eaten – why, of course!

It's the eve of our departure. No work today. We took our
suitcases to school (a dress and a few underclothes; we're only
staying two days).

Tomorrow morning, we all meet at half past nine and go

123

off in old Racalin's evil-smelling omnibus which will cart us off to the station.

It's over. We returned from the main town yesterday, triumphant all except (naturally) poor Marie Belhomme, who was ploughed. Mademoiselle Sergent is thoroughly puffed-up over such a success. I must tell the whole story.

On the morning of our departure, we were piled into old Racalin's omnibus. He happened to be dead-drunk and drove us crazily, zigzagging from one ditch to the other, asking us if he was taking us all to be married, and congratulating himself on the masterly way he was bumping us about: 'Be going ever sho eashy, bean't I? . . .' while Marie uttered shrill cries and turned green with terror. At the station, they parked us in the waiting-room. Mademoiselle Sergent took our tickets and lavished tender farewells on the beloved who had come along to accompany her thus far. The beloved, in a frock of unbleached linen, and wearing a big, artless hat under which she looked fresher than a convolvulus (that bitch of an Aimée!) excited the admiration of three cigar-smoking commercial travellers who, amused at this departure of a batch of schoolgirls, had come into the waiting-room to dazzle us with their rings and their witticisms, for they found it irresistible to let out the most shocking remarks. I nudged Marie Belhomme to warn her to listen; she strained her ears but could not understand: however I couldn't draw diagrams to help her out! The gawky Anaïs understood perfectly well and wore herself out in adopting graceful attitudes and making vain efforts to blush.

The train puffed and whistled: we grabbed our suitcases and surged into a second-class carriage. It was overheated to the point of suffocation; luckily the journey only lasted three hours! I installed myself in a corner so as to be able to breathe a little and we didn't talk at all on the way, it was so entertaining to watch the landscape flying past. Little Luce, nestling beside me, slipped her arm under mine but I extricated myself, saying: 'Let go, it's too hot.' Yet I had on a dress of cream tussore, very straight and smocked like a baby's, clasped at the waist with a leather belt that was wider than my hand and had a square opening in front. Anaïs, brightened up by a red linen frock, looked her best; so did Marie Belhomme, who was in half-mourning, wearing mauve linen with a black flower-pattern. Luce Lanthenay had kept to her black uniform and wore a black hat with a red bow. The two Jauberts continued to be non-existent and drew out of their pockets some lists of questions that Mademoiselle Sergent, disdainful of this excessive zeal, made them put back again. They couldn't get over it!

Factory chimneys appeared, then scattered white houses that suddenly huddled closer together and became a crowd; the next moment, we were at the station and were getting out. Mademoiselle Sergent hustled us towards an omnibus and soon we were bumping along over grievous cobblestones, like cats' skulls, towards the Hôtel de la Poste. Idlers were strolling about the streets, which were gay with bunting, for tomorrow it was St Someone-or-other's day – a great local feast – and the Philharmonic would be in full blast in the evening.

The manageress of the hotel, Mme Cherbay, a fat, gushing woman who came from the same part of the country as Mademoiselle Sergent, fussed over us. There were endless staircases, then a corridor and . . . three rooms for six. That had never occurred to me! Who would they put to share with me? It's stupid; I hate sleeping with other people!

The manageress left us to ourselves, at last. We burst out chattering and asking questions; we opened our suitcases. Marie had lost the key of hers and was bewailing the fact: I sat down, tired already. Mademoiselle said ruminatively: 'Let's see, I must get you fixed up . . .' She stopped, trying to find the best way of installing us in pairs. Little Luce slid silently up to me and squeezed my hand: she hoped they would thrust us both into the same bed. The Headmistress made up her mind. 'The two Jauberts, you'll sleep together. You, Claudine, with . . .' (She looked at me in a pointed way but I neither flinched nor fluttered an eyelash) '. . . with Marie Belhomme, and Anaïs with Luce Lanthenay. I think that will work out quite well.' Little Luce was not at all of this opinion! She picked up her luggage with a crestfallen look and went off sadly with the gawky Anaïs to the room opposite mine. Marie and I settled ourselves in; I tore off most of my clothes so as to wash off the dust of the train and we wandered about ecstatically in our chemises behind the shutters that were closed because of the sun. A chemise, *that* was the only rational, practical dress!

There was singing in the courtyard. I looked out and saw the fat proprietress sitting in the shade with the hotel servants and some young men and girls; they were all bawling sentimental songs: 'Manon, behold the sun!' as they made paper roses and garlands of ivy to decorate the front of the building, tomorrow. The courtyard was strewn with pine-branches; the painted iron table was loaded with bottles of beer and glasses; the earthly paradise, in fact!

Someone knocked: it was Mademoiselle Sergent. I let her come in, she didn't embarrass me. I received her in my chemise while Marie hurriedly pulled on a petticoat, out of respect. However, she didn't look as if she had noticed it, and merely told us to hurry up: luncheon was ready. We all went downstairs. Luce complained about their room; it was lit from above, they hadn't even the resource of looking out of the window!

The hotel's set luncheon was bad.

As the written exam took place next day, Mademoiselle Sergent enjoined us to go up to our rooms and make one last final revision of what we felt weakest on. What point in being here just for *that*? I'd much rather have gone to see Papa's charming friends, the Xs, who were excellent musicians . . . She added: 'If you're good, tonight you shall come down with me after dinner and we'll make roses with Madame Cherbay and her daughters.' There were murmurs of joy: all my companions exulted. But not me! I felt no intoxication at the prospect of making paper roses in a hotel courtyard with that fat manageress who looked as if she were made of lard. Probably I let this be seen, for the Redhead went on, suddenly irritated:

'I'm not forcing anyone, naturally; if Mademoiselle Claudine thinks she ought not to join us . . .'

'Honestly, I *would* rather stay in my room, Mademoiselle. I'm afraid I'd be so totally useless!'

'Stay there, then, we'll do without you. But, in that case, I fear I shall be forced to take the key of your room with me. I am responsible for you.'

This detail had not occurred to me and I did not know what to reply. We went upstairs again and we yawned all the afternoon over our books, our nerves frayed with the suspense of waiting for tomorrow. It would have been much better for us to go out for a walk, for we didn't do any good, none at all . . .

And to think that tonight I was going to be locked in! Locked in! Anything that's in the least like imprisonment makes me rabid: I lose my head as soon as I'm shut up. (When I was a child, they could never send me to boarding-school because I used to fall into swoons of rage at realizing that I was forbidden to go out of the door. They tried twice when I was nine. Both times, on the very first night, I dashed to the windows like a stunned bird; I screamed, bit and scratched, then fell down unconscious. They had to set me at liberty again and I could only 'stick it' at this fantastic school in Montigny because there, at least, I didn't feel 'trapped' and I slept in my own bed at home.)

Certainly, I wasn't going to let the others see it, but I was sick with nervous tension and humiliation. I wasn't going to beg to be let off; she'd be far too pleased, that beastly Redhead! If she'd only leave me the key on the inside! But I wasn't going to ask her for anything at all, I didn't want to! I only prayed the night would be short . . .

Before dinner, Mademoiselle Sergent took us for a walk along the river: little Luce, quite overcome with pity, tried to console me for my punishment:

'Listen, if you asked her to let you come downstairs, I'm sure she would, if you asked her nicely . . .'

'Don't worry! I'd rather be triple-locked in for eight months, eight days, eight hours and eight minutes.'

'You're awfully silly not to want to! We'll make roses and we'll sing – and we'll . . .'

'Such pure pleasures! I shall pour some water on your head!'

'Ssh! Be quiet! But truly, you've spoilt our day. I shan't feel a bit gay tonight, because you won't be there.'

'Don't get sentimental. I shall sleep, I shall gather strength for the "great day" tomorrow.'

We dined again at the common table with commercial travellers and horse-dealers. The gawky Anaïs, obsessed with the idea of getting herself noticed, gesticulated wildly and upset her glass of wine and water over the white cloth. At nine, we went upstairs again. My companions armed themselves with little shawls against the coolness that might come later and, as for me – I went back into my room. Oh, I put a good face on it, but I listened with far from kindly feelings to the key that Mademoiselle Sergent turned in the door and carried off in her pocket . . . There, I was all alone . . . Almost at once, I heard them in the courtyard. I could have had an excellent view of them from my window but not for anything in the world would I have admitted my regrets by showing any curiosity. Very well, what then? There was nothing to do but go to bed.

I had already taken off my belt when, suddenly, I stood stock-still before the dressing-table in front of the communicating door that it blocked. That door opened into the neighbouring room (the bolt was on my side) and the neighbouring room gave on to the corridor . . . I recognized the finger of Providence in this, it was undeniable . . Never mind, come what might, I didn't want the Redhead to be able to triumph and say to herself: 'I shut her in!' I buckled on my belt again and put on my hat. I wasn't going to be so silly as to go into the courtyard, I was going to see Papa's friends, those charming hospitable Xs, who would give me a warm welcome. Ouf! How heavy that dressing-table was! It made me hot. The bolt was hard to push back, it needed exercise, and the door grated as it opened, but it *did* open. The room I entered, holding my candle high, was empty; there were no sheets on the bed. I ran to the door, the blessed door which was not locked and which opened angelically on to the adorable corridor . . . How easily one breathes when one is

128

not under lock and key! I mustn't let myself get caught! But there wasn't a soul on the stairs, not a soul at the reception-desk . . . everyone was making roses. Go on making roses, good people, go on making roses without me!

Outside, in the warm darkness, I laughed very softly; but I had to get to the X's house . . . The trouble was that I didn't know the way, especially at night. Pooh! I would ask. First of all, I resolutely followed the course of the river, then, under a lamp-post, I decided to ask a passing gentleman 'the way to the Place du Théâtre, please?' He stopped and leant down to have a good look at me: 'But, my lovely chid, allow me to take you there, you'll never find it all by yourself . . .' Botheration! I turned on my heels and fled precipitately into the shadows. At last I asked a grocer's boy, who was pulling down the iron curtain of his shop with a tremendous din, and then, after walking street after street, often pursued by a laugh or a cheeky call, I arrived in the Place du Théâtre. I rang the bell of the house I knew.

My entrance interrupted the trio for violin, 'cello, and piano which two fair-haired sisters and their father were playing: they all got up excitedly: 'You here? How? Why? All alone!' – 'Wait, let me explain and do forgive me.' I told them about my imprisonment, my escape, and the Certificate tomorrow; the little fair girls laughed like mad. 'Oh, that's funny! No one but you would think of such marvellous stunts!' Their Papa laughed too, indulgently: 'Come along, don't be frightened. We'll take you back, we'll obtain your forgiveness.' Thoroughly nice people!

So we went on making music, with no remorse. At ten o'clock, I thought I ought to go and I managed to persuade them to let only an old servant take me back . . . Nevertheless I wondered what on earth the peppery Redhead would say to me!

The servant came into the hotel with me and I discovered that my companions were still in the courtyard, occupied in crumpling up roses and drinking beer and lemonade. I could have returned to my room unnoticed but I preferred to stage a little effect so I presented myself modestly to Mademoiselle who leapt to her feet at the sight of me. 'Where have you come from?' With my chin, I indicated the servant accompanying me and she meekly produced her set speech: 'Mademoiselle spent the evening at the Master's with the young ladies.' Then she murmured a vague good night and vanished. I was left alone (one, two, three!) with . . . a fury! Her eyes blazed, her eyebrows knitted together till they touched, while my stupefied classmates remained standing, their half-finished roses in their hands. From Luce's brilliant glances and Marie's scarlet cheeks, and Anaïs's feverish appearance, it looked to me as if they were a little tight; of course, there was no harm in *that*. Mademoiselle Sergent did not utter a word; either she was trying to find adequate ones or else she was forcibly controlling herself so as not to explode. At last she spoke, but not to me. 'Let us go upstairs, it's late.' So it was in my room that she was going to burst out? Very well, then . . . On the stairs, all the girls stared at me as if I had the plague: little Luce questioned me with her imploring eyes.

In the room, there was, at first, a portentous silence; then the Redhead interrogated me with weighty solemnity:

'Where were you?'

'You know very well . . . at the X's . . . some friends of my father's.'

'How did you dare leave your room?'

'How? You can see for yourself. I pulled out the dressing-table that barred that door.'

'This is the most odious insolence! I shall inform your father of your monstrous behaviour. No doubt it will give him intense pleasure.'

'Papa? He'll say: "Good gracious, yes, that child has a passion for liberty", and he'll wait impatiently for you to finish your story so that he can eagerly bury himself again in the *Malacology of Fresnois*.'

She noticed that the others were listening and turned on her heels. 'Off to bed, all of you! If your candles aren't out in a quarter of an hour, you'll have me to deal with! As to Mademoiselle Claudine, she is no longer my responsibility and she can elope this very night, if she pleases!'

Oh! shocking! Really, Mademoiselle! The girls had dis-

130

appeared like frightened mice and I was left alone with Marie Belhomme who declared:

'It's absolutely true that they can't shut you up. But do stir your stumps a little so that she doesn't come back to blow out the candle.'

One sleeps badly in a strange bed and, besides, I glued myself all night against the wall so as not to brush against Marie's legs.

In the morning, they woke us up at half past five: we got up in a state of torpor and I drenched myself in cold water to rouse myself a little. While I was splashing, Luce and the lanky Anaïs came in to borrow my scented soap, ask for a corkscrew, etc. Marie begged me to start plaiting her chignon for her. They were an amusing sight, all those little creatures, still half-asleep and wearing next to nothing.

We exchanged views on ingenious precautions to take against the examinations. Anaïs had copied out all the history dates she wasn't sure of on the corner of her handkerchief (I should need a tablecloth!). Marie Belhomme had contrived to make a minute atlas which could be slipped into the palm of her hand. On her white cuffs, Luce had written dates, fragments of royal reigns, arithmetic theorems – a whole manual. The Jaubert sisters had also put down quantities of useful information on strips of thin paper which they rolled up in the tubes of their penholders. They were all very anxious concerning the examiners themselves; I heard Luce say: 'In arithmetic, it's Lerouge who takes the oral questions; in physics and chemistry, it's Roubaud . . . apparently he's an absolute beast; in literature, it's old Sallé . . .'

I broke in:

'Which Sallé? The one who used to be Principal of the college?'

'Yes, that's the one.'

'What luck!'

I was delighted that I was to be questioned by this extremely kind old gentleman whom Papa and I knew very well; he would be good to me.

Mademoiselle Sergent appeared, concentrated and taciturn at this zero hour before battle.

'You haven't forgotten anything? Let's be off.'

Our little squad crossed the bridge, mounted through various steep streets and lanes, and eventually arrived in front of a battered old porch, on whose door an almost-effaced inscription proclaimed it to be the Rivoire Institute. It had once been the Girls' Boarding-School, but had been deserted for the past two or three years on account of its decrepitude. (Why did they park us *there*?) In the courtyard that had lost half its paving-stones, some sixty girls were chattering vivaciously, in well split-off groups; the schools didn't mix with each other. There were some from Villeneuve, from Beaulieu, and from a dozen country-towns in the district; all of them clustered in little groups round their respective Headmistresses and making copious and far from charitable remarks about the other schools.

The moment we arrived, we were stared out of countenance and criticized from top to toe. I was singled out for particularly sharp scrutiny on account of my white dress with blue stripes and my big floppy lace hat which stood out against the black of the uniforms. As I smiled insolently at the candidates who were glaring at me, they turned away in the most contemptuous way imaginable. Luce and Marie flushed under the stares and shrank back into their shells: the gawky Anaïs exulted in the consciousness of being so hypercritically examined. The examiners had not arrived yet; we were merely marking time. I was getting bored. A little door without a latch yawned open on a dark corridor, lit at the far end by a luminous pane. While Mademoiselle Sergent was exchanging icily polite remarks with her colleagues, I slipped quietly into the passage: at the end was a glass door – or the remains of one – I lifted the rusty latch and found myself in a little square courtyard, by a shed. It was overgrown with jasmine and clematis, and there was a little wild plum-tree and all sorts of charming weeds, growing unchecked. On the ground – admirable find! – some strawberries had ripened and smelt delicious.

I promptly decided to call the others to show them these marvels! I went back to the playground without attracting attention and I informed my companions of the existence of this unknown orchard. After nervous glances at Mademoiselle Sergent who was talking to an elderly headmistress, at the door which had still not opened on the examiners (they sleep late, those chaps), Marie Belhomme, Luce Lanthenay, and the lanky Anaïs made up their minds, but the Jauberts refrained. We ate the strawberries, we plundered the clematis, we shook the plum-tree; then, hearing an even louder hullabaloo in the front courtyard, we guessed that our torturers had arrived.

As fast as our legs could carry us, we dashed back along the corridor; we arrived just in time to see a file of black-clad gentlemen, by no means handsome ones, entering the ancient building in solemn silence. In their wake, we climbed the staircase, the sixty-odd of us making a noise like a squadron of cavalry. But, on the first floor, they halted us on the threshold of a deserted study-room; we had to allow their Lordships to instal themselves. They sat down at a big table, mopped their brows, and deliberated. What about? the advisability of allowing us to enter? But no, I was certain they were exchanging observations about the weather and chatting about their trifling affairs while we were held back with difficulty on the landing and the stairs on to which we overflowed.

Being in the front rank, I was able to observe these great men: a tall, greying one with a gentle, grandfatherly expression – kind old Sallé, twisted and gouty, with his hands like gnarled vines – a fat short one, his neck swathed in a shot-silk cravat worthy of Rabastens himself – that was Roubaud, the terrible, who would question us tomorrow in 'science'.

At last, they decided to tell us to come in. We filled this ugly old room, with its indescribably dirty plaster walls, scored all over with inscriptions and pupils' names. The tables were appalling too, scarred with penknives and black and purple from inkpots upset over them in former days. It was shameful to intern us in such a hovel.

One of the gentlemen proceeded to allot us our places; he held a big list in his hand and carefully mixed all the schools, separating the girls from the same district as widely as possible, so as to avoid any communication between them.

(Didn't he realize one could always convey information?) I found myself at the end of a table, by a small girl, in mourning, with large, serious eyes. Where were my classmates? Far away, I caught sight of Luce who was sending me despairing signs and looks; Marie Belhomme was fidgeting about at a table just in front of her. They would be able to pass information to each other, those two weak vessels . . . Roubaud was going round distributing large sheets of writing-paper, stamped in blue on the top left-hand corner, and sealing-wafers. We all understood the routine; we had to write our names in the corner, along with that of the school where we had done our studies, then to fold over this corner and seal it. (The idea was to reassure everyone about the impartiality of the criticisms.)

This little formality over, we waited for them to be kind enough to dictate something to us. I looked about me at the little unknown faces, several of which made me feel sorry for them, they were already so strained and anxious.

Everyone gave a start; Roubaud had broken the silence and spoken: 'Spelling test, young ladies, be ready to take it down. I shall repeat the sentence I dictate only once.'

There was a great hush of concentration. No wonder! Five-sixths of these little girls had their whole future at stake. And to think that all of those would become schoolmistresses, that they would toil from seven in the morning till five in the afternoon and tremble before a Headmistress who would be unkind most of the time, to earn seventy-five francs a month! Out of those sixty girls, forty-five were the daughters of peasants or manual labourers; in order not to work in the fields or at the loom, they had preferred to make their skins yellow and their chests hollow and deform their right shoulders. They were bravely preparing to spend three years at a Training College, getting up at five a.m. and going to bed at eight-thirty p.m. and having two hours recreation out of the twenty-four and ruining their digestions, since few stomachs survived three years of the college refectory. But at least they would wear hats and would not make clothes for other people or look after animals or draw buckets from the well, and they would despise their parents. And what was I,

Claudine, doing here? I was here because I had nothing else to do and so that, while I was undergoing the ordeal of being questioned by these professors, Papa could mess about in peace with his slugs. I was also there 'for the honour of the School', to obtain one more Certificate for it, one more glory for this unique, incredible, delightful School . . .

They had crammed this dictation with so many participles and laid so many traps of ambiguous plurals and all the sentences were so twisted and inverted that the piece ended by making no sense at all. It was puerile!

I was pretty sure I had made no mistakes; all I had to do was to be careful about the accents, for they counted stray accents hovering in the wrong place over words as half-mistakes and quarter-mistakes. While I was reading it through again, a little ball of paper, very deftly aimed, landed on my exam sheet; the lanky Anaïs had written to me asking: 'Should there be an s to *trouvés*, in the second sentence?' She hadn't the faintest idea, that Anaïs! Should I lie to her? No, I disdained her own usual methods. Raising my head, I signalled an imperceptible 'Yes' and, calmly, she made the correction.

'You have five minutes for revision,' announced the voice of Roubaud; 'the handwriting test will follow.'

A second and larger ball of paper arrived. I looked about me: it came from Luce whose anxious eyes were seeking mine. But . . . but she was asking for four words! If I sent back the ball, I was sure it would get pinched. I had an inspiration, a really brilliant one: I took the black leather satchel containing pencils and charcoal (the candidates had to provide everything themselves) and, using a bit of plaster torn off the wall as chalk, I wrote down the four words that were worrying Luce. Then I suddenly lifted the satchel above my head, with its virgin side turned towards the examiners who, in any case, weren't paying much attention to us. Luce's face lit up; she made some hurried corrections: my neighbour, the girl in mourning, who had observed the scene, spoke to me:

'I say, you, aren't you frightened?'

'Not much, as you see. Got to help one another a bit.'

'Yes . . . of course. Still, I wouldn't dare. You're called Claudine, aren't you?'

'Yes. How did you know?'

'Oh, you've been "talked of" for quite a time. I'm from the school at Villeneuve; our mistresses used to say about you: "She's an intelligent girl but as impudent as a cock-sparrow and her tomboyishness and the way she does her hair set a very bad example. All the same, if she chooses to take the trouble to exert herself, she'll be a redoubtable competitor in the exam." You're known at Bellevue too; they say you're a bit crazy and more than a bit eccentric.'

'Charming women, your teachers! But they're more interested in me than I am in them. So tell them they're only a pack of old maids who are furious because they're running to seed. Tell them that from me, will you?'

Scandalized, she said no more. Besides, Roubaud was promenading his plump little pot-belly between the tables and gathering up our papers which he carried up to the others of his species.

Then he distributed other sheets of paper to us for the handwriting test and went off to inscribe four lines on the blackboard in a 'beautiful hand'.

Tu t'en souviens, Cinna, tant d'heur et tant de gloire, etc., etc. . . .

'Young ladies, you are asked to execute a line of thick cursive, one of medium cursive, one of fine cursive, one of thick round-hand, one of medium round-hand, one of fine round-hand, one of thick slanting-hand midway between round and cursive, one of medium, and one of fine. You have one hour.'

It was an hour of rest, that hour. The exercise was not tiring and they were not very exacting about handwriting. The round-hand and the slanting suited me all right because they almost amounted to drawing; my cursive is vile; my looped letters and my capitals have considerable difficulty in keeping the prescribed number of 'bodies' and 'half-bodies'. Never mind! I was feeling hungry when we got to the end of the period.

We fairly flew out of that depressing, musty room into the playground to rejoin our anxious teachers who were clustered in the shade that was not even cool. Promptly there was a torrential outburst of words and questions and laments: 'Did it go well? What was the subject for dictation? Did you remember the difficult phrases?'

'It was this – that – I put *indication* in the singular – *I* put it in the plural – the participle was invariable, wasn't it, Mademoiselle? I wanted to correct it, and then, after all, I left it – such a difficult dictation! . . .'

It was past twelve and the hotel was so far away . . .

I was yawning from starvation. Mademoiselle Sergent took us to a nearby restaurant, as our hotel was too far away to walk back there in this oppressive heat. Marie Belhomme wept and wouldn't eat, disheartened by three mistakes she had made (and every mistake took off two marks!). I told the Headmistress – who seemed to have forgotten all about my escapade of last night – our methods of communicating; she laughed over them, delighted, and merely cautioned us not to do too many rash things. During examinations, she egged us on to the worst kinds of cheating; all for the honour of the school.

While we were waiting for the period of French Composition, we were nearly all of us dozing on our chairs, overcome with heat. Mademoiselle was reading the illustrated papers and got up, after a glance at the clock: 'Come along, children, we must go . . . Try not to make yourselves out too stupid in the paper you're just going to do. And you, Claudine, if you're not marked eighteen out of twenty for French Composition, I'll throw you in the river.'

'I'd be cooler there, at least!'

What dolts these examiners were! The most obtuse mind would have grasped that, in this crushing heat, we should have written more lucid French essays in the morning. But not they. Whatever we were capable of, at *this* hour?

Though full, the playground was more silent than this morning and their Lordships were keeping us waiting again! I went off by myself into the walled garden: I sat down under the clematis, in the shade, and I closed my eyes, drunk with drowsiness . . .

There were shouts and calls: 'Claudine! Claudine!' I started up, only half-awake for I had been well and truly asleep, to find myself faced with Luce, looking terrified as she shook me to my feet and dragged me along with her. 'But you're crazy! But you don't know what's happening! My dear, we went in a quarter of an hour ago! They've dictated the synopsis of the essay and then at last Marie Belhomme and I plucked up courage to say you weren't there . . . they looked for you . . . Mademoiselle Sergent! out in the fields – and I thought maybe you were strolling about here . . . My dear, you aren't half going to catch it, up there!'

I dashed up the staircase, Luce after me: a mild hullabaloo arose at my entrance and their Lordships, red from a prolonged luncheon, turned towards me:

'You had forgotten all about it, Mademoiselle? Where were you?' It was Roubaud who had spoken to me, half amiable, half thoroughly nasty.

'I was in the garden over there. I was having a siesta.' A pane of the open window showed me my dim reflection; I had mauve clematis petals in my hair, leaves on my frock, a little green insect and a lady-bird on my shoulder; my hair was in wild disarray . . . The general effect was not unattractive . . . At least, I could only presume so, for their Lordships considered me at length and Roubaud asked me point-blank:

'You don't know a picture called *Primavera*, by Botticelli?'

Aha! I was expecting that.

'Yes, I do, Sir . . . I've been told that already.'

I had cut the compliment off short and he pinched his lips with annoyance. The black-coated men laughed among themselves; I went to my place, escorted by these reassuring words mumbled by Sallé, a worthy man, although he was too short-sighted to recognize me, poor fellow: 'In any case, you're not late. Copy the synopsis written on the blackboard, your companions have not begun yet.' There, there, he needn't have been frightened – I wasn't going to scold him!

Forward, French Composition! This little adventure had given me new heart.

'*Synopsis* – Develop the thoughts and comments aroused in you by these words of Chrysale: "What matter if she fails to observe the laws of Vaugelas," etc.'

By unheard-of-luck, it was not too stupid or too repellent a

138

subject. All round me I could hear anxious and agonized questions, for most of these little girls had never heard of Chrysale nor of *Les Femmes savantes*. They were going to make a splendid hash of it! I couldn't help laughing over it in advance. I prepared a little lubrication that wasn't too silly, adorned with various quotations to prove that one knew one's Molière tolerably well; it went quite well and I ended up by being quite oblivious to what was going on about me.

As I looked up in search of a recalcitrant word, I noticed that Roubaud was deeply absorbed in sketching my portrait in a little notebook. I was quite agreeable, and I resumed the pose without appearing to do so.

Paf! Yet another little ball had dropped. It was from Luce: 'Can you write me one or two general ideas? I'm in a hopeless mess, I'm simply wretched. I send you a kiss from the distance.' I looked at her and saw her poor little face was all blotched and her eyes red. She answered my look by a despairing shake of the head. I scribbled down everything I could for her on a bit of tracing-paper and launched the ball, not in the air – too dangerous – but along the ground in the aisle that separated the two rows of tables, and Luce deftly put her foot on it.

I titivated up my final version, developing the things that pleased them and displeased me. Ouf! Finished! I could have a look at what the others were doing . . .

Anaïs was working without raising her head, sly and secretive, her left arm curved over her paper to prevent her neighbour from copying. Roubaud had finished his sketch and it was getting late, though the sun was almost as high as ever. I was exhausted: tonight I would go to bed virtuously with the others, with no music. I went on observing the class-room; a whole regiment of tables in four ranks, extending right down to the end; the bent black figures of little girls of whom all one could see were smooth chignons or hanging plaits, tight as ropes; very few light dresses, only those of elementary schools like ours; the green ribbons at the necks of the boarders from Villeneuve made a splash of colour. There was a great hush, disturbed only by the faint rustle of paper being turned over or by a sigh of weariness . . . At last,

Roubaud folded up the *Fresnois Monitor*, over which he had dozed a little, and took out his watch: 'Time is up, young ladies. I will collect your papers!' A few faint groans were heard; the little things who hadn't finished took fright and asked for five minutes' grace which was granted them; then the examiners collected up the fair copies and left us. We all stood up, yawning and stretching, and, before we had reached the bottom of the staircase, the groups had re-formed. Anaïs rushed up to me:

'What did you put? How did you begin?'

'You bore me stiff . . . You don't imagine I learnt all that stuff by heart?'

'But your rough?'

'I didn't do one – only a few sentences that I licked into shape before I wrote them down.'

'My dear, you'll get a terrific scolding! *I've* brought my rough out to show to Mademoiselle.'

Marie Belhomme had also brought her rough out, so had all the others, including all the girls from other schools; it was always done.

In the playground, still warm from the sun that had now withdrawn from it, Mademoiselle Sergent was sitting on a little low wall, reading a novel: 'Ah! Here you are at last! Your roughs, quick . . . let me see that you haven't made too many howlers.'

She read them and pronounced on them: Anaïs's, it seemed, was 'not devoid of merit'; Luce's 'had good ideas' (mine, to be exact) 'not sufficiently developed'; Marie's was 'full of padding, as usual'; the Jauberts' essays were 'very presentable'.

'Your rough, Claudine?'

'I didn't do one.'

'My dear child, you must be mad! No rough on an examination day! I give up all hope of ever getting any rational behaviour out of you . . . Well, was your essay bad?'

'Oh no, Mademoiselle, I don't think it was bad.'

'It's worth what? Seventeen?'

'Seventeen? Oh, Mademoiselle, modesty forbids me . . . seventeen, that's a lot . . . After all, they ought to give me at least eighteen!'

My companions stared at me with envious spite. 'That Claudine, she isn't half lucky to be able to foretell what marks she'll get! Let's hasten to add that it's no merit to her, she's naturally good at it and that's that; she does French essays as easily as anyone else fries eggs' . . . and so on and on!

All about us, candidates were chattering in a shrill key, showing their roughs to their teachers, exclaiming, giving 'Ahs' of regret at having missed out an idea . . . twittering like little birds in an aviary.

That night, instead of escaping into the town, I lay in bed, side by side with Marie Belhomme, discussing this great day with her.

'The girl on my right,' Marie told me, 'comes from a convent school. Just imagine, Claudine, this morning, when they were giving out the papers before Dictation, she brought a rosary out of her pocket and was saying it under the table. Yes, my dear, a rosary with huge round beads, something like a pocket abacus. It was to bring her luck.'

'Pooh! If that doesn't do any good, it doesn't do any harm either . . . What's that I hear?'

What I heard, or thought I heard, was a tremendous row in the room opposite ours, the one where Luce and Anaïs slept. The door opened violently and Luce, in a brief chemise, flung herself into the room, distracted:

'Please, *please* . . . protect me . . . Anaïs is being so *horrid* . . .'

'What's she been doing to you?'

'First she poured water in my boots, and then, in bed, she kicked me and she pinched my thighs, and, when I complained she told me I could sleep on the bedside mat if I wasn't satisfied!'

'Why don't you call Mademoiselle?'

'All very well, call Mademoiselle! I went to the door of her room, she wasn't there, and the girl who was going along the passage told me that she'd gone out with the manageress . . . So now what am I going to do?' She was crying, poor kid! She was so small in her daytime chemise that showed her slim arms and her pretty legs. Decidedly, she would be much more

141

seductive quite naked and with her face veiled. (Two holes for eyes, perhaps?) But this was not the moment to speculate about such matters; I jumped out of bed and ran across to the room opposite. Anaïs occupied the middle of the bed, with the blanket pulled right up to her chin: she was wearing her wickedest face.

'Look here, what's come over you? Won't you let Luce sleep with you?'

'I don't say that. Only she wants to take up all the room, so I pushed her.'

'Rot! You pinched her – and you poured water in her boots.'

'Sleep with her yourself, if you want to. *I'm* not keen to.'

'Anyway her skin's much fresher than yours! True that's not saying much.'

'Oh go on, go on. Everyone knows you're as keen on the little sister as you are on the big one!'

'You just wait, my girl. I'm about to change your ideas.'

Only in my chemise as I was, I hurled myself on the bed, tore off the sheets and grabbed the lanky Anaïs by her two feet. In spite of the nails she silently dug into my shoulders, I dragged her down from the bed on her back, with her feet still in my hands and I called out: 'Marie, Luce, come and look!'

A little procession of white chemises ran in on bare feet and everyone was scared. 'Hi! Separate them! Call Mademoiselle!' Anaïs did not scream; she waved her legs and threw me devouring glances, desperate to hide what I was revealing as I dragged her along the floor – yellow thighs and a pear-shaped behind. I had such a frantic desire to laugh that I was frightened I would let go of her. I explained the situation:

'The fact is that this great gawk Anaïs I'm holding doesn't want to let little Luce sleep with her, that she pinches her, that she puts water in her boots and that I want to make her keep quiet.'

There was silence and a marked chill. The Jauberts were too prudent to lay the blame on either of us two. At last I let go of Anaïs's ankles and she got up, hastily pulling down her chemise.

'Into bed with you now, and try and leave this kid in peace or you'll get a thrashing that'll tan your hide.'

Still silent and furious, she ran to her bed, and huddled down into it, her face to the wall. She's an incredible coward and blows are the only thing in the world she fears. While the little white ghosts were scurrying back to their rooms, Luce got timidly into bed beside her persecutor, who was now as motionless as a sack. (My protégée told me next day that Anaïs had not stirred all night, except to fling her pillow on the floor out of rage.)

No one mentioned the story to Mademoiselle Sergent. We were far too busy thinking about the day that lay before us! Arithmetic and drawing tests and, in the evening, they would put up the lists of the candidates admitted to the oral exam.

After gulping down some chocolate, we made a hurried departure. It was already warm at seven o'clock. Feeling more used to things, we took our places ourselves and we chattered, with decent moderation, while we waited for their Lordships. Already we felt more at home; we slipped ourselves in without banging ourselves between the bench and the table; we arranged our pencils, pen-holders, india-rubbers and scrapers in front of us with an air of being quite accustomed to doing so; it was remarkably convincing, that air. We very nearly displayed personal fads.

The masters of our destinies made their entrance. They had already lost some of their prestige; the least shy ones looked at them tranquilly, as if they knew them quite well. Roubaud, who was sporting a pseudo-panama hat in which he obviously fancied himself very smart, became quite fidgety and said impatiently: 'Come along, young ladies, come along! We're late this morning, we must make up for lost time.' I liked that! So, just now, it had been our fault that they hadn't been able to get up in good time. At top speed, the tables were strewed with sheets of paper; hurriedly we sealed the corners to hide our names; hurriedly the revved-up Roubaud broke the seal of the big yellow envelope bearing the official stamp of the Examining Faculty and drew out of it the redoubtable statement of the problems:

143

'*First Question*. – A certain man bought 3½ per cent stock at the rate of 94 francs, 60 centimes, etc.'

I longed for hail to batter through his pseudo-panama! Operations on the Bourse drive me frantic: there are brokerages of ⅛ per cent that I have all the torment in the world not to forget.

'*Second Question*. – The Theory of Divisibility by 9. You have one hour.'

My goodness, that was none too much. Luckily I'd learnt divisibility by 9 for so long that it had finally stuck in my mind. Once again I'd have to put in order all the necessary and sufficing conditions – what a bore!

The other candidates were already absorbed and alert; a faint whispering of numbers, of muttered calculations, arose above the bent heads.

The first problem was finished. After having begun each calculation all over again twice (I so often make mistakes!) I obtained a result of 22,850 francs as the gentleman's profit: a pretty profit! I had confidence in this round and reassuring number but all the same, I wanted the support of Luce who conjures with figures in a masterly way. Several competitors had finished and I could see none but satisfied faces. In any case most of these little daughters of grasping peasants or shrewd seamstresses are gifted for arithmetic to an extent that has often amazed me. I might have asked my dark-haired next-door neighbour, who had also finished, but I mistrusted her discreet and serious eyes, so I therefore concocted a ball, which flew off and fell under Luce's nose, bearing the figure 22,850. The child joyfully signalled me a 'Yes' with her head. Satisfied, I then asked my neighbour: 'How much have you got?' She hesitated and murmured, with reserve: 'I've over 20,000 francs.'

'So've I, but how much more?'

'I told you . . . more than 20,000 francs . . .'

'All right, I'm not asking you to lend me them! Keep your 22,850 francs, you're not the only one who's got the right result. You're like a black ant – for various reasons!'

A few girls near us laughed; my interlocutor, not even offended, folded her hands and lowered her eyes.

144

'Have you finished, young ladies?' bellowed Roubaud. 'I restore you your liberty. Be in good time for the drawing test.'

We returned at five minutes to two to the ex-Rivoire Institute. What disgust, what a desire to run away the sight of that dilapidated prison induced in me!

In the best-lit part of the classroom, Roubaud had disposed two circles of chairs; in the centre of each, a stand. What were they going to put on it? We were all eyes. The examiner-cum-factotum disappeared and returned bearing two glass jugs with handles. Before he had placed them on the stand, all the girls were whispering: 'My dear, it's going to be frightfully difficult, because of being transparent!'

Roubaud announced:

'Young ladies, for the drawing test, you are at liberty to sit where you choose. Reproduce these two utensils (utensil yourself!) in line, the sketch in charcoal, the finished outline in drawing-pencil. You are strictly forbidden to use a ruler or anything whatever that resembles one. The sheets of cardboard that you should all have brought with you will serve you as drawing-boards.'

He had not finished speaking before I had already flung myself into the chair I had my eye on, an excellent place from which one saw the jug in profile, with the handle at the side. Several followed my example and I found myself between Luce and Marie Belhomme. 'Strictly forbidden to use a ruler for the lines of construction?' Nonsense, everyone knew what *that* meant! My companions and I had in reserve strips of stiff paper a decimetre long and marked off in centimetres, very easy to conceal.

We had permission to talk, but we made little use of it; we preferred to make grimaces, arm outstretched and one eye shut, in order to take measurements with the charcoal-holder. With a little dexterity, nothing was simpler than to draw the construction-lines with a ruler (two strokes which divided the sheet cross-wise and a rectangle to enclose the belly of the jug).

From the other circle of chairs came a sudden small commotion, stifled exclamations and Roubaud's severe voice: 'It wouldn't need more than that, Mademoiselle, to have yourself excluded from the examination!' It was a wretched girl, a skimpy, puny little thing, who had got caught, ruler in hand, and was now sobbing into her handkerchief. Roubaud became extremely nosy and examined us at close quarters, but the marked strips of paper had disappeared as if by magic. In any case, we didn't need them any more.

My jug was coming on beautifully, with a well-curved belly. While I was complacently considering it, our invigilator, distracted by the timid entry of the schoolmistresses who had come to find out 'if the French composition had been good on the whole', left us alone, Luce gave me a gentle tug: '*Do* tell me if my drawing's all right; it looks to me as if something's wrong with it.'

After examining it, I explained to her:

'Why, of course – it's got the handle too low. It makes it look like a whipped dog that's tucking its tail in.'

'What about mine?' asked Marie from the other side.

'*Yours* is hunchbacked on the right side: put an orthopaedic corset on it.'

'A what?'

'I'm telling you you ought to put some cottonwool on the left, it's only got "advantages" on one side. Ask Anaïs to lend you one of her false bosoms.' (For the lanky Anaïs inserts two handkerchiefs in the gussets of her stays and all our gibes haven't succeeded in making her decide to give up this childish padding.)

This back-chat threw my neighbours into a state of uncontrolled gaiety. Luce flung herself back in her chair, exposing all the fresh teeth in her little cat-like jaw as she laughed. Marie blew out her cheeks like the bellows of a bagpipe. Then suddenly they both stopped, petrified in the midst of their joy – for the terrible pair of blazing eyes belonging to Mademoiselle Sergent had cast a Medusa look at them from the far end of the room. And the session was concluded in irreproachable silence.

They put us out, feverish and noisy at the thought that, this very evening, we should read, on a big list nailed to the door,

146

the names of the candidates who had qualified for the Orals next day. Mademoiselle Sergent had difficulty in restraining us: we were making an intolerable noise chattering.

'Are you coming to look at the names, Marie?'

'Gracious, no! If I wasn't on it, the others would jeer at me.'

'*I'm* coming,' said Anaïs. 'I want to see the faces of those who haven't qualified.'

'And suppose you were one of them yourself?'

'All right then, I don't have my name written on my forehead. I'd know how to put on a beaming expression so that the others wouldn't look pitying.'

'That's enough! You're bursting my eardrums,' said Mademoiselle Sergent sharply. 'You'll see what you'll see – and take care I don't come alone, this evening, to read the names on the door. To begin with, we're not going back to the hotel; I've no desire to make that trek twice more; we'll dine at the restaurant.'

She asked for a private room. In the species of bathroom they allotted to us where the light fell drearily from above, our effervescence petered out. We ate like so many little wolves, without saying a word. Our hunger appeased, we took it in turn to ask, every ten minutes, what time it was. Mademoiselle tried vainly to calm our jangled nerves by assuring us there were too many entrants for their Lordships to have been able to read all the essays before nine o'clock; we went on seething all the same.

We did not know what to do with ourselves in this cellar! Mademoiselle Sergent would not take us out of doors; I knew why: the garrison was off duty at that hour and the red-trousered soldiers, out to cut a dash, did not stand on ceremony. Already on the way to dinner, our little band had run the gauntlet of smiles, tongue-clickings, and the sound of blown kisses; these manifestations had exasperated the Headmistress who had machine-gunned these audacious infantrymen with her scowls, but it would have needed more than that to reduce them to order!

The declining day, and our impatience, made us peevish and ill-natured; Anaïs and Marie had already exchanged spiteful remarks, their feathers ruffled like two fighting hens;

the two Jauberts appeared to be meditating on the ruins of Carthage and I had thrust little Luce away with a sharp elbow when she wanted to be cuddled. Luckily, Mademoiselle, whose nerves were almost as much on edge as ours, rang, and asked for some light and two packs of cards. Good idea!

The brightness of the two gas-jets restored our morale a little and the packs of cards made us smile.

'I say, let's play *trente-et-un*!''

'Come on, then!'

The two Jauberts did not know how to play! All right, they could go on reflecting the frailty of human destiny; we others were going to play cards while Mademoiselle read the papers.

We had quite fun. We played badly and Anaïs cheated. And, every now and then, we stopped in the middle of a game, our elbows on the table and our faces strained, to ask: 'Whatever time is it?'

Marie gave vent to the opinion that, as it was dark, we shouldn't be able to read the names; we should have to take matches with us.

'Silly, there'll be street-lamps.'

'So there will! . . . But suppose that, just in that very place, there wasn't one?'

'All right,' I said very low, 'I'll steal a candle from the candlesticks on the mantelpiece and you bring the matches . . . Let's go on playing . . . Knave of Clubs and two aces!'

Mademoiselle Sergent drew out her watch; we did not take our eyes off her. She stood up; we followed her example so abruptly that chairs fell over. All our excitement surged up again, we danced over to get our hats, and, while I was looking in the glass to put mine on, I pinched a candle.

Mademoiselle Sergent put herself to unheard-of trouble to prevent us from running; passers-by laughed at this swarm of girls which was forcing itself not to gallop and we laughed back at the passers-by. At last, the door glittered before our eyes. When I say glittered, I am using the word in a literary way . . . for, after all, there actually wasn't a lamp-post! In front of that closed door, a crowd of agitated shadows was screaming, jumping for joy or lamenting; they were our competitors from the other schools. Sudden, brief match-flares, soon extinguished, and flickering candle-flames lit up a great white sheet pinned to the door.

Nothing would stop us: we dashed forward, brutally shoving away the small, milling silhouettes; no one paid the least attention to us.

Holding the stolen candle as straight as I could, I read and divined, guided by the initials in alphabetical order: 'Anaïs, Belhomme, Claudine, Jaubert, Lanthenay.' All of us! All! What joy! And now came the verifying of the number of marks. The minimum of marks required was 45; the total was written beside the names, the detailed marks between two brackets. Mademoiselle Sergent, in ecstasy, transcribed in her notebook: 'Anaïs 65, Claudine 68 – what did the Jauberts get? 63 and 64, Luce 49, Marie Belhomme 44½. What? 44½? But you've not qualified then? Whatever's this you're telling me?'

'No, Mademoiselle,' said Luce, who had just gone up to verify. 'It's 44¾ . . . she's qualified with a quarter of a mark short . . . by a special favour of those gentlemen.'

Poor Marie, quite out of breath from the terrible fright she had just had, gave a long sigh of relief. It was decent of those chaps to have overlooked her quarter of a mark but I was afraid she would make a mess of the Oral. Anaïs, once her first joy was over, charitably held up a light for the new arrivals, while spattering them with melted wax, horrid girl!

Mademoiselle could not calm us, not even by dousing us with the cold water of this sinister prediction: 'You're not at the end of your troubles yet. I should like to see your faces tomorrow night after the Oral.'

With difficulty she got us back to the hotel, skipping about and singing in the moonlight.

And later on, when the Headmistress was in bed and asleep, we got out of our beds and danced, Anaïs, Luce, Marie and I (not the Jauberts, of course). We danced wildly, our hair flying, holding out our brief chemises as if for a minuet.

Then, at a fancied noise from the direction of the room where Mademoiselle reposed, the dancers of this unseemly quadrille fled with suppressed giggles and a rustling of bare feet.

*

The next morning, waking up too early, I ran in to scare the life out of the Anaïs–Luce couple which was sleeping in an absorbed, conscientious way. I tickled Luce's nose with my hair; she sneezed before she opened her eyes and her dismay woke Anaïs who grumbled and sat up, cursing me. I exclaimed, with immense seriousness: 'But don't you know what time it is? Seven o'clock, my dear, and the Oral's at half past.' I let them hurl themselves out of bed and put on their stockings and I waited till they'd buttoned up their boots before telling them it was only six, that I'd seen it wrong. This didn't annoy them as much as I'd hoped.

At a quarter to seven, Mademoiselle hustled us, hurried us over our chocolate, insisted on our casting a glance through our history summaries while we ate our slices of bread and butter and finally pushed us out into the sunlit street, completely dazed. Luce was armed with her pencilled cuffs, Marie with her tube of rolled-up paper, Anaïs with her miniature atlas. They clung to these little life-saving planks even more than yesterday for today they had to talk; talk to their Lordships whom they did not know; talk in front of thirty pairs of malicious little ears. Anaïs was the only one who looked cheerful; she did not know the meaning of intimidation.

In the dilapidated courtyard, there were far fewer candidates today; so many had fallen by the wayside between the written exam and the oral! (That was good; when they admit a lot to the written, they turn down a lot for the oral.) Nearly all of them looked pale, yawned nervously and complained, like Marie Belhomme, of a tight feeling in their stomachs . . . that disturbing stage-fright!

The door opened to admit the black-garbed men: we followed them silently to the room upstairs, stripped today of all its chairs. In each of the four corners, behind black tables (or rather, tables that had once been black) an examiner seated himself, solemn, almost lugubrious. While we were taking in this stage-setting, feeling both curious and fearful, as we stood massed in the doorway, embarrassed by the vast space we had to cross, Mademoiselle gave us a push: 'Go on! Go on, for goodness' sake! Are you going to take root here?'

150

Our group advanced more boldly, in a bunch: old Sallé, gnarled and shrivelled, stared at us without seeing us, he was so incredibly short-sighted; Roubaud was playing with his watch-chain, his eyes abstracted; the elderly Lerouge was waiting patiently and consulting the list of names; and, in the embrasure of a window, a fat lady, Mademoiselle Michelet, was enthroned, with sol-fa charts in front of her. I nearly forgot another one, the bad-tempered Lacroix, who was grumbling and furiously shrugging his shoulders as he turned over the pages of his books and seemed to be having a fierce argument with himself; the girls, terrified, were telling each other he must be 'an absolute beast'! He was the one who made up his mind to growl out a name: 'Mademoiselle Aubert!'

The said Aubet, an overgrown girl, limp and stooping, started like a horse, squinted and promptly became stupid. In her desire to do the right thing, she bounded forward, shouting in trumpet-like tones, and with a strong peasant accent: 'But here I be, Surr!' We all burst out laughing and that laugh we hadn't thought of repressing raised our spirits and cheered us up.

That bulldog of a Lacroix had frowned when the unfortunate girl had bellowed her 'But here I be!' of distress and had replied: 'Who's denying it?' As a result, she was in a pitiable state.

'Mademoiselle Vigoureux!' called Roubaud. *He* was taking the alphabet by the tail. A plump little thing hurried forward; she wore the white hat, wreathed in daisies, of the Villeneuve school.

'Mademoiselle Mariblom!' barked old Sallé, who thought he was taking the middle of the alphabet and was reading it all wrong. Marie Belhomme advanced, crimson, and seated herself on the chair opposite old Sallé; he stared at her and asked her if she knew what the Iliad was. Luce, just behind me, sighed: 'At least, she's begun – the great thing is to begin!'

The unoccupied competitors, of whom I was one, dispersed shyly, scattered themselves about the room and went to listen to their colleagues sitting on the stool of repentance. I myself went off to the examination of the Aubert girl to give myself a little entertainment. At the moment I approached, old Lacroix was asking her: 'So you don't know who married Philip the Handsome?'

Her eyes were starting out of her head and her face was red and glistening with sweat; her mittens revealed fingers like sausages: 'He married . . . no, he didn't marry . . . Surr, Surr,' she cried all of a sudden, 'I've forgotten. Everything!' She was trembling; big tears rolled down her cheeks. Lacroix looked at her, vicious as the plague. 'You've forgotten everything? With what remains, you get a nice zero.'

'Yes, yes,' she stammered. 'But it doesn't matter, I'd rather go off back home, I don't care . . .'

They took her away, hiccuping with great sobs. Through the window, I heard her outside, telling her mortified teacher: 'Honest I'd rather look after Dad's cows, so I would. An' I'll never come back here, I won't. An' I'll take the two o'clock train, so I will.'

In the classroom, her schoolmates were discussing the 'regrettable incident', grave and disapproving. 'My dear, can you imagine her being so idiotic! My dear, if they'd asked me a question as easy as that, I'd have been only too pleased, my dear!'

'Mademoiselle Claudine!'

It was old Lerouge who was asking for me! Ugh! Arithmetic . . . Luckily he looked like a kindly Papa . . . I saw at once that he wouldn't do me any harm.

'Let's see, my child, now could you tell me something about right-angled triangles?'

'Yes, Sir, though, actually, I don't much care for them.'

'Now, now! You make them out worse than they are. Let's see, construct me a right-angled triangle on this blackboard, and then you'll give it its dimensions and then you'll talk to me nicely about the square on the hypotenuse . . .'

One would have to be pretty determined, to get oneself ploughed by a man like that! So I was as meek as a lamb with a pink ribbon round its neck and I said everything I knew. Actually, it didn't take long.

'But you're getting along splendidly. Tell me, as well, how

one recognizes that a number is divisible by 9, and I'll let you off any more.'

I rattled off: 'sum of the digits . . . necessary condition . . . adequate condition.'

'You can go, my child, that's enough.'

I stood up with a sigh of relief and found Luce behind me. She said: 'You're lucky, I'm so glad you were.' She said it charmingly: for the first time, I stroked her neck without laughing at her. Goodness! It was me again! One hadn't time to breathe!

It was the porcupine, Lacroix; things were getting hot! I installed myself; he looked at me over the top of his eyeglasses and said: 'Ha! What was the War of the Two Roses?' After the names of the leaders of the two factions, I stopped dead.

'And then? And then? And then?'

He irritated me. I burst out:

'And then, they fought like ragamuffins for a long time, but that hasn't stuck in my memory.'

He stared at me, amazed. I'd get something thrown at my head in a moment!

'Is that how you learn history, my good girl?'

'Pure chauvinism, Sir. I'm only interested in the history of France.'

Incredible luck: he laughed!

'I'd rather deal with impertinent girls than stupefied ones. Tell me about Louis XV (1742).'

'All right. That was the period when Madame de la Tournelle was exercising a deplorable influence over him . . .'

'Good heavens! You're not being asked about that!'

'Excuse me, Sir, it's not my own invention, it's the simple truth . . . the best historians . . .'

'What d'you mean? the best historians . . .'

'Yes, Sir, I read it in Michelet – with full details!'

'Michelet! but this is madness! Michelet, get this into your head, wrote a historical novel in twenty volumes and he dared to call that the *History of France*! And you come here and talk to me of Michelet!'

He was excited, he banged on the table, but I stood up to him. The young candidates round us stood transfixed, not believing their ears; Mademoiselle Sergent had approached, gasping, ready to intervene . . . When she heard me declare:

'Anyway, Michelet's less boring than Duruy! . . .'

She flung herself against the table and protested in anguish:

'Sir, I implore you forgive . . . this child has lost her head: she will withdraw at once . . .'

He interrupted her, mopped his brow and panted:

'Let her alone, Mademoiselle, there's no harm done. I hold to my own opinions, but I'm all in favour of others holding to theirs. This young person has false ideas and bad reading-habits, but she is not lacking in personality – one sees so many dull ones! – Only you, my peruser of Michelet, try and tell me how you would go, by boat, from Amiens to Marseilles or I'll chuck you a 2 that will give you a painful surprise!'

'Leaving Amiens by embarking on the Somme, I go up . . . etc., etc., . . . canals . . . etc., and I arrive at Marseilles only after a period varying between six months and two years.'

'That isn't *your* business. Mountain-system of Russia, and step lively.'

Alas, I cannot say that I shine outstandingly in the knowledge of the mountain-system of Russia, but I got through it more or less except for some gaps which seemed regrettable to the examiner.

'And the Balkans . . . you're cutting them out, then?'

The man spat out his words like a fire-cracker.

'Certainly not, Sir, I was keeping them as a final titbit.'

'That's all right. Be off with you.'

People drew back rather indignantly to let me through. Those dear little pets!

I relaxed; no one had summoned me, so I listened with horror to Marie Belhomme who was answering Roubaud that 'to prepare sulphuric acid, you pour water on lime and then that begins to boil; then you collect the gas in a balloon-flask'. She wore the expression that always meant enormous howlers and boundless stupidities; her huge, long, narrow hands gripped the table; her eyes, like those of a brainless bird, rolled and glittered; she poured out monstrous ineptitudes with extreme volubility. There was nothing to be done; even if one had whispered in her ear, she wouldn't have heard!

154

Anaïs was listening to her too and enjoying herself with all her kindly soul. I asked her:

'What have you got through, already?'

'Singing, history, joggraphy.'

'Nasty old Lacroix?'

'Yes. What a swine! But he asked me easy ones, Thirty Years' War, the Treaties . . . I say, Marie's off the rails!'

'Off the rails seems to me putting it mildly.'

Little Luce, excited and astounded, came up to us:

'I've passed joggraphy, and history, I answered well . . . Oh, I *am* bucked!'

'Hullo, twirp! I'm going to have a drink at the pump, I can't hold out any longer. Anyone comin' too?'

Not one of them was; either they weren't thirsty or they were afraid of missing a summons. Downstairs, in a kind of parlour, I found the Aubert girl, her cheeks still blotched with red from her recent despair and her eyes swollen. She was writing to her family, at a little table, calm now and pleased to be going back to the farm. I said to her:

'Look here, didn't you *want* to know anything just now?'

She raised her calf's eyes.

'Makes me frightened, all that do, and gets me in ever such a state, it do. Mother sent me to boarding-school, father he didn't want it, he said I'd do best looking after the house like my sisters, and doing the washing and digging the garden. Mother, she didn't want it – it was her as they listened to. They made me ill, trying to make me learn – and you see how I come over today. I said as it would happen! Now they'll have to believe me!'

And she went on tranquilly writing her letter.

Upstairs, in the classroom it was hot enough to kill one. The girls, nearly all red and shiny (lucky I haven't any tendency to redness!), were scared and tense, straining their ears to hear their names called and obsessed with the idea of not making stupid answers. Wouldn't it soon be twelve o'clock so that we could go?

Anaïs returned from physics and chemistry; *she* wasn't red, how could she be red? I believe that, even in a boiling cauldron, she would remain yellow and cold.

'Well, everything all right?'

'Thank goodness, I've finished. You know Roubaud's taking English into the bargain: he made me read sentences and translate; I don't know why he squirmed when I read in English . . . isn't he idiotic?'

It was the pronunciation! Bother! It was pretty obvious now that Mademoiselle Aimée Lanthenay, who gave the lessons, did not speak English with excessive purity. And, as a result, any moment now that imbecile of a Professor was going to make fun of me because *I* didn't pronounce better! Still another delightful episode! I was enraged to think that idiot was going to laugh at me.

Midday at last. Their Lordships rose and we proceeded to the usual shindy of our departure. Lacroix, his hair bristling and his eyes starting out of his head, announced that the merry little party would begin again at 2.30. Mademoiselle sorted us out with difficulty from the swirling tide of chattering young things and took us off to the restaurant. She was still stiff with me on account of my 'odious' conduct with old Lacroix; but I didn't care! The heat weighed down on me; I was tired and mute . . .

Oh, the woods, the dear woods of Montigny! At that very hour, how well I knew how they hummed! The wasps and flies that tippled in the flowers of the limes and the elders made the whole forest vibrate like an organ; and the birds did not sing, for, at midday, they perched upright on the branches, seeking the shade, preening their feathers and peering into the undergrowth with bright, shifting eyes. I would be lying at the edge of the Fir Plantation from which I could see the whole town down there below me with the warm wind in my face, half dead with well-being and laziness.

. . . Luce saw me far away, completely in another world, and tugged my sleeve, giving me her most fetching smile. Mademoiselle was reading the papers; my classmates were exchanging sleepy scraps of conversation. I complained and Luce protested gently:

'And you never talk to me any more, either! All day we're passing exams, in the evening we go to bed and at meals

156

you're in such a bad temper that I don't know when to find you any more!'

'Perfectly simple! Don't look for me!'

'Oh, that's not a bit nice of you! You don't even notice all my patience in waiting for you, the way I put up with your always pushing me away . . .'

The gawky Anaïs laughed like a door that needed oiling and the little thing stopped, highly intimidated. All the same it is true that she has unshakeable patience. And to think that so much constancy won't avail her in the least; sad! sad!

Anaïs was pursuing an idea of her own: she had not forgotten Marie Belhomme's incoherent answers and, amiable bitch, she kindly asked the poor wretch who was sitting dazed and motionless:

'What question did they ask you in physics and chemistry?'

'It's of no importance,' growled Mademoiselle crossly. 'Whatever they asked her, she'll have given nonsensical answers.'

'I can't remember now,' said poor, flummoxed Marie. 'Sulphuric acid, I think . . .'

'And what did you say?'

'Oh, luckily I knew a bit, Mademoiselle; I said that you poured water on lime and that the bubbles of gas that form were sulphuric acid . . .'

'You said that?' articulated Mademoiselle, gritting her teeth as if she were longing to bite . . .

Anaïs gnawed her nails with delight. Marie, thunderstruck, did not utter another word and the Headmistress, rigid and red in the face, marched us off, walking very fast. We trotted behind her like little dogs, practically hanging our tongues out under the sun that beat down on us.

We no longer paid the least attention to our alien competitors and they did not look at us either. The heat and our jangled nerves had taken away all desire to show off and all animosity. The girls from Villeneuve School, the 'apple-greens' as we called them – because of the green ribbons round their necks, that appalling harsh green which is the special prerogative of boarding-schools – still put on prudish, disgusted airs when they came anywhere near us (why? we shall never know); but everyone was settling down and relaxing. Already we were thinking about our departure tomorrow morning and brooding deliciously on how we'd rile our rejected schoolmates, the ones who hadn't been able to enter on account of 'general weakness'. How the gawky Anaïs was going to preen and strut and talk about the Training College as if she owned it! Pooh! I hadn't enough shoulders to shrug.

The examiners reappeared at least; they were mopping their faces and looked ugly and shiny. Heavens, I should hate to be married in weather like this! The mere idea of sleeping with a man who was as hot as they were . . . (In any case, in summer, I should have two beds . . .) Moreover, the smell in that overheated room was appalling; it was obvious that a great many of those little girls were anything but fastidious about their underclothes. I would have done anything to get away.

I collapsed on a chair and vaguely listened to the others as I awaited my turn; I saw the girl, the luckiest one of all, who had 'finished' first. She had endured all the questioning; now she could breathe again as she crossed the room to the accompaniment of compliments, envious glances and cries of 'You're jolly lucky!' Soon another one followed her and joined her in the playground where the 'released' were resting and exchanging their impressions.

Old Sallé, slightly unbent by this sun which warmed his gout and his rheumatics, was taking a forced rest as the girl he was waiting for was occupied elsewhere. Suppose I risked a tentative assault on his virtue? Very quietly, I went up and sat down on the chair opposite him.

'Good morning, Monsieur Sallé.'

He stared at me, settled his glasses, blinked – and still did not recognize me.

'Claudine, you know?'

'Ah . . . fancy that! Good morning, my dear child! Is your father well?'

'Very well, thank you.'

'Well now, how's the exam going? Are you satisfied? Will you soon be finished?'

'Alas, I'd like to be! But I've still got to get through physics and chemistry, literature – which is your department – English and music. Is Madame Sallé well?'

'My wife's gadding about in Poitou; she'd do much better to be looking after me but . . .'

'Listen, Monsieur Sallé, now you've got me here, do get me over the literature.'

'But I haven't got to your name, not nearly! Come back a little later on . . .'

'Monsieur Sallé, whatever would it matter?'

'Matter? It would matter that I was enjoying a moment's respite and that I had thoroughly deserved it. And besides, it's not in the programme; we mustn't break the alphabetical order.'

'Monsieur Sallé, be a dear. You need hardly ask me anything. You know that I know much more than the syllabus demands about books that count as literature. I'm a bookworm in Papa's library.'

'Er . . . yes, that's true. I can certainly do that for you. I had intended to ask you what were the bards and the troubadours and the *Roman de la rose*, and so on.'

'You can set your mind at rest, Monsieur Sallé. The troubadours, I know all about *them*. I always see them in the poem of the little Florentine Singer, like this . . .'

I stood up and struck the pose; my body leaning forward on the right leg and old Sallé's green umbrella doing duty as a mandoline. Luckily we were quite alone in that corner! Luce stared at me from the distance and gaped with surprise. Poor gouty old man, it amused him a little and he laughed.

'And they wore a velvet cap and curly hair, very often even a piebald costume (in blue and yellow, it looks particularly well); their mandoline hung on a silken cord and they sang that little thing out of the *Passer-By*: "My sweet one, April's here." That, Monsieur Sallé, is how I see the troubadours. We have also the First Empire troubador.'

'My child, you're a little crazy but I find you refreshing. Just Heaven! What on earth can you possibly call troubadors of the First Empire? Speak very low, my little Claudine – if their Lordships saw us . . .'

'Ssh. The First Empire troubadors, I knew all about them from the songs Papa used to sing. Listen carefully.'

I hummed very softly:

'Burning with love, setting forth to the wars,
His helm on his head and his lyre in his hand,
A troubador sings to the maid he adores,
Looking his last on his dear native land:
"My country, she calls me,
My sweetheart enthrals me,
For love and for glory, I'd gladly be slain,
Such is the troubador's merry refrain."'

Old Sallé roared with laughter:
'Good Lord, how absurd those people were! Of course I know we shall be just as absurd in twenty years' time, but that idea of a troubador with a helmet and a lyre! . . . Run away quick, child, you'll get a good mark; kind regards to your father, tell him I'm devoted to him and that he teaches his daughter fine songs!'

'Thank you, Monsieur Sallé, good-bye. Thank you again for not asking me any questions. I won't say a word – don't worry!'

What a thoroughly nice man! This had slightly restored my courage and I looked so cheerful that Luce asked me:

'Did you answer well, then? What did he ask you? Why did you take his umbrella?'

'Ah! I'll tell you! He asked me very difficult things about the troubadors, about the shape of the instruments they used; luckily I happened to know all those details!'

'The shape of the instruments . . . no, honest, I shudder at the thought he might have asked me that! The shape of the . . . but it's not in the syllabus! I shall tell Mademoiselle!'

'Right, we'll make a formal complaint. Have *you* finished?'

'Yes, thanks! I've finished. I've got a hundred pounds weight off my chest, I assure you! I think there's only Marie left to go through it now.'

'Mademoiselle Claudine!' said a voice behind us. Aha! It was Roubaud. I sat down in front of him, decorous and reserved. He assumed a pleasant manner – he is the most

160

polished of the local professors – and I talked back, but he still had a grudge against me, vindictive creature, for having too hastily brushed aside his Botticellian compliment. It was in a slightly peevish voice that he asked me:

'You haven't fallen asleep under the leaves today, Mademoiselle?'

'Is that a question that forms part of the programme Monsieur?'

He gave a slight cough. I had made a shocking blunder to vex him. Well, it couldn't be helped:

'Kindly tell me how you would set about procuring yourself ink.'

'Good heavens, Sir, there are lots of ways: the simplest would be just to go and ask for some at the stationer's on the corner . . .'

'A pleasant joke, but not enough to obtain you lavish marks . . . Will you try and tell me what ingredients you would use to fabricate ink?'

'Nut gall . . . tannin . . . iron monoxide . . . gum . . .'

'You don't know the proportions?'

'No.'

'Pity! Can you tell me something about mica?'

'I've never seen it anywhere except in the little panes in the doors of stoves.'

'Really? Once more, a pity! The lead in pencils, what is it made of?'

'Graphite, a soft stone that is cut into thin rods and enclosed between two halves of a wooden cylinder.'

'Is that the only use of graphite?'

'I don't know any others.'

'As usual, what a pity! Only pencils are made with it?'

'Yes, but a great many are made; there are some mines in Russia, I think. People consume a fabulous quantity throughout the entire world, especially examiners who sketch portraits of candidates in their notebooks . . .'

(He blushed and fidgeted.)

'We will pass on to English.'

Opening a little collection of Miss Edgeworth's *Tales*, he said:

'Please translate a few sentences for me.'

'Translate, yes, but read . . . that's another matter!'

'Why?'

'Because our English mistress pronounces it in a ridiculous way. And I don't know how to pronounce it otherwise.'

'Pooh! What does that matter?'

'It matters that I don't like making a fool of myself.'

'Read a little, I'll pull you up at once.'

I read but in a very low voice, hardly articulating the syllables and I translated the sentences before I had uttered the last words. Roubaud burst out laughing, in spite of himself, at such eagerness not to display my deficiency in English and I felt like scratching his face. As if it were my fault!

'Good. Will you give me some instances of irregular verbs, with their form in the present tense and in the past participle?'

'To see, I saw, seen. To be, I was, been. To drink, I drank, drunk. To . . .'

'That's enough, thank you, Good luck, Mademoiselle.'

'Too kind of you, Sir.'

I discovered the next day that that hypocrite had given me extremely bad marks, three below the average, so that I would have been ploughed if my marks for written work, especially for French Composition, hadn't pleaded in my favour. Beware of these underhand men in pretentious neckties who stroke their moustaches and pencil your portrait while giving you surreptitious looks! It was true that I had annoyed him, but the fact remains that straightforward bulldogs like old Lacroix are worth a hundred of him!

Delivered from physics and chemistry as well as English, I sat down and busied myself with making my disordered hair look slightly more artistic. Luce made a bee-line for me and obligingly rolled my curls round her finger, kittenish and cuddling as usual! She certainly had courage, in a temperature like that!

'Where are the others, baby?'

'The others? Oh, they've all finished, they're down in the playground with Mademoiselle. And all the girls from the other schools who've finished are down there too.'

The room was, in fact, rapidly emptying.

That fat, kind Mademoiselle Michelot summoned me at last. She was red and exhausted enough to make Anaïs herself feel sorry for her. I sat down; she studied me with big, puzzled, good-natured eyes, without saying a word.

'You are . . . musical, Mademoiselle Sergent told me.'

'Yes, Mademoiselle, I play the piano.'

She threw up her arms and exclaimed:

'Then you know much more about it than I do.'

It was a cry from the heart; I couldn't help laughing.

'Dear me, now! Listen . . . I'm going to make you read at sight and that'll be all. I'll find you something difficult, you'll get through it without any trouble.'

The 'something difficult' she found was a fairly simple exercise which, being all in semiquavers, with seven flats in the key-signature, had seemed to her 'black' and redoubtable. I sang it *allegro vivace*, surrounded by a circle of admiring little girls who sighed with envy. Mademoiselle Michelot nodded her head, and, without further insistence, awarded me a 20 which made the audience turn green.

Ouf! So it was actually over! Soon I would be back in Montigny; I would return to school, run about the woods, watch the frolics of our instructresses (poor little Aimée, she must be languishing, all by herself!). I tore down to the playground; Mademoiselle Sergent was only waiting for me and stood up as soon as she saw me.

'Well! Is it all over?'

'Yes, thank the Lord! I've got twenty for music.'

'Twenty for music!' ·

My companions shouted the words in chorus, unable to believe their ears.

'It only needed that – that you should *not* have got twenty for music,' said Mademoiselle, with an air of detachment, but secretly flattered.

'All the same,' said Anaïs, annoyed and jealous, 'twenty for music, nineteen for French Composition . . . if you've got a lot of marks like those!'

'Don't worry, sweet child, the elegant Roubaud will have marked me extremely stingily!'

'Because?' inquired Mademoiselle, promptly uneasy.

'Because I didn't have much to say to him. He asked me what wood they made flutes out of, no, pencils, something of that sort, and then something or other about ink . . . and about Botticelli . . . Quite frankly, the two of us didn't "click".'

The Headmistress's brow darkened again.

'I should have been extremely surprised if you *hadn't* done something idiotic! You'll have no one but yourself to blame if you fail.'

'Alas, who knows? I shall blame it on Monsieur Antonin Rabastens – he has inspired me with a violent passion and my studies have suffered deplorably as a result.'

At this, Marie Belhomme clasped her midwife's hands and declared that, if she had a lover, she would not say it so brazenly. Anaïs looked at me out of the corner of her eye to find out if I were joking or not, and Mademoiselle, shrugging her shoulders, took us back to the hotel, lagging and dropping behind and dawdling so much that she invariably had to wait for someone at every turning. We had dinner; we yawned. At nine o'clock we were smitten again with the fever of going to read the names of the elect on the gates of that ugly Paradise. 'I shan't take any of you,' declared Mademoiselle, 'I shall go alone and you will wait here.' But there arose a concert of groans that she relented and let us come.

Once again we took candles as a precaution, but this time they were not needed; a benevolent hand had hung a big lantern over the white notice on which our names were inscribed . . . there, I'm going a little too fast in saying 'our' . . . suppose mine wasn't to be found in the list? Anaïs would have fainted from joy! Luckily in the midst of exclamations, shoves from behind and much clapping of hands, I read out: Anaïs, Claudine, etc . . . All of us, in fact! Alas, no, not Marie: 'Marie's failed,' murmured Luce. 'Marie's not on it,' whispered Anaïs, hiding her malicious delight with considerable difficulty.

Poor Marie Belhomme remained rooted to the spot, her face quite white, in front of the cruel sheet which she studied with her glittering, birdlike eyes huge and round: then the corners of her mouth pulled down and she burst into noisy tears . . . Mademoiselle took her away, annoyed; we followed, without giving a thought to the passers-by who looked back. Marie was moaning and sobbing out loud.

'Come, come, little girl,' said Mademoiselle. 'You're being unreasonable. You can try again in October, you'll have better luck . . . Why think, that gives you two more months to work in . . .'

'Oh, oh!' wailed the other, inconsolable.

'You'll pass, I tell you! Look, I promise you that you'll pass! Now are you satisfied?'

This affirmation did, indeed, have a happy result. Marie no longer did more than give little grunts, like a month-old puppy when you stop it from sucking the teat, and walked along dabbing her eyes.

Her handkerchief was wringing wet and she ingenuously wrung it out as we walked over the bridge. That bitch of an Anaïs said in an undertone: 'The papers announce a high rise in the river Lisse.' Marie, who had heard, burst into uncontrollable laughter mixed with the remains of sobs, and we all laughed wildly too. And, in a flash, the unstable head of the ploughed candidate had veered round to joy, like a weathercock; she thought how she was going to pass in October and became positively gay. And nothing seemed more appropriate to us, that heavy, sultry night, than to take a skipping-rope and skip and skip in the square (all of us, yes, even the Jauberts!) up till ten o'clock under the moon.

The next morning, Mademoiselle had already come round and shaken us in our beds at six o'clock, though the train didn't leave till ten! 'Get up, get up, you little ticks; you've got to pack your things and have your breakfast; you'll have none too much time!' She was throbbing with violent trepidation, her sharp eyes gleamed and sparkled; she hustled Luce who was staggering with sleep and pommelled Marie Belhomme who, in her nightdress and slippers, was rubbing her eyes without regaining any clear consciousness of the everyday world. *We* were all utterly exhausted but who would have recognized in Mademoiselle the duenna who had chaperoned us these last three days? Happiness transfigured her; she was going to see her little Aimée again. From sheer joy, she kept smiling beatifically at nothing in the omnibus that took us back to the station. Marie seemed a little melancholy about her failure, but I think it was only out of duty that she put on a contrite expression. And we chattered wildly, all at once, each one telling the story of her exam to five others who were not listening.

'Old thing!' screeched Anaïs. 'When I heard that he was asking me the dates of the . . .'

'I've forbidden you a hundred times to call each other "old thing",' broke in Mademoiselle.

'Old thing,' went on Anaïs under her breath, 'I only just had time to open my little notebook in my hand; the most terrific thing is that he saw it – cross my heart he did – and he didn't say a word!'

'Oh, you liar of liars!' cried the honest Marie Belhomme, her eyes starting out of her head. 'I was there, I was watching, he didn't see anything at all – he'd have taken it away from you . . . they certainly took the ruler away from one of the Villeneuve girls . . .'

'You'd better keep your mouth shut! Or run along and tell Roubaud that the Dog's Grotto is full of sulphuric acid!'

Marie hung her head, turned red and began to cry again at the remembrance of her misfortunes. I made the gesture of opening an umbrella and Mademoiselle once more emerged from her 'delicious anticipation':

'Anaïs, you're a pest! If you torment one single one of your companions, I'll make you travel alone in a separate compartment.'

'The smoking compartment, naturally,' I observed.

'*You* were not being asked your opinion. Pick up your bags and wraps, don't stand there like stuffed dummies!'

Once in the train, she paid no more attention to us than if we did not exist; Luce went to sleep, with her head on my shoulder; the Jauberts became absorbed in the contemplation of the fields that slipped past and of the white and dappled sky; Anaïs bit her nails; Marie declined into a doze, along with her affliction.

At Bresles, the last station before Montigny, we began to fidget a little; ten minutes more and we should be there.

Mademoiselle pulled out her little pocket-mirror and verified the set of her hat, the disorder of her rough frizzy red hair, the cruel crimson of her lips. Absorbed and palpitating with excitement, her expression was almost demented. Anaïs pinched her cheeks in the wild hope of bringing a faint touch of red to them; I put on my immense, riotous hat. For whom we were taking so much pains? Not for Mademoiselle Aimée, certainly, in the case of us small fry . . . Oh, well! for no one, for the station officials, for the omnibus-driver, old Racalin, a sixty-year-old drunkard, for the half-wit who sold the papers, for the dogs who would be trotting along the road.

There was the Fir Plantation, and the Bel Air Wood, and then the common, and the goods station; then, at long last, the brakes squeaked! We jumped out behind Mademoiselle who had already rushed to her little Aimée, who was hopping gaily about on the platform. She had crushed her in such a fierce embrace that the frail assistant-mistress had suddenly turned red, stifled by it. We ran up to her and welcomed her in the manner of good little schoolgirls: '. . . 'morning, Mmmselle! . . . H'are you, Mmmmselle?'

As it was fine and we were in no hurry, we stuffed our suitcases into the omnibus and returned on foot, strolling the whole way between the high hedges where milkwort blossomed, blue and winey pink, and *Ave Marias* with their flowers like little white crosses. Happy to be off the leash, to have no French History to revise or maps to colour, we ran in front of and behind those ladies who walked arm in arm, close together and keeping in perfect step. Aimée had kissed her sister and given her a tap on the cheek, saying: 'There, you see now, little canary-bird, one gets through somehow, in spite of everything!' And, after that, she had only eyes and ears for her tall friend.

Disappointed once again, poor Luce attached herself to my person and followed me like a shadow, muttering jeers and threats: 'It's truly worth while splitting one's head to get compliments like that! . . . What a couple of guys those two look; my sister hanging on the other like a basket! . . . In front of all the people going by, it's enough to make you weep!' They couldn't have cared less about the people going by.

167

Triumphal return! Everyone knew not only where we came from but the results of the examination which Mademoiselle had telegraphed: people were standing in their doorways and made friendly signs to us ... Marie felt her distress increasing and effaced herself as much as possible.

The fact of having left the School for a few days made us see it more clearly on returning to it. It was finished, perfect to the last detail, white and spotless. The Town Hall stood in the middle, flanked by the two schools, boys' and girls'; there lay the big playground, whose cedars they had mercifully spared, with its small, formal, typically French clumps of shrubs, and the heavy iron gates – far too heavy and too redoubtable – that shut us in. There stood the water-closets with six compartments, three for the big girls, three for the little ones (in a touching concession to modesty, the big girls' lavatories had full doors and the little ones' half-doors); upstairs were the handsome dormitories whose shining window-panes and white curtains were visible from outside. The unfortunate ratepayers would be paying for it for years to come. Anyone might think it was a barracks, it was so handsome!

The girls gave us a noisy welcome. Since Mademoiselle Aimée had kindly confided the supervision of her own pupils and that of the First Class to the chlorotic Mademoiselle Griset during her little trip to the station, the classrooms were strewn with papers, and littered with sabots that had been used as missiles and the cores of wind-fallen apples ... At a frown from Mademoiselle Sergent, everything was restored to order; creeping hands picked up the apple-cores and feet stretched out and silently resumed possession of the scattered sabots.

My stomach was crying out and I went off to lunch, delighted to see Fanchette again, and the garden, and Papa; my white Fanchette, who had been baking herself and growing thinner in the sunshine, welcomed me with sharp, surprised mews; the green garden, neglected and overgrown with plants which had strained upward and grown immensely tall to find the sunlight the great trees hid from them; and Papa who welcomed me with a hearty, affectionate slap in the hollow under my shoulder:

'What on earth's become of you? I never see you these days!'

'But, Papa, I've just come back from passing my exam.'

'What exam?'

I assure you there is no one like him! Obligingly, I recounted to him the adventures of the last few days, while he tugged his great red and white beard. He seemed pleased. No doubt, his experiments in cross-breeding slugs had furnished him with unhoped-for results.

I allowed myself four or five days of rest and of wandering over to the Matignons where I found Clare, my co-First Communicant, dripping with tears because her lover had just left Montigny without even deigning to inform her. In a week she will possess another fiancé who will leave her at the end of three months; she is not cunning enough to hold the boys and not practical enough to get herself married. And, as she obstinately insists on remaining virtuous, this may go on for a long time.

Meanwhile, she was looking after her twenty-five sheep, a slightly comic-opera, slightly absurd little shepherdess, with the big mushroom hat that protected her complexion and her chignon (the sun fades one's hair, my dear!), her tiny blue apron embroidered in white, and the white novel, with its title *En Fête!* lettered in red, that she concealed in her basket. (It was I who had lent her the works of Auguste Germain to initiate her into Life! Alas, maybe I shall be responsible for all the appalling errors she'll commit.) I was convinced that she found herself poetically unhappy – a pathetic, deserted fiancée – and that, when she was by herself, she delighted in assuming nostalgic poses, 'her arms dropped, like useless weapons', or her head bowed, half-buried under her dishevelled hair. While she was telling me the meagre news of the past four days, along with her misfortunes, it was I who kept an eye on the sheep and urged the bitch after them: 'Fetch them, Lisette! Fetch them over there!' and I who uttered the warning 'Prrr . . . my beauty!' to stop them from touching the oats: I'm used to it.

'When I found out what train he was leaving by,' sighed Claire, 'I arranged to leave my sheep with Lisette and I went

169

down to the level crossing. At the barrier, I waited for the train – it doesn't go too fast there because it's uphill. I saw him, I waved my handkerchief, I blew him kisses, I *think* he saw me . . . Listen, I'm not certain, but it looked to me as if his eyes were red. Perhaps his parents forced him to come back home . . . Perhaps he'll write to me . . .'

Keep it up, romantic little thing, hope costs nothing. If I tried to dissuade you, you wouldn't believe me.

After five days of loafing about the woods, scratching my arms and legs on brambles, bringing home armfuls of wild pinks, cornflowers and campions, and eating bitter wild cherries and gooseberries, curiosity seized me again and I felt a homesick longing for the School. So I went back to it again.

I found them all – that is the big ones – sitting on benches in the shade, working lazily at 'exhibition pieces'; the little ones, under the covered-in part, were in process of splashing each other at the pump; Mademoiselle was in a wicker armchair, her Aimée at her feet on an inverted flower-box, lounging and whispering. At my arrival, Mademoiselle Sergent started and swung round in her seat.

'Ah, there you are! That's lucky! You've certainly taken your time! Mademoiselle Claudine runs wild in the fields without giving a though to the fact that the prizegiving is approaching and that the pupils don't know a note of the part-song they're supposed to be singing at it!'

'But . . . isn't Mademoiselle Aimée a singing-teacher then? Isn't Monsieur Rabastens (Antonin) one either?'

'Don't talk nonsense! You know perfectly well that Mademoiselle Lanthenay can't sing, her voice is too delicate to permit her to. As to Monsieur Rabastens, apparently they've been gossiping in the town about his visits and his singing-lessons. Good heavens, what a filthy hole this is for tittle-tattle! The long and short of it is, he won't be coming back. We can't do without you for the part-songs and you take advantage of the fact. This afternoon, at four o'clock, we will divide up the parts and you will copy out the verses on the blackboard.'

'*I'm* perfectly willing. What's the song this year?'

'The *Hymn to Nature*. Marie, go and get it – it's on my desk. Claudine is going to begin to din it into you.'

It was a chorus in three parts, the typical kind of thing that schoolgirls sing. The sopranos twittered earnestly:

> *'O'er the distant fields they ring,*
> *As the morning hymn they sing,*
> *Echoing sweetly to the sky . . .'*

Meanwhile, the mezzos, echoing the rhymes in 'ing', repeat 'ding, ding, ding' to imitate the Angelus bell. The audience would love it.

So that delightful life was about to begin; a life consisting in shouting myself hoarse, in singing the same tune three hundred times over, in returning home voiceless, in losing my temper with those little girls who were congenitally lacking in the faintest sense of rhythm. If at least they gave me a present for doing all this!

Anaïs, Luce, and a few others luckily had a good aural memory and, after the third repetition, could follow me with their voices. We stopped because Mademoiselle said: 'Enough for today' – it would have been too cruel to make us sing for long in that African temperature.

'And, one other thing,' added Mademoiselle. 'It's forbidden to hum the *Hymn to Nature* between lessons. Otherwise you'll murder it, you'll distort it out of all knowledge and you'll be incapable of singing it properly at the prizegiving. Get on with your needlework now and don't let me hear you talking too loud.'

They kept us big ones out of doors so that we could execute in greater comfort the marvellous pieces of needlecraft destined for the exhibition of *hand work*! (Could these works be done in any way except 'by hand'? I don't know of any 'foot work'.) For, after the distribution of prizes, the entire town would come and admire the display of our work. Two classrooms would be filled with samples of lace, tapestry, and beribboned lingerie laid out on the study-tables. The walls would be hung with open-work curtains, crochet bedspreads mounted on coloured linings, bedside rugs of green wool

171

moss (in brushed-up knitting) dotted with imitation red and pink flowers, also in wool and with chimney-piece borders in embroidered plush . . . These grown-up little girls liked the underclothes they displayed to be glamorous, so their main exhibits consisted of sumptuous pieces of lingerie – batiste chemises embroidered with tiny flowers, with marvellous yokes; frilly drawers gartered with ribbons; camisoles scalloped top and bottom – all displayed over linings of red, blue, and mauve paper with labels on which the maker's name was inscribed in beautiful round handwriting. All along the walls were ranged stools worked in cross-stitch on which reposed either the horrible cat whose eyes were made of four green stitches with a black one in the middle or the dog with the crimson back and the purplish paws, from whose mouth lolled a turkey-red tongue.

Obviously it was the underclothes that principally interested the boys who came, like everyone else, to see the exhibition. They lingered over the flowered chemises and the beribboned knickers, nudged each other, laughed and whispered monstrous comments.

It is only fair to say that the Boys' School boasted its own exhibition, rivalling our own. If they did not offer exciting lingerie for public admiration, they displayed other marvels; cleverly-turned table-legs, twisted columns (my dear! they're the most difficult of all), samples of woodwork in 'dovetailing', cardboard boxes dripping with glue, and, above all, clay models – the joy of the Headmaster who modestly christens this room *Sculpture Section* – models which claim to reproduce the friezes of the Parthenon and other bas-reliefs but are all blurred, bloated and pitiable. The *Drawing Section* is no more consoling: the heads of the Brigands of the Abruzzi squint, the King of Rome has a boil, Nero grimaces horribly, and President Loubet in a tricolour frame (woodwork and paste-board combined) obviously wants to be sick (because he's thinking about his minister, explains Dutertre, still furious at not being a Deputy). On the walls, grubby wash-drawings, architectural plans, and the 'anticipated (*sic*) general view of the Exhibition of 1900' – a water-colour which deserves the prize of honour.

So, during the time that still separates us from the holidays, we shall leave all our books on the shelf, we shall work lazily in the shade of the walls, incessantly washing our hands – a pretext to go for a stroll – so as not to stain light wools and white fabrics – with damp fingers. All I am exhibiting is three pink lawn chemises, cut like a baby's, with matching knickers – closed ones. This last detail scandalizes my companions who unanimously find it 'indecent' – on my word of honour!

I installed myself between Luce and Anaïs who herself was sitting next to Marie Belhomme for, from force of habit, we keep together in a little group. Poor Marie! She had to work again for the exam in October . . . Since she was fretting to death in the classroom, Mademoiselle took pity on her and let her come with us; she sat there reading Atlases and Histories of France; when I say 'reading' – her book was open on her knees, she bent her head and glanced sideways in our direction, straining her ears to catch everything we said. I could foresee the result of the October exam!

'I'm parched with thirst! Have you got your bottle?' Anaïs asked me.

'No, didn't think of bringing it, but Marie's sure to have hers.'

Still another of our immutable, absurd customs, those bottles. As soon as the weather turned really hot, it was agreed that the water in the pump became undrinkable (it is at any season), and each one brought along a bottle of some cool drink at the bottom of her little basket – sometimes in her leather satchel or her canvas bag. There was great rivalry as to who could produce the most fantastic mixture and the most unnatural liquid. No cocoa, that was for the baby class! For us water mixed with vinegar which blanches the lips and gnaws at the stomach; acid lemonades; mint drinks, confected oneself with the fresh leaves of the plant; brandy, pinched from home and thickened with sugar; the astringent juice of green gooseberries that made one's mouth water. The lanky Anaïs bitterly deplored the departure of the chemist's daughter who at one time used to provide us with bottles of spirits of peppermint diluted with far too little water, or sometimes with a patent concoction called eau de Botot. I myself, being a simple nature, confined myself to drinking white wine with a dash of Seltzer water, sugar, and a little lemon. Anaïs indulged too freely in vinegar and Marie in extract of liquorice, so concentrated that it was almost black.

As the use of bottles was forbidden, each one, I repeat, brought her own, stoppered with a cork through which was thrust a quill. This arrangement allowed us to drink by bending forward on the pretext of picking up a cotton-reel, without displacing the bottle lying in its basket, its beak sticking out. At the little quarter-of-an-hour recreation (at half past nine and half past three), everyone rushed to the pump to pour water over the bottles and cool them a little. Three years ago, a little girl fell down with her bottle and blinded herself in one eye; her eye is all white now. After this accident, they confiscated all the receptacles, every single one, for the space of a week . . . then someone brought hers back, an example followed by someone else the next day . . . and, a month later, the bottles were functioning regularly again. Perhaps Mademoiselle did not know of this accident which happened long before her arrival – or else she preferred to shut her eyes so that we should leave her in peace.

Nothing has been happening, to tell the truth. The heat has taken away all our high spirits. Luce besieges me less with her importune caresses; inclinations to quarrel hardly arise before they die down at once; it is general slackness, of course, and the sudden storms of July that catch us unawares in the playground and sweep us away under tremendous downpours of hail. An hour later, the sky is cloudless.

We played a wicked joke on Marie Belhomme, who had boasted of coming to school without any drawers on, on account of the heat.

There were four of us, one afternoon, sitting on a bench in the following order:

Marie – Anaïs – Luce – Claudine.

After having had my plan duly explained to them in undertones, my two neighbours got up to wash their hands and the

174

middle of the bench remained empty, leaving Marie at one end and me at the other. She was half asleep over her arithmetic. I got up suddenly; the bench tipped over: Marie, startled awake, fell, her legs in the air, with one of those squawks like a slaughtered hen which are her personal speciality, and showed us . . . that she was, indeed, wearing no drawers. There was an outburst of howls and tremendous laughs; the Headmistress wanted to lecture us but could not, being in fits of laughter herself. Aimée Lanthenay preferred to take herself off so as not to present her pupils with the sight of herself writhing like a poisoned cat.

Dutertre had not been here for ages. He was said to be at some bathing-resort where he was basking in the sun and flirting (but where did he get the money?). I could just see him in white flannels, wearing belts that were too broad and shoes that were too yellow; he adores those rather flashy get-ups. He would look very much of a flashy adventurer himself in those light colours – his face too sun-tanned and his eyes too bright – with his pointed teeth and his black moustache that has a rusty look as if it has been singed. I have never given another thought to his sudden attack in the glass-paned corridor; the impression had been sharp, but short – and besides, with him, one knows perfectly well that it means nothing! I am probably the three hundredth little girl he has tried to lure to his house; the incident is of no interest either to him or to me. It would have been if the attempt had succeeded, that's all.

Already, we were giving a great deal of thought to what we should wear for the prizegiving. Mademoiselle was getting herself a black silk dress embroidered by her mother, an exquisite needlewoman, who was working a design all over it, in satin-stitch; a pattern of big bundles of flowers and slender garlands that ran round the hem of the skirt and branches that climbed over the bodice – all in subtle, muted shades of violet silk. It was an extremely distinguished affair, a little 'old-ladyish' perhaps, but impeccably cut. Always dressed in dark, simple things, the chic of our Headmistress's clothes eclipses all the lawyers' and tax-collectors' and shopkeepers' and retired businessmen's wives' in the place! It is her little

175

revenge – the revenge of an ugly woman with an excellent figure.

Mademoiselle Sergent was also concerned about dressing her little Aimée charmingly for this great day. They had ordered samples of stuff from the Louvre and the Bon Marché and the two friends, deeply absorbed, made their selection together in our presence, in the playground where we sat working in the shade. I thought that this was going to be a dress that would not cost Mademoiselle Aimée much; really, she would be very wrong to act otherwise. It was not with her seventy-five francs a month – from which she had to deduct thirty francs for her board (which she did not pay), another thirty for her sister's (which she saved), and twenty francs she sent to her parents, as I knew from Luce – it was not, I declare, with these emoluments that she would pay for the charming dress of white mohair of which I had seen the pattern.

Among the schoolgirls, it was very much the thing not to seem in the least concerned about what one was going to wear for the prizegiving. All of them were brooding over it a month in advance and tormenting their Mamas to be allowed ribbons or lace or at least alterations which would bring last year's dress up to date – but it was considered good taste to say nothing about it. We asked each other with detached curiosity, as if out of politeness: 'What's your dress going to be like?' And we appeared hardly to listen to the answer, made in the same off-hand contemptuous tone.

The gawky Anaïs had asked me the routine question, her eyes elsewhere and her face vacant. With an absent-minded look, and sounding quite indifferent, I explained: 'Oh, nothing startling . . . white muslin . . . a crossed fichu on the bodice, with the neck cut down to a point . . . and Louis XV sleeves with a muslin frill, stopping at the elbows . . . That's all.'

We were always all in white for the prizegiving, but the dresses were trimmed with light ribbons; these rosettes, bows and sashes whose colour, which we insisted on changing every year, greatly preoccupied us.

'The ribbons?' inquired Anaïs in an artificial manner.

(I had been expecting that.)

'White too.'

'My dear, a real bride then! You know, lots of them are going to look as black in all that white as fleas on a sheet.'

'True. Luckily, white suits me quite well.'

(Fume, dear child! Everyone knows that with your yellow skin, you're forced to put red ribbons or orange ones on your white frock so as not to look like a lemon.)

'What about you? Orange ribbons?'

'Goodness, no! I had *them* last year! Louis XV ribbons, striped, in two materials, faille and satin, ivory and scarlet. My dress is cream wool.'

'Me,' announced Marie Belhomme, who had not been asked anything. 'It's white muslin with periwinkle-blue ribbons, a mauvey blue, awfully pretty!'

'Me,' said Luce, as usual, nestling in my skirts or couched in my shadow, 'I've got the dress, only I don't know what ribbons to put on it; Aimée would like them blue . . .'

'Blue? Your sister's a dolt, saving the respect I owe her. With green eyes like yours, one doesn't choose blue ribbons – that sets one's teeth on edge. The hat-shop in the square sells very pretty ribbons, in green and white glacé . . . your dress is white?'

'Yes . . . white muslin.'

'Good! Now, bully your sister into buying you green ribbons.'

'No need to. I'm the one who's buying them.'

'Better still. You'll see, you'll look charming; there won't be three who'll dare risk green ribbons, they're too difficult to wear.'

That poor kid! At the least kind thing I say to her without meaning to, her face lights up . . .

Mademoiselle Sergent, in whom the forthcoming exhibition inspired certain anxieties, hustled us and hurried us up; it snowed punishments, punishments that consisted in doing twenty centimetres of lace, a metre of hem or twenty rows of knitting after class. She herself was working, too, at a pair of magnificent muslin curtains which she embroidered very prettily indeed: when her Aimée left her time to. That charming sluggard of an Assistant, lazy as a cat as she is, sighed and yawned over fifty tapestry stitches, in front of all the pupils and Mademoiselle told her, without daring to scold her, that 'it was a deplorable example to us'. Whereupon the *in*subordinate tossed her work in the air, looked at her friend with sparkling eyes and flung herself on her, nibbling her hands. The big ones smiled and nudged each other; the little ones did not raise an eyebrow.

A large paper, bearing the seal of the Prefecture and the stamp of the Town Hall, which Mademoiselle found in the letter-box, has greatly disturbed this morning which happens, for once, to be cool. All heads are busy about it – and all tongues. The Headmistress unfolded it; read it, re-read it, and said nothing. Her giddy little companion, impatient at not being in the know, snatched it with lively, insistent paws and uttered such cries of 'Ah!' and 'That's going to cause a lot of fuss' that we were violently intrigued and positively palpitating.

'Yes,' Mademoiselle said to her, 'I was told about it, but I was waiting for the official confirmation; he's a friend of Doctor Dutertre's . . .'

'But that's not all. You must tell the school, because they're going to hang out the flags, they're going to have illuminations, they're going to have a banquet . . . Just look at them, they're sizzling with impatience!'

Sizzling? Weren't we just!

'Yes, we must announce it to them . . . Young ladies, try and listen to me and to take in what I say! The Minister of Agriculture, Monsieur Jean Dupuy, is coming to the main town on the occasion of the forthcoming Agricultural Show, and he will take advantage of this to come and officially open the new schools: the town will be decorated with flags and bunting and illuminated; there will be a reception at the station . . . and now I'm bored with you all – you'll soon know all about it because the town-crier will announce it. Only try and "get a move on" more than you're doing at the moment so that your samples of work will be ready.'

Profound silence. And then babel broke loose! Ejaculations burst out, everyone talked at once and the tumult grew, pierced by a shrill little voice: 'Is the Minister going to ask us questions?'

We howled down Marie Belhomme, the duffer who had asked that.

Mademoiselle made us get into line, although it wasn't time yet, and left us screeching and chattering while she went off to sort out her ideas and make arrangements in view of the unheard-of event which was brewing.

'Old thing, what have *you* got to say about that?' Anaïs asked me in the street.

'I say that our holidays will begin a week earlier. That's no joy for me. I'm bored stiff when I can't come to school.'

'But there's going to be celebrations and balls and fun and games in the square.'

'Yes, and heaps of people to parade in front of, I know just what's in your mind! You know, we shall be very much in the public eye. Dutertre, who's an intimate friend of the new Minister (it's because of him that this newly-fledged Excellency's risking himself in a hole like Montigny), will put us forward . . .'

'No! D'you really think so?'

'Definitely! It's a plot he's hatched to get the Deputy pushed out!'

She went off radiant, dreaming of official celebrations during which ten thousand pairs of eyes would contemplate her admiringly!

The town-crier had announced the news: we were promised endless joys: arrival of the ministerial train at nine o'clock; the municipal authorities, the pupils of the two Schools would await the Minister near the station, at the entrance to the town and would conduct him through the decorated streets to the bosom of the Schools. There, on a platform, he would speak! And in the great reception-room of the Town Hall he would banquet, along with a numerous company. After that, distribution of prizes to grown-up people (for Monsieur Jean Dupuy was bringing along a few little green and purple ribbons for those to whom Dutertre was under an obligation – a master-stroke the latter had brought off). In the evening, a great ball in the banqueting room. The brass band of the principal town of the district (something very special!) would graciously lend its assistance. Finally the Mayor invited the inhabitants to hang out flags and bunting on their dwellings and to decorate them with greenery. Ouf! What an honour for us!

This morning, in class, Mademoiselle solemnly announced to us – we saw at once that great things were brewing – the visit of her dear Dutertre who would give us, with his customary obligingness, ample details about the way in which the ceremony was to be ordered.

Whereupon, he did not come.

It was only in the afternoon, just before four o'clock, at the moment when we were folding away our lace and knitting and tapestry-work into our little baskets that Dutertre arrived, as usual, like a whirlwind, without knocking. I had not seen him since his 'attempt'; he had not changed. He was dressed with his usual carefully thought-out negligence – coloured shirt, almost white jacket and trousers, a big, light-coloured, sailor-knotted tie tucked into the cummerbund that served him as a waistcoat. Mademoiselle Sergent, like Anaïs, like Luce, like Aimée Lanthenay, like all of them, found his taste in clothes supremely distinguished.

While he was talking to those ladies, he let his eyes wander in my direction, long eyes, tilting up at the outer corners – the eyes of a vicious animal, which he knew how to make gentle. He won't catch me again letting him take me out into the corridor; those days are over!

'Well, little ones,' he exclaimed. 'You're pleased to be seeing a Minister?'

We answered in vague, respectful murmurs.

'Attention! You're going to give him an elegant reception at the station, all in white! That's not all, you must offer him bouquets, three of the big ones, one of whom will recite a little compliment; yes, definitely!'

We exchanged looks of feigned shyness and untruthful fright.

'Don't behave like little geese! There must be one in pure white, one in white with blue ribbons, one in white with red ribbons, to symbolize a flag of honour. Sh! Eh! not a bad little

flag at all! You're in it, of course, in the flag, you (that was *me*)
... you're decorative and besides I want you to be seen. What
are your ribbons for the prizegiving like?'

'As it happens, this year, I'm white all over.'

'That's fine, you little virginal type, you'll be the middle of
the flag. And you'll recite a speech to my friend the Minister.
He won't be bored looking at you, you know!' (He was
completely crazy to let out things like that here! Mademoiselle
Sergent would kill me!)

'Who's got red ribbons?'

'Me!' shrieked Anaïs who was palpitating with hope.

'Right, you then. I'm quite agreeable.'

It was a half-lie on the part of Anaïs, who was determined
at all costs to be in the picture, since her ribbons were striped.

'Who's got blue ones?'

'Me, S-sir,' stammered Marie Belhomme, choking with
terror.

'That's fine, you won't make a repulsive trio. By the way,
about the ribbons, don't spoil the ship for a ha'porth of tar,
let yourselves go, I'm doing the paying! (Hum!) Magnificent
sashes, fine dashing bows – and I'm buying you bouquets to
match your colours!'

'So far ahead!' I observed. 'They'll have plenty of time to
get faded.'

'Be quiet, you little hoyden, you'll never develop the bump
of reverence. I like to think you've already developed two
others more pleasantly situated!'

The entire class burst into enthusiastic giggles; Mademoiselle
gave a sickly smile. As to Dutertre, I could have sworn he was
drunk.

They threw us out before he left. I was bombarded with
cries of: 'My dear, there's no denying it, you're always the
lucky one!' 'All the honours for you, as usual!' 'It wouldn't
have been anyone else, no fear!' I did not answer a word but
went off to comfort poor little Luce who was heartbroken at
not having been chosen as one of the flag. 'There, there, green
will suit you better than anything . . . And, besides, it's your
own fault. Why didn't you put yourself forward like Anaïs?'

'Oh,' sighed the little thing, 'it doesn't matter. I lose my head in front of lots of people and I should have done something silly. But I'm glad that you're reciting the compliment and not that great gawk Anaïs.'

Papa, when informed of the glorious part I was to play in the opening of the schools, wrinkled his Bourbon nose and inquired:

'Ye gods! Am I going to have to show myself over there?'

'Certainly not, Papa. You remain in the shadow!'

'Then you really mean I haven't got to bother about you?'

'Really and truly not, Papa. Don't change your usual ways!'

The town and the School are upside down. If it goes on like this, I shall no longer have time to describe anything in my diary. This morning we were in class by seven o'clock, though class was hardly the word! The Headmistress had had enormous parcels of tissue-paper sent over from the main town; pink, pastel blue, red, yellow, and white. In the central classroom, we gutted the parcels – the biggest girls were constituted chief assistants – and off we went, counting the huge flimsy sheets, folding them in six lengthwise, cutting them into six strips and tying these strips in little bundles which were carried to Mademoiselle's desk. She scalloped them along the edges with pinking-shears, then Mademoiselle Aimée distributed them to the entire First Class and the entire Second Class. Nothing to the Third; those kids were too little – they would ruin the paper, the pretty paper of which every strip would become a crumpled, bloated rose at the end of a wire stalk.

We lived in a state of ecstasy! Text-books and exercise-books slept in closed desks and it was a question of who could get up first and rush off at once to the School, now transformed into a florist's workroom.

I no longer lingered lazily in bed and I was in such a hurry to get there in good time that I fastened my belt in the street. Sometimes we were all assembled in the classrooms already when their Ladyships came down at last. They were taking things easy too, in the matter of costume! Mademoiselle Sergent displayed herself in a red cotton dressing-gown (without any corsets, proudly); her winsome assistant followed her, in bedroom slippers, her eyes sleepy and tender. The atmosphere has become completely homely; the day before yesterday, Mademoiselle Aimée, having washed her hair, appeared in the morning with her hair down and still damp. Her golden hair was as fine as silk, rather short and curling softly at the ends; she looked like a scamp of a little page and her Headmistress, her kind Headmistress, devoured her with her eyes.

The playground was deserted; the drawn serge curtains enveloped us in a blue, fantastic twilight. We made ourselves comfortable; Anaïs left off her apron and turned up her sleeves like a pastry-cook; little Luce, who hopped and ran behind me all day long, had pulled up her dress and her petticoat like a washerwoman, a pretext for displaying her rounded calves and slender ankles. Mademoiselle, moved to pity, had allowed Marie Belhomme to shut away her books. Wearing a linen blouse with black and white stripes and looking, as usual, rather like a Pierrot, she flapped around with us, cutting the strips crooked, making mistakes, catching her feet in the wire, in utter despair or swooning with joy all in the same minute, but so gentle and inoffensive that we didn't even tease her.

Mademoiselle Sergent stood up and with a brusque gesture drew the curtain on the side that overlooked the boys' playground. We could hear, from the school opposite, the braying of harsh, badly-pitched young voices; it was Monsieur Rabastens teaching his pupils a Republican song. Mademoiselle waited a moment or two, then waved her arm. The obliging Antonin promptly came running up, bareheaded, with a La France rose adorning his buttonhole.

'Would you be kind enough to send two of your boys over to the workshop and make them cut this brass-wire into lengths of twenty-five centimetres?'

'Rright away, Mademoiselle! Are you still working at your flowers?'

'We shan't be finished for a long time; it needs five thousand roses for the school alone and we're also commissioned to decorate the banqueting room!'

Rabastens went off, running bareheaded under the

ferocious sun. A quarter of an hour later, there was a knock on our door which opened to admit two big boobies of fourteen or fifteen, bringing back the lengths of wire. Not knowing what to do with their lanky bodies, they stood there, red-faced and stupid, excited to find themselves in the midst of fifty little girls who, bare-necked and bare-armed, with their bodices undone, laughed mischievously at the two boys. Anaïs brushed against them in passing, I gently stuffed serpentine trails of paper into their pockets; they escaped at last, both pleased and sorry, while Mademoiselle was prodigal of 'Shs's' to which we paid scant attention.

Along with Anaïs, I was a folder and cutter; Luce tied up the bundles and carried them to the Headmistress; Marie put them in a heap. At eleven in the morning, we left everything and formed into a group to rehearse the *Hymn to Nature*. Towards five o'clock, we smartened ourselves up a little; tiny mirrors emerged from pockets; some smaller fry of the Second Class obligingly stretched their black aprons behind the panes of an open window and, in front of this sombre looking-glass, we put on our hats again, I fluffed up my curls, Anaïs pinned up her collapsing chignon, and we went off home.

The town was beginning to be as stirred-up as we were; just think, Monsieur Jean Dupuy was arriving in six days' time! The boys went off in the morning in carts, singing at the top of their lungs and whipping the sorry steed in the shafts with all their might. They went out into the municipal wood – and into private woods too, I'm quite sure – to choose their trees and mark them; firs in particular, elms and velvety-leaved aspens would perish in hundreds; at all costs, honour must be done to this newly-made Minister! In the evening, in the square and on the pavements, the girls crumpled paper roses and sang to attract the boys to come and help them. Good heavens, how they must speed the task! I could see them from here, going at it with both hands!

Carpenters removed the mobile screens from the great room in the Town Hall where the banquet was to be held; a huge platform sprouted in the courtyard. The district Doctor-Superintendent Dutertre made brief and frequent appearances, approved everything that was being built, slapped the men on the back, chucked the women under the chin, stood drinks all round and disappeared, soon to return. Happy countryside! During this time, the woods were ravaged, poaching went on day and night, there were brawls in the taverns and a cow-girl at Chêne-Fendu gave her newborn child to the pigs to eat. (After a few days, they stopped the prosecution, Dutertre having succeeded in proving that the girl was not responsible for her actions . . . Already, no one bothered any more about the affair.) Thanks to these methods, he was poisoning the countryside but, out of a couple of hundred scoundrels, he had constituted himself a bodyguard who would murder and die for him. He would be made a Deputy. What else mattered!

As for us, good heavens! *We* made roses. Five or six thousand roses is no light matter. The little ones' class was busy to the last child making garlands of pleated paper in pastel colours which would float all over the place at the whim of the breeze. Mademoiselle was afraid that these preparations would not be finished in time and gave us provisions of tissue paper and wire to take away every afternoon when school was over. We worked at home, after dinner, before dinner, without respite; the tables in all our houses were loaded with roses – white, blue, red, pink, and yellow ones – full-blown, crisp and fresh on the end of their stalks. They took up so much room that one didn't know where to put them; they overflowed everywhere, blooming in multi-coloured heaps, and we carried them back in the morning in sheaves, looking as if we were going to wish relatives a happy birthday.

The Headmistress, bubbling over with ideas, also wants to construct a triumphal arch at the entrance to the Schools: the side-pillars are to be built up with pine-branches and dishevelled greenery, stuck with quantities of roses. The pediment is to bear this inscription, in letters of pink roses on a ground of moss:

WELCOME TO OUR VISITORS!

Charming, isn't it?

I've had my inspiration too. I have suggested the idea of crowning the flag – meaning us three – with flowers.

'Oh, yes,' Anaïs and Marie Belhomme screeched delightedly.

'That's fixed then. (Hang the expense!) Anaïs, you'll be crowned with poppies; Marie, you'll be diademmed with cornflowers and, as for me, whiteness, candour, purity, I shall wear . . .'

'What? Orange blossom?'

'I've still a right to it, Miss! More than *you* have, no doubt!'

'Do lilies seem immaculate enough to you?'

'You make me *sick*! I shall choose marguerites; you know perfectly well the tricolour bouquet is made up of marguerites, poppies, and cornflowers. Let's go down to the milliner's.'

Looking disdainful and superior, we made our choice. The milliner took our head measurements and promised 'the very best that could be made'.

The next day we received three wreaths which grieved me to the heart; diadems that bulged in the middle like the ones country brides wear; how on earth could one look pretty in that? Marie and Anaïs, enraptured, tried theirs on in the midst of an admiring circle of juniors; *I* said nothing, but I took my accessory home where I quietly took it to pieces. Then, on the same wire frame, I reconstructed a fragile, slender wreath with the big, starry marguerites placed as if by chance, ready to drop away; two or three flowers hung in bunches about my ears, a few trailed behind in my hair; then I tried my creation on my head. I'm only telling you that much! No danger of my letting the two others in on it!

An additional job has descended on us: the curl-papers! You don't know, you couldn't be expected to know. Learn then, that, at Montigny, a schoolgirl could not assist at a prize-giving, or at any solemnity, without being duly curled or waved. Nothing strange in that, certainly, although those stiff corkscrews and excessive twistings make the hair resemble teasled brooms more than anything else. But the Mammas of all these little girls, seamstresses, women market-gardeners, wives of labourers and shopkeepers have neither the time, nor

186

the wish, nor the skill to put all those heads in curl-papers. Guess to whom this work, sometimes far from appetizing, reverts? To the teachers and to the pupils of the First Class! Yes, it's crazy, but you see it's the custom and that word is the answer to everything. A week before the prizegiving, juniors badger us and inscribe themselves on our lists. Five or six for each of us, at least! And for one clean head with pretty, supple hair, how many greasy manes – not to mention inhabited ones!

Today we began to put these creatures, ranging from eight to eleven years old, in curl-papers. Squatting on the ground, they abandoned their heads to us and, for curlers, we used pages from our old exercise-books. This year, I was only willing to accept four victims and chosen, moreover, among the clean ones; each of the other big girls was being hair-dresser to six little ones! A far from easy job, since nearly all girls in the country round here possess great bushy manes. At midday, we summoned our docile flock: I began with a fair-haired little thing with fluffy hair that curled softly by nature.

'Why, whatever are you doing here? With hair like that, you want me to frizz it in curl-papers? It would be a massacre!'

'Fancy! But of *course* I want it curled for me! Not curled, on a Prizeday, on a day a Minister's coming! Whoever heard of such a thing!'

'You'll be as ugly as the fourteen deadly sins! You'll have stiff hair, sticking out all round your head like a scarecrow . . .'

'I don't care. At least I'll be curled.'

Since she insisted! And to think that they all felt as she did; I was prepared to bet that Marie Belhomme herself . . .

'I say, Marie, you who've got natural corkscrews, I'm sure *you'll* stay as you are, won't you?'

She screeched with indignation at the idea:

'Me? Stay as I am? Don't you think it! I'd arrive at the prizegiving with a flat head!'

'But *I'm* not going to frizz myself.'

'My dear, you curl tight enough. And besides your hair goes into a "cloud" quite easily . . . and besides everyone knows your ideas are never the same as everyone else's.'

As she spoke she was vivaciously – too vivaciously – rolling the long locks, the colour of ripe wheat, of the little girl who was sitting in front of her, buried in her hair – a bush from which there occasionally issued shrill squeaks.

Anaïs, not without deliberate malice, was maltreating her patient, who was howling.

'Well, she's got that much hair, this one,' she said, by way of excuse. 'When you think you've finished, you're only half-way. You wanted it – you're here – try not to scream!'

We curled, we curled . . . the glass-paned corridor was filled with the rustle of the folded paper we twisted into the hair . . . Our work achieved, the juniors stood up with a sigh of relief and displayed heads bristling with wisps of paper on which one could still read: 'Problems . . . morals . . . Duc de Richelieu . . .' During the next four days they will go about the streets and the School, looking utter little frumps, without the least shame. But it's the custom and that's that . . . Our life had become completely disorganized. We were always out of doors, trotting hither and thither, carrying home or bringing back roses, begging – we four, Anaïs, Marie, Luce and I – requisitioning flowers, real ones this time, to decorate the banqueting-hall. Sent by Mademoiselle, who counted on our innocent young faces to disarm the conventional, we went into the houses of people we had never seen. It was thus we paid a visit to Paradis, the Registrar, because rumour accused him of being the possessor of dwarf rose-trees, little marvels. All shyness gone, we burst into his peaceful office with: 'Good morning, Monsieur! We've been told you have some lovely rose-trees, it's for the flower-stands in the banqueting-hall, you know, we've been sent by etc., etc.' The poor man muttered something into his great beard and led us out, armed with a pair of secateurs. We departed with our arms loaded with pots of flowers, laughing, chattering, cheekily answering back the people who, at the entrance to each street, were all busy erecting the framework of triumphal arches. They called out to us: 'Hi! You nice little pieces, there! Want someone to lend a hand? We'll find you one, all right . . . Hoy! look out! There's one just going to fall! You're losing something, pick it up!' Everyone knew each other; everyone addressed each other familiarly as *tu* ...

Today and yesterday, the boys went off in the carts at dawn and did not come back till sunset, buried under branches of box, larch and *arbor vitae*, under cartloads of green moss that smelt of the bogs; afterwards they went off drinking, as usual. I have never seen these gangs of ruffians in such a state of excitement; normally they don't care a fig about anything, even politics. Now they emerged from their woods, their hovels, from the bushes where they spied on the girls who looked after the cows, to embower Jean Dupuy! It was beyond all comprehension! Louchard's gang, six or seven ne'er-do-wells who had pillaged the forests, went by, singing, invisible under heaps of ivy that trailed behind them, rustling softly.

The streets fought among themselves in rivalry; the Rue du Cloître erected three triumphal arches because the Grande-Rue had planned two, one at each end. But the Grande-Rue, put on its mettle, constructed a marvellous affair, a medieval castle, all in pine-branches trimmed even with shears, with pepper-pot turrets. The Rue des Fours-Barraux, just by the School, came under the rural-arty influence of Mademoiselle Sergent. It confined itself to covering the houses on either side with a complete tapestry of long-tressed, dishevelled branches and then putting battens across from each house to the one opposite and covering this roof with hanging masses of intertwining ivy. The result was a delicious arbour, dusky and green, in which voices were muted as if in a thickly-curtained room; people walked to and fro under it for sheer pleasure. Furious at this, the Rue du Cloître lost all restraint and linked its three triumphal arches together with clusters of mossy garlands stuck with flowers so as to have *its* arbour too. Whereupon, the Grande-Rue calmly set to and took up its pavements and erected, in their stead, a wood! Yes, honestly, a real little wood on either side with young trees that had been uprooted and replanted. It would only have needed a fortnight of this furious emulation for everyone to be cutting each other's throats.

The masterpiece, the jewel, was our School – rather our

Schools. When it was all finished, not a square inch of wall would be visible under the greenery, the flowers, and the flags. Mademoiselle had requisitioned an army of young men; the bigger boys and the assistant-masters, all of whom she directed with a rod of iron; they obeyed her without a murmur. The triumphal arch at the entrance had now seen the light of day; standing on ladders, the two mistresses and the four of us had spent three hours 'writing' in pink roses on the pediment:

WELCOME TO OUR VISITORS!

while the boys amused themselves by ogling our calves. From up above, from the roofs and windows and all the rough surfaces of the walls, there flowed and rippled such a cascade of branches, of red, white, and blue material, of ropes masked with ivy, of hanging greenery and trailing roses, that the huge building seemed to undulate from base to summit in the light wind and to be gently swaying. You entered the School by lifting a rustling curtain of flower-decked ivy and the fairy-like atmosphere continued inside. Ropes of roses outlined the corners, were festooned from wall to wall and hung at the windows: it was adorable.

In spite of our activity, in spite of our bold incursions on garden-owners, this morning we saw ourselves on the point of being short of flowers. General consternation! Curl-papered heads bent forward agitatedly around Mademoiselle who was brooding, with knitted brows.

'All the same, I've got to have some!' she exclaimed. 'The whole stand on the left hasn't any at all; we must have flowers in pots. You Rovers, come here at once!'

'Here, Mademoiselle!'

We sprang up, all four of us (Anaïs, Marie, Luce, Claudine); we sprang forth from the buzzing throng, ready to dash away.

'Listen. You're to go and see old Caillavaut . . .'

'Oh!!! . . .'

We hadn't let her finish. You must realize that old Caillavaut is a miser, a regular Harpagon, slightly mad, spiteful as the plague and immensely rich. He owns a magnificent house and grounds which no one is allowed to enter but himself and his gardener. He is feared for being extremely malicious, hated for being a miser, and respected as a living mystery. And Mademoiselle wanted us to go and ask him for flowers! She couldn't have realized what she was doing!

'. . . Now, now, now! anyone would think I was sending off lambs to the slaughterhouse! You'll soften his gardener's heart and you won't even *see* old Caillavaut himself. Anyway, what if you do? You've got legs to run away with, haven't you? Off you go!'

I took the three others off, though they were far from enthusiastic, for I was conscious of a burning desire, tinged with vague apprehension, to penetrate into this old maniac's domain. I urged them on: 'Come on, Luce, come on, Anaïs! We're going to see terrific things, we'll be able to tell the others all about it . . . Why, they can be counted on the fingers of one hand, the people who've been inside old Caillavaut's place!'

Confronted with the great green door, where flowering, over-scented acacias overhung the wall, no one dared to pull the bell-chain. Finally, I gave it a violent tug, thereby setting off a terrifying tocsin; Marie took three steps towards flight, and Luce, trembling, hid bravely behind me. Nothing happened; the door remained shut. A second attempt was equally unsuccessful. I then lifted the latch, which yielded, and, like mice, we crept in one by one, uneasily, leaving the door ajar. A great gravel courtyard, beautifully kept, lay in front of the fine white house whose shutters were closed against the sun; the courtyard expanded into a green garden, rendered deep and mysterious by its thick clumps of trees . . . Rooted to the spot, we stared without daring to move; still no one to be seen and not a sound. To the right of the house were greenhouses, closed and full of marvellous plants . . . The stone staircase widened out gently as it descended to the level of the gravel courtyard; on each step there were flaming geraniums, calceolarias with little tiger-striped bellies, dwarf rose-trees that had been forced into too much bloom.

The obvious absence of any owner restored my courage.

'I say, are you coming or not? We're not going to take root in the gardens of the Sleeping-Miser-in-the-Wood!'

'Ssh!' whispered Marie in terror.

'What d'you mean, ssh? On the contrary, we must call out! Hi, over there! Monsieur Caillavaut! Gardener!'

No answer; all remained silence. I went over to the greenhouses, and, pressing my face against the panes, I tried to make out what was inside; a kind of dark emerald forest, dotted with splashes of brilliant colour that must certainly be exotic flowers . . .

The door was locked.

'Let's go,' whispered Luce, ill at ease.

'Let's go,' repeated Marie, even more anxious. 'Suppose the old man jumped out from behind a tree!'

This idea made them flee towards the door; I called them back at the top of my voice.

'Don't be such dolts! You can see there isn't anyone here. Listen . . . you're each going to choose two or three pots, the best ones on the stone steps. We'll carry them off back there, without saying anything and I think we'll have a huge success!'

They did not budge; definitely tempted, but nervous. I seized two clumps of 'Venus's slippers', speckled like tit's eggs, and I made a sign that I was waiting. Anaïs decided to imitate me and loaded herself with two double geraniums; Marie imitated Anaïs, Luce too, and we all four walked discreetly away. Near the door, absurd terror seized us again; we crowded each other like sheep in the narrow opening of the door and we ran all the way to the School where Mademoiselle welcomed us with cries of joy. All at once, we recounted our Odyssey. The Headmistress, startled, remained in perplexity for a moment, then concluded light-heartedly:

'Well, well, we shall see! After all, it's only a loan . . . a slightly forced one.' We've never, never heard one mention of it since, but old Caillavaut has put up a bristling defence of spikes and broken tiles on his walls (this theft earned us a certain prestige; they're connoisseurs in brigandage here). Our flowers were placed in the front row and then, goodness me!, in the whirlwind of the ministerial arrival, we completely forgot to return them; they now embellish Mademoiselle's garden.

For a good long time now, this garden has been the one single subject of discord between Mademoiselle and that great fat woman, her mother. The latter, who has remained an out-and-out peasant, digs, weeds, tracks snails to their last retreats, and has no other ideal than to grow beds of cabbages, beds of leeks, beds of potatoes – enough to feed all the boarders without buying anything, in fact. Her daughter's refined nature dreams of deep arbours, flowering shrubs, pergolas wreathed in honeysuckle – in short, of useless plants! As a result, one could alternately see Mother Sergent giving contemptuous hacks with her hoe at the little lacquer-trees and weeping birches and Mademoiselle stamping an irritated heel on the borders of sorrel and the odorous chives. This battle convulses us with joy. I must be just and also admit that, everywhere else except in the garden and in the kitchen, Madame Sergent effaces herself completely, never pays us a visit, never gives her opinion in discussions, and bravely wears her goffered peasant's bonnet.

The most amusing thing, in the few hours that now remained to us, was arriving at the School and going home again through the unrecognizable streets, transformed into forest paths and parklike landscapes, all fragrant with the penetrating smell of cut firs. It was as if the woods that encircled Montigny had invaded it, had come in and almost buried it . . . One could not have dreamed of a prettier, more becoming decoration for this little town lost among the trees . . . I cannot bring myself to say more 'adequate', it's a word I simply loathe.

The flags, which will make all these green alleys ugly and commonplace, will all be in place tomorrow, not to mention the Venetian lanterns and the fairy-lights. What a pity!

No one felt embarrassed with us; the women and boys called out to us as we passed: 'Hi! you there, you've got the trick of it! Come on, come and 'elp us a bit sticking in these roses!'

We ''elped' willingly. We climbed up ladders: my

companions let themselves – all for the Minister's sake, of course! – be tickled around the waist and sometimes on the calves: I must say that no one ever allowed themselves those little pranks on the daughter of the 'Gentleman of the slugs'. In any case, with these boys who don't give it another thought once their hand is removed, it's offensive and not even annoying; I can understand the girls from the School falling in with the general behaviour. Anaïs allowed all liberties and yearned after still more; Féfed carried her down from the top of the ladder in his arms. Touchard, known as Zero, stuffed prickly branches of pine under her skirts; she gave little squeaks, like a mouse caught in a door, and half closed swooning eyes, without strength even to pretend to put up a defence.

Mademoiselle let us rest a little, for fear we should be too limp and tired on the great day. Beside, I really could not see what remained to be done; everything was decked with flowers, everything was in place; the cut flowers were soaking their stalks in buckets of cool water in the cellar; they would be scattered all over the place at the last moment. Our three bouquets arrived this morning in a big, fragile packing-case; Mademoiselle did not want us even to unnail it completely: she removed one slat, and slightly lifted up the tissue-paper which shrouded the patriotic flowers and the cotton wool from which came a damp smell: then Old Madame Sergent promptly took the light case, in which rattled crystals of some salt that I don't know and that prevents flowers from fading, down to the cellar.

Nursing her principal subjects, the Headmistress sent us off, Anaïs, Marie, Luce and me, to rest in the garden under the hazels. Slumped in the shade on the green bench, our minds were almost blank; the garden hummed. As if stung by a fly, Marie Belhomme gave a start and suddenly began to unwind one of the big curl-papers that, for three days, had been quivering round her head.

'. . . 't 'you doing?'

'Seeing if it's curled, of course!'

'And supposing it isn't curled enough?'

'Why, I'll wet it tonight when I go to bed. But you can see – it's very curly – it's fine!'

Luce followed her example and gave a little cry of disappointment.

'Oh! It's as if I hadn't done anything to it at all! It corkscrews at the end, and nothing at all higher up – or next to nothing!'

She had, in fact, the kind of hair that is supple and soft as silk and that escapes and slips out of one's fingers and out of ribbons and will only do what it wants to do.

'So much the better,' I told her. 'That'll teach you. Look at you . . . thoroughly miserable at not having a head like a bottle-brush!'

But she refused to be comforted, and, as I was weary of their voices, I went further off and lay down on the gravel, in the shade of the chestnut trees. I hadn't any distinct notions in my head; I was aware only of heat, of lassitude . . .

My dress was ready, it was a success . . . I should look pretty tomorrow, prettier than the gawky Anaïs, prettier than Marie: that wasn't difficult, but it pleased me all the same . . . I was going to leave school; Papa was sending me to Paris to a rich, childless aunt; I should make my début in the world, and a thousand blunders at the same time . . . How should I do without the country; with this hunger for green, growing things that never left me? It seemed insane to me to think that I should never come here again, that I should never see Mademoiselle any more, or her little Aimée with the golden eyes, or the scatterbrained Marie, or the bitch Anaïs, or Luce, always greedy for blows and caresses . . . I should be unhappy at not living here any more. Moreover, now that I had the time, I might as well admit something to myself; that, in my heart of hearts, Luce attracted me more than I liked to own. It's no good reminding myself that she has hardly any real beauty, that her caressing ways are those of a treacherous little animal, that her eyes are deceitful; none of this prevents her from possessing a charm of her own, the charm of oddity and weakness and still innocent perversity – as well as a white skin, slender hands, rounded arms and tiny feet. But she will never know anything about it! She suffers on account of her sister whom Mademoiselle Sergent took away from me by main force. Rather than admit anything, I would cut out my tongue!

Under the hazels, Anaïs was describing her dress for tomorrow to Luce. I walked towards them, in an ill-natured mood, and I heard:

'The collar? There isn't any collar! It's open in a V in front and at the back, edged with a runner of silk muslin and finished with a cabbage-bow of red ribbon . . .'

'"Red cabbages, known as curly cabbages, demanded a meagre, stony soil", the ineffable Bérillon teaches us. That fills the bill perfectly, eh, Anaïs? Scarlet runners, cabbages . . . that's not a dress, it's a kitchen-garden.'

'My lady Claudine, if you've come here to say such witty things, you can stay on your gravel. We weren't pining for your company!'

'Don't get in a temper. Tell us how the skirt's made, what vegetables are being used to give it a relish? I can see it from here – there's a fringe of parsley all round!'

Luce was highly amused; Anaïs wrapped herself in her dignity and stalked off; as the sun was getting low, we got up too.

Just as we were shutting the garden gate, we heard bursts of silvery laughter. They came nearer and Mademoiselle Aimée passed us, giggling as she ran, pursued by the amazing Rabastens who was pelting her with flowers fallen from the bignonia bush. This ceremonial opening by the Minister authorizes pleasant liberties in the streets – and in the School too, apparently! But Mademoiselle followed behind, frowning and turning pale with jealousy: further on, we heard her call out: 'Mademoiselle Lanthenay, I've asked you twice whether you've told your class to assemble at half past seven.' But the other, in wild spirits, enchanted to be playing with a man and annoying her friend, ran on without stopping and the purple flowers caught in her hair and glanced off her dress . . . There would be a scene tonight.

At five o'clock, the two ladies assembled us with considerable difficulty, scattered all over the building as we were. The Headmistress decided to ring the dinner-bell, thereby interrupting a furious galop that Anaïs, Marie, Luce and I were dancing in the banqueting-room under the flower-decked ceiling.

'Girls,' she cried, in the voice she used for great occasions, 'you're to go home at once and get to bed in good time! Tomorrow morning, at half past seven, you're all to be assembled here, dressed and your hair done, so that we don't have to bother about you any more! You will be given your streamers and banners; Claudine, Anaïs, and Marie will take their bouquets . . . All the rest . . . you'll see when you get here. Be off with you now, don't ruin the flowers as you go through the doors and don't let me hear so much as a mention of you till tomorrow morning!'

She added:

'Mademoiselle Claudine, you know your complimentary speech?'

'Do I know it! Anaïs has made me rehearse it three times today.'

'But . . . what about the prizegiving?' risked a timid voice.

'Oh! the prizegiving, we'll fit that in when we can! In any case, it's probable that I shall just give you the books here and that this year there will be no public prizegiving, on account of the opening.'

'But . . . the songs, the *Hymn to Nature*?'

'You'll sing them tomorrow, before the Minister. Now, vanish!'

This speech had caused consternation to quite a number of little girls who looked forward to the prizegiving as a unique festive occasion in the year; they went off perplexed and discontented, under arches of flower-decked greenery.

The people of Montigny, exhausted but proud, were taking a rest, sitting on their doorsteps and contemplating their labours; the girls used the rest of the dying day to sew on a ribbon or to put some lace round an improvised low neck – for the great ball at the Town Hall, my dear!

Tomorrow morning, as soon as it was light, the boys would strew the route of the procession with cut grass and green leaves, mingled with flowers and rose-petals. And if the Minister Jean Dupuy wasn't satisfied, he must be extremely hard to please, so he could go to blazes!

The first thing I did when I got up this morning was to run to the looking-glass; goodness, one never knew, suppose I'd grown a boil overnight? Reassured, I made my toilet very carefully: I was admirably early, it was only six o'clock: I had time to be meticulous over every detail. Thanks to the dryness of the air, my hair went easily into a 'cloud'. My small face is always rather pale and peaky, but, I assure you, my eyes and mouth are not at all bad. The dress rustled lightly; the underskirt of plain unspotted muslin swayed to the rhythm of my walk and brushed softly against my pointed shoes. Now for the wreath. Ah, how well it suited me! A little Ophelia, hardly more than a child, with those amusing dark shadows round the eyes! . . . Yes, they used to tell me, when I was little, that I had a grown-up person's eyes; later, it was eyes that were 'not quite respectable': you can't please everyone and yourself as well. I prefer to please myself first of all . . .

The tiresome thing was that tight around bouquet which was going to ruin the whole effect. Pooh! it didn't matter since I was to hand it over to His Excellency . . .

All white from head to foot, I set off to the School through the cool streets; the boys, in process of 'strewing' called out coarse, monstrous compliments to the 'little bride' who fled in shyness.

I arrived ahead of time, but I found about fifteen of the juniors already there, little things from the surrounding countryside and the distant farms; they were used to getting up at four in summer. They were comical and touching; their heads looked enormous with their hair frizzed out in harsh twists and they remained standing up so as not to crumple their muslin dresses, rinsed out in too much blue, that swelled out stiffly from waists encircled by currant-red or indigo sashes. Against all this white their sunburnt faces appeared quite black. My arrival had provoked a little 'ah!' from them, hastily suppressed. Now they stood silent, greatly awed by their fine clothes and their frizzed hair, rolling an elegant handkerchief, on which their mother had poured some 'smell-nice', in their white-cotton-gloved hands.

Our two lady mistresses had not appeared but, from the upper floor, I could hear little footsteps running . . . Into the playground came pouring a host of white clouds, beribboned in pink, in red, in green and in blue; in ever-increasing numbers the girls arrived – silent for the most part, because they were extremely busy eyeing each other, comparing themselves and pinching their lips disdainfully. They looked like a camp of female Gauls, those flying, curly, frizzy, overflowing manes, nearly all of them golden . . . A clattering troop poured down the staircase; it was the boarders – always a hostile and isolated band – for whom their First Communion dresses still did duty on festive occasions. Behind them came Luce, dainty as a white Persian, charming with her soft, fluttering curls and her complexion like a newly-opened rose. Didn't she only need a happy love-affair, like her sister, to make her altogether beautiful?

'How love you look, Claudine! And your wreath isn't a bit like the two others. Oh, you *are* lucky to be so pretty!'

'But, kitten, do you know I find *you* amusing and desirable in your green ribbons? You certainly are an extremely odd little animal! Where's your sister and her Mademoiselle?'

'Not ready yet. Aimée's dress does up under the arm, just fancy! It's Mademoiselle who's hooking it up for her.'

'I see. That may take quite a time.'

From above, the voice of the elder sister called: 'Luce, come and fetch the pennants!'

The playground was filled with big and little girls and all this white, in the sunlight, hurt one's eyes. (Besides, there were too many different whites that clashed with each other.)

There was Liline, with her disturbing Gioconda smile under her golden waves, and her sea-green eyes; and that young beanpole of a 'Matilde', covered to the hips in a cascade of hair the colour of ripe corn; there was the Vignale family, five girls ranging from eight to fourteen, all tossing exuberant manes that looked as if they had been dyed with henna. There was Nannette, a little sly-boots with knowing eyes, walking on two deep blonde plaits as long as herself and as heavy as dull gold – and so many, many others. Under the dazzling light, all these fleeces of hair blazed like burning bushes.

Marie Belhomme arrived, appetizing in her cream frock and blue ribbons, quaint under the crown of cornflowers. But, good heavens, how big her hands were under the white kid!

At last, here came Anaïs, and I sighed with relief to see how awful her hair looked in stiff, corrugated waves; her wreath of crimson poppies, too close to her forehead, made her complexion look like a corpse's. With touching accord, Luce and I ran to meet her and burst out into a concert of compliments: 'My dear, how nice you look! Honest, my dear – *definitely* – there's nothing so becoming to you as red! It's a complete success!'

A little mistrustful at first, Anaïs dilated with pleasure and we staged a triumphal entry into the classroom where the children, their numbers now complete, greeted the living tricolour flag with an ovation.

A religious silence descended: we were watching our two mistresses walk slowly and deliberately, step by step, down the stairs, followed by two or three boarders loaded with pennants on the end of long, gilded lances. As to Aimée, frankly I had to admit it; one could have eaten her alive, she was so attractive in her white dress of glistening mohair (merely a slim sheath with no seam at the back!) and her rice-straw hat trimmed with white gauze. Away with you, little monster!

And Mademoiselle looked at her with fond, brooding eyes, moulded, herself, in the black dress embroidered with mauve sprays that I have already described to you. *She* can never be pretty, that bad-tempered Redhead, but her dress fitted her like a glove and one was only aware of the eyes that sparkled from under the fiery waves crowned by an extremely smart black hat.

'Where is the flag?' she demanded at once.

The flag came forward, modest and pleased with itself.

'That's good! That's . . . very good! Come here, Claudine . . . I knew you'd be at your best. And now, seduce that Minister for me!'

She rapidly reviewed her white battalion, arranged a curl here, pulled a ribbon there, did up Luce's skirt which was gaping, slid a reinforcing hairpin into Anaïs's chignon and, having scrutinized everything with her redoubtable eye, seized the bundle of various inscriptions: *Long live France! Long live the Republic! Long live Liberty! Long live the Minister! . . .* etc., twenty pennants in all which she distributed to Luce, to the Jauberts, to various chosen souls who crimsoned with pride and held the shaft upright like a candle, envied by the mere mortals who were fuming.

Our three bouquets, tied with a shower of red, white and blue ribbons, were taken with infinite precautions out of their cotton wool like jewels. Dutertre had used the money of the secret funds to advantage; I received a bunch of white camellias, Anaïs one of red camellias; the big bouquet of great velvety cornflowers fell to Marie's share, since nature, not having foreseen ministerial receptions, had neglected to produce blue camellias. The little ones pushed forward to see and already slaps were being exchanged, along with shrill complaints.

'That's enough!' cried Mademoiselle. 'Do you think I've got time to be a policeman? Come here, flag! Marie on the left, Anaïs on the right, Claudine in the middle, and forward march. Hurry up and get down into the playground! It would be a fine thing if we missed the arrival of the train! Banner-bearers, follow in fours, the tallest in front . . .'

We descended the steps into the courtyard without waiting to hear more; Luce and the tallest ones walked behind us, the pennants of their lances flapped lightly above our heads; followed by a trampling like sheep, we passed under the arch of greenery – WELCOME TO OUR VISITORS!

The whole crowd which awaited us outside, a crowd in its Sunday best, excited and ready to shout 'Long live – it doesn't matter what!' let out a huge 'Ah!' at the sight of us, as if we were fireworks. Proud as little peacocks, our eyes lowered, but inwardly bursting with vanity, we walked delicately, our bouquets in our clasped hands, treading on the strewn leaves and flowers that kept down the dust. It was only after some minutes that we exchanged sidelong looks and rapturous smiles, in a daze of bliss.

'We're having a gorgeous time!' sighed Marie, gazing at the green paths along which we proceeded slowly between two hedges of gaping onlookers, under the leafy arches which filtered the sunshine, letting a charming, artificial daylight sift through, as if in the depths of a wood.

'We certainly are! You'd think all the festivities were for us!'

Anaïs did not breathe a word, too absorbed in her dignity, too busy searching out among the crowd, that made way before us, for boys whom she knew and who she imagined thought she was dazzling. Not beautiful today, nevertheless, in all that white – no, certainly *not* beautiful! . . . but her narrow eyes sparkled with pride all the same. At the crossroads of the Market, they shouted to us: 'Halt!' We had to let ourselves be joined by the boys' school, a whole dark procession which was only kept in regular ranks with infinite difficulty. The boys seemed thoroughly contemptible to us today, sunburnt and awkward in their best suits; their great, clumsy hands held up flags.

During the halt, we all three turned round, in spite of our importance: behind us Luce and her like leant like warriors on the spears of their pennants; the little thing was radiant with vanity and held herself straight, like Fanchette when she is showing off; she kept laughing low from sheer pleasure! And, as far as eye could see, under the green arches, with their starched, full-skirted dresses and their bushy manes, stretched the deep ranks of the army of female Gauls.

'Forward march!' We set off again, light as wrens; we went down the Rue du Cloître and eventually we passed that green wall made of trimmed yew that represented a fortified castle. As the sun struck hot on the road, they halted us in the shade of a little acacia wood just outside the town, there to await the arrival of the ministerial carriages. We relaxed a little.

'Is my wreath keeping on all right?' inquired Anaïs.

'Yes . . . see for yourself.'

I passed her a little pocket-mirror that I had prudently brought and we made sure that our head-dresses were in position . . . The crowd had followed us, but too tightly packed in the road, it had broken down the hedges that bordered it and was trampling down the fields, regardless of the second crop. The boys, delirious with excitement, carried bunches of flowers and flags, not to mention bottles! (I was sure of this because I had just seen one stop, throw back his head and drink from the neck of one that held a litre.)

The 'Society' ladies had remained at the gates of the town and were seated, some on the grass, some on camp-stools, and all under parasols. They would wait there, it was more refined; it was unbecoming to show too much enthusiasm.

Over there, flags floated over the red roofs of the station, towards which the crowd was hurrying; the noise of it retreated into the distance. Mademoiselle Sergent, all in black, and her Aimée, all in white, already out of breath from supervising us and trotting beside us, sat down on the grass, lifting up their skirts so as not to get green stains on them. We waited, standing. We had no desire to talk – I went over in my head the rather absurd little complimentary speech, composed by Antonin Rabastens, that I should have to recite in a moment.

Mr Minister, – The children of the schools of Montigny, bearing the flowers of their native countryside . . .
 (If anyone has ever seen fields of camellias here, let them say so!)
 . . . come to you, full of gratitude . . .

Boom!!! A fusillade bursting out at the station brought our mistresses to their feet.

The shouts of the populace came to us in a muffled roar, that suddenly grew louder and came nearer, with a confused din of joyous cries, the tramp of innumerable feet and the gallop of horses' hooves . . . Tense, we all watched the spot where the road turned . . . At last, at last, the vanguard came in sight: dusty urchins trailing branches and bawling; then floods of people; then two broughams that glittered in the sun and two or three laudaus from which emerged arms waving hats . . . We watched them, all eyes . . . The carriages approached at a slowed-down trot; they were there, in front of us.

A young man in black evening clothes jumped out and offered his arm to support the Minister of Agriculture. The great man had not a ha'porth of distinction, in spite of the pains he took to appear imposing to us. I even found him slightly ridiculous, this haughty little gentleman, stout as a bullfinch, who was mopping his undistinguished brow and his hard eyes and his short, reddish beard for he was dripping with sweat. After all, *he* wasn't dressed in white muslin – and cloth in this heat! . . .

A minute of interested silence greeted him, then, immediately, came extravagant cries of 'Long live the Minister! Long live Agriculture! Long live the Republic! . . .' Monsieur Jean Dupuy thanked them with a cramped, but adequate gesture. A fat gentleman, embroidered in silver, wearing a cocked hat, his hand on the mother-of-pearl hilt of a little sword, came and placed himself on the left of the illustrious man; an old general with a little white goatee, a tall, bent man, flanked him on the right. And the imposing trio came forward, escorted by a troop of men in black evening clothes adorned with red ribbons, rows of decorations or military medals. Between the heads and shoulders I made out the triumphant face of that blackguard of a Dutertre. He was acclaimed by the crowd who made much of him being both the Minister's friend and the future Deputy.

I sought Mademoiselle's eyes and asked, with my chin and my eyebrows: 'Should I get on with the little speech?' She signalled 'Yes' and I advanced with my two acolytes. A startling silence suddenly descended; – Heavens! How was I going to dare to speak in front of all these people? If only I wasn't choked with that beastly stage-fright! – first of all, keeping well together, we dived into our skirts in a magnificent curtsy that made our dresses frou-frou and I began, my ears buzzing so much that I couldn't hear my own voice:

Mr Minister, – The children of the schools of Montigny, bearing the flowers of their native countryside, come to you, full of gratitude . . .

And then my voice suddenly became firmer and I went on, clearly articulating the prose in which Rabastens guaranteed our 'unshakeable loyalty to Republican institutions', as calm now as if I were reciting Eugène Manuel's *The Dress* in class.

In any case, the official trio wasn't listening to me; the Minister was reflecting that he was dying of thirst and the two other great personages were exchanging appreciative remarks in whispers:

'Mr Prefect, wherever does that little peach spring from?'

'Not the faintest idea, General. She's as pretty as a picture.'

'A little Primitive (he too!). If she looks in the least like a Fresnois girl, I'll eat my . . .'

'Pray accept these flowers of our maternal soil!' – I concluded, offering my bouquet to His Excellency. Anaïs, looking supercilious as she always does when she is aiming at being distinguished, handed hers to the Prefect, and Marie Belhomme, crimson with emotion, presented hers to the General.

The Minister mumbled a reply in which I caught the words 'Republic . . . solicitude of the Government . . . confidence in the loyalty'; he got on my nerves. Then he remained motionless and so did I; everyone was waiting expectantly, then Dutertre bent down to his ear and prompted him: 'Come on, you must kiss her!'

Thereupon he kissed me, but clumsily (his harsh beard scratched me). The brass band of the main town blared the *Marseillaise*, and, doing an about-turn, we marched towards the town, followed by the banner-bearers; the rest of the Schools made way for us and, leading the majestic procession, we passed under the 'fortified castle', and returned once more under the leafy arches. All about us, people were shouting in a shrill, frenzied way, but we honestly gave no sign that we heard anything! Erect and crowned with flowers, it was the three of us they were acclaiming, quite as much as the Minister . . . Ah! if I had any imagination, I should have seen us at once as three king's daughters, entering some 'loyal town' with their father; the girls in white would be our ladies-in-waiting, we would be being escorted to the tournament where the noble knights would dispute for the honour of . . . Heaven send that those wretched boys hadn't overfilled the little coloured lamps with oil earlier this morning! With the jolts those urchins were giving to the posts on which they were perched, yelling, we should be a nice sight! We did not talk, we had nothing to say to each other; we had quite enough to do throwing out our chests the way people do in

Paris and leaning our heads in the direction of the wind to make our hair stream out . . .

We arrived in the front-courtyard of the Schools, we halted and massed in close formation. The crowd surged in on all sides, beat up against the walls and climbed up on to them. With the tips of our fingers, we rather icily pushed away our companions who were over-anxious to surround us and overwhelm us. There were sharp exchanges of 'Do be careful!' 'Well, *you* needn't look as much as if butter wouldn't melt in your mouth! You've had enough people staring at you all the morning!' The lanky Anaïs greeted these jeers in disdainful silence; Marie Belhomme became fidgety; I restrained myself with great difficulty from pulling off one of my strapless shoes and applying it to the face of the bitchier of the two Jauberts who had slyly jostled me.

The Minister, escorted by the General, the Prefect and a host of councillors, secretaries, and I don't know what else (I'm not up in that world) who had forced a way for him through the crowd, had mounted the platform and installed himself in the handsome, over-gilded armchair that the Mayor had specially provided from his own drawing-room. A meagre consolation for the poor man who was tied to his bed with gout on that unforgettable day! Monsieur Jean Dupuy sweated and mopped himself; what would he not have given for it to be tomorrow! Still, that's what he's paid for . . . Behind him, in concentric semi-circles, sat the district councillors and the municipal council of Montigny . . . all those perspiring people couldn't smell very agreeable . . . Well, and what about us? Was it over, our glory? Were we to be left down there, without anyone so much as offering us a chair? That was really too much! 'Come on, all of you, we're going to sit down.' Not without difficulty, we made ourselves a gangway as far as the platform, we, the flag, and all the pennant-bearers. There, lifting my head, I hailed Dutertre in an undertone – he was chatting, leaning over the back of the Prefect's chair right at the edge of the platform. 'Sir, hi, Sir! Monsieur Dutertre, I say! . . . Doctor!' He heard that appeal better than the others and bent down, smiling and showing his fangs: 'It's you! What do you want? My heart? I give it to you!' I was quite sure he was drunk already.

'No, Sir, I'd much rather have a chair for myself and some others for the girls with me. They've abandoned us there all by ourselves, with the mere mortals – it's heart-rending.'

'That cries out for justice, pure and simple. You shall all sit in tiers on the steps so that the populace can at least refresh its eyes while we're boring them with our speeches. Up with the lot of you!'

We did not wait to be asked twice. Anaïs, Marie, and I climbed up first, with Luce, the Jauberts, and the other pennant-bearers behind us. Their lances got caught and entangled in each other and they tugged them furiously, their teeth gritted and their eyes lowered because they thought the crowd was laughing at them. A man – the sacristan – took pity on them and obligingly collected the little flags and carried them away; no doubt the white dresses, the flowers, and the banners gave the good fellow the illusion that he was assisting at a slightly more secular Corpus Christi procession, and, from long force of habit, he removed our candles – I mean our flags – at the end of the ceremony.

Installed and enthroned, we gazed at the crowd at our feet and the Schools in front of us, those Schools so charming today under the curtains of greenery and flowers, under all that quivering decoration that hid their bleak, barrack-like look. As to the vulgar herd of our schoolmates, left standing below, who stared at us enviously, and nudged each other and gave sickly smiles, we disdained them.

On the platform, there was a scraping of chairs and some coughing: we half-turned round to see the orator. It was Dutertre; he was standing up, in the middle, lithe and bowing, and preparing to speak without notes, empty-handed. A deep hush descended. One could hear, as at High Mass, the shrill weeping of a small child who was pining to get away, and, just as at High Mass, it raised a laugh. Then:

Mr Minister,

....

He did not speak for more than two minutes; his speech was deft and ruthless, packed with fulsome compliments and

subtle scurrilous allusions, of which I probably only understood a quarter. It was savage against the Deputy and
charming towards all the rest of humanity; towards his
glorious Minister and dear friend – they must have done some
dirty deals together – towards his dear fellow-citizens,
towards the Headmistress, 'so unquestionably of the very
highest order, Gentlemen, that the number of awards and
certificates gained by her pupils dispenses me from any other
encomium', . . . (Mademoiselle Sergent, seated down below,
modestly lowered hear head beneath her veil); even, believe it
or not, towards *us*: 'flowers carrying flowers, a feminine flag,
patriotic and enchanting'. At this unexpected thrust, Marie
Belhomme lost her head and covered her eyes with her hand,
Anaïs renewed her vain efforts to blush, and I could not
prevent myself from rippling my spine. The crowd looked at
us and smiled at us, and Luce winked at me . . .

   . . . *of France and of the Republic!*

The clapping and the shouts of applause lasted five minutes,
so violent that they went *bzii* in one's ears; while they were
dying down, the lanky Anaïs said to me:
  'My dear, d'you see Monmond?'
  'Where? . . . Yes, I see him. Well, what about him?'
  'He keeps staring all the time at that Joublin girl.'
  'Does that give you corns?'
  'No, but honest! He must have queer tastes! Just look at
him! He's making her stand on a bench and he's holding her
up! I bet he's feeling if she's got firm calves.'
  'Probably. Poor Jeannette, I wonder whether it's only the
arrival of the Minister that's put her in such a state of
excitement! She's as red as your ribbons and she's trembling
all over . . .'
  'Old thing, do you know who Rabastens is getting off
with?'
  'No.'
  'Look at him, you'll soon see.'
  It was true; the handsome assistant-master was fixedly
gazing at someone . . . and that someone was my incorrigible

Claire, dressed in pale blue, whose lovely, rather melancholy eyes were dwelling with satisfaction on the irresistible Antonin . . . Good! My First Communion partner was caught again! It wouldn't be long before I should be hearing romantic descriptions of meetings, of delights, of desertions . . . Lord, how hungry I was!

'Aren't you hungry, Marie?'

'Yes, I am a bit.'

'*I'm* dying of starvation. I say, do you like the milliner's new dress?'

'No, I think it's loud. She thinks the more a dress shrieks at you, the smarter it is. The Mayoress ordered hers from Paris, did you know?'

'Fat lot of good *that's* done her! She wears it like a dog dressed-up. The watchmaker's wife has got on the same bodice she wore two years ago!'

'Yes, I know! Bet she wants to give her daughter a dowry so she's got good reason, poor thing!'

The revered little Jean Dupuy had stood up and was beginning his reply in a dry voice, wearing an air of importance that was highly diverting. Luckily, he did not speak for long. Everyone clapped, including ourselves, as loud as we could. It was amusing, all those heads waving, all those hands beating in the air down there at our feet, all those black mouths yelling . . . And what glorious sunshine over it all! a trifle too hot . . .

There was a scuffling of chairs on the platform; all their Lordships were getting up. They signed to us to go down; they led the Minister away to feed; now we could go off to lunch!

With great difficulty, tossed about in the crowd which kept pushing in opposite directions, we managed at last to get out of the courtyard into the square where the cohorts were thinning out a little. All the little girls in white were going off, alone or with immensely proud Mammas who were waiting for them; the three of us were going to separate, too.

'Did you enjoy yourself?' asked Anaïs.

'Certainly I did. It went off very well – it was great fun!'

'Well, to my mind . . . Somehow, I thought it would have been more amusing . . . It needed a bit of livening-up, in fact!'

'Shut up, you give me a pain! I know what *you* thought it needed. You'd have liked to stand up and sing something, all by yourself on the platform. Then the whole thing would have immediately seemed much gayer to you.'

'Go on, you can't hurt *my* feelings. Everyone knows what those polite remarks mean from *you*!'

'As for me,' confessed Marie, 'I've never enjoyed myself so much in my life. Oh! What he said about us . . . I didn't know where to hide myself! . . . What time do we have to be back?'

'Two o'clock precisely. That means half past two, you can be quite sure the banquet won't be finished before that. Goodbye, see you very soon!'

At home, Papa inquired with interest:

'Did he speak well, Méline?'

'Méline! Why not Sully? It's Jean Dupuy, you know, Papa!'

'Why, yes.'

But he found his daughter pretty and looked at her with satisfaction.

After lunch, I tidied myself up; I rearranged my wreath of marguerites, I shook the dust off my muslin skirts and I waited patiently for two hours, fighting off with all my might a violent desire to take a siesta. Heavens, how hot it would be down there! – 'Fanchette, don't touch my skirt, it's muslin. No, I'm not going to catch flies for you, can't you see I'm receiving the Minister?'

I went out once again; the streets were already humming and rang with the sound of footsteps, all of which were going downhill towards the Schools. Nearly all my schoolmates were already there when I arrived; red faces, muslin skirts already limp and crumpled; the crisp freshness of this morning had gone. Luce was stretching and yawning; she had eaten her lunch too fast; she was sleepy; she was too hot; she could 'feel herself growing claws'. Anaïs alone remained the same; just as pale, just as cold, neither languid nor excited.

Our two mistresses came down at last. Mademoiselle Sergent, her cheeks burning, was scolding Aimée who had stained the hem of her skirt with raspberry juice; the spoilt little thing sulked and shrugged her shoulders and turned away, refusing to see the tender beseeching in her friend's eyes. Luce eagerly watched all this, fuming and sneering.

'Now, now, are all of you here?' scolded Mademoiselle, who, as usual, was visiting her personal resentments on our innocent heads. 'Whether you are or not, we're leaving now. I've no desire to hang . . . to wait about here for an hour. Get into line – and quicker than lightning!'

We needn't have hurried! Up there, on that enormous platform, we marked time for ages, for the Minister lingered endlessly over his coffee and all that went with it. The crowd, herded like sheep down below, looked up at us and laughed, with the sweating faces of people who have lunched heavily . . . The 'Society' ladies had brought campstools; the innkeeper from the Rue du Cloître had set out benches, which he was hiring out at two sous a place; and the boys and girls had piled on to them, shoving each other; all those people, tipsy, coarse, and cheerful, waited patiently, exchanging loud ribaldries which they shouted to each other from a distance with tremendous laughs. From time to time, a little girl in white forced her way through to the steps of the platform, climbed up and got herself hustled and pushed into the back rows by Mademoiselle whose nerves were on edge from all these delays and who was champing her bit under her eye-veil. She was even more furious on account of little Aimée who was making great play with her long lashes and her lovely eyes at a group of draper's assistants who had bicycled over from Villeneuve.

A great 'Ah!' heaved the crowd towards the doors of the banqueting-room which had just opened to let out the Minister, even redder and more perspiring than this morning, followed by his escort of black dress-suits. Already people made way for him with more familiarity, with smiles of recognition: if he stayed here three days, the rural policemen would be tapping him on the stomach, asking him for a tobacconist's shop for his daughter-in-law who's got three children, poor girl, and no husband.

Mademoiselle massed us on the right-hand side of the platform, for the Minister and his confederates were going to sit on this row of seats, the better to hear us sing. Their Lordships installed themselves; Dutertre, the colour of Russia leather, was laughing and talking too loud, drunk, as if by accident. Mademoiselle threatened us under her breath with appalling punishments if we sang out of tune, and off we went with the *Hymn to Nature*:

> 'Lo, *the sky is tinged with morning,*
> *Glowing beams grow brighter yet:*
> *Haste, arise! the day is dawning,*
> *Honest toil demands our sweat!*'

(If it's not content with the sweat of the official cortège, honest toil must demand a great deal!)

The small voices were a little lost in the open air; I did my very utmost to superintend the 'seconds' and the 'thirds' simultaneously. Monsieur Jean Dupuy vaguely followed the beat by nodding his head; he was sleepy, dreaming of the report in the *Petit Parisien*. The whole-hearted applause woke him up; he stood up, went forward and clumsily complimented Mademoiselle Sergent who promptly turned shy, stared at the ground and retired into her shell . . . Queer woman!

We were dislodged and the pupils of the boys' School took our place. They had come to bray in chorus a completely imbecile song:

> 'Sursum corda! Sursum corda!
> *Up all hearts! this noble order*
> *Be the cry that spurs our soul!*
> *Rally, brothers, thrust aside*
> *All that might our wills divide,*
> *March on firmly to the goal!*
> *Fling cold selfishness away,*
> *Traitors, who for wealth betray,*
> *Are not such a bitter foe*
> *To the burning love we owe*
> *As patriots to . . . etc., etc . . .*'

After them, the brass-band of the main town, 'The Friendly Club of Fresnois', came to shatter our ears. It was excessively

212

boring, all this! If I could only find a peaceful corner . . . And then, since no one was paying the least attention to us, upon my word, I left without telling anyone. I went back home, I undressed and I lay down till dinnertime. Why not? I should be fresher at the ball!

At nine o'clock, I was standing on the steps in front of the house, breathing in the coolness that was falling at last. At the top of the street, under the triumphal arch, ripened paper balloons in the shape of huge coloured fruits. All ready, my gloves on, a white hood under my arm, a white fan clasped in my fingers, I waited for Marie and Anaïs who were coming to fetch me . . . Light footsteps and well-known voices were heard approaching down the street, it was my two friends . . . I protested:

'Are you mad? To leave for the ball at half past nine! But the room won't even be lit up – it's ridiculous!'

'My dear, Mademoiselle said: "It'll begin at half past eight. In this part of the world, they're like that, you can't make them wait. They'll rush off to the ball as soon as they've wiped their mouths!" That's what she *said*.'

'All the more reason not to imitate the boys and girls round here! If the "dress-suits" dance tonight, they'll arrive about eleven, as people do in Paris, and we shall already have lost our bloom from dancing! Come into the garden for a little with me.'

They followed me, much against their wills, into the dusky tree-lined paths where my cat Fanchette, dressed in white, like us, was dancing after moths, capering like a crazy creature . . . She mistrusted the sound of strange voices and climbed up into a fir-tree, from which her eyes followed us, like two tiny green lanterns. In any case, Fanchette despised me these days: what with the examination, and the opening of the Schools, I was never there any more. I no longer caught her flies, quantities of flies, that I impaled in a row on a hatpin and which she picked off delicately in order to eat them, coughing occasionally because of a wing stuck uncomfortably in her throat; I hardly ever gave her coarse cooking-chocolate now or the bodies of butterflies, which she adored, and sometimes, in the evening, I went so far as to forget to 'make her room' between two volumes of Larousse – patience, Fanchette darling! Soon I shall have all the time in the world to tease you and make you jump through a hoop because, alas! I shall never be going back to the School . . .

Anaïs and Marie could not keep still and only answered me with absent-minded *Yeses* and *Noes* – their legs were itching to dance. All right, we would go since they were so desperately keen to be off! 'But you'll see that our lady mistresses won't even have come downstairs!'

'Oh! You know, they've only got to come down the little inside staircase to find themselves right in the ballroom; they'll take a peep now and then through the little door to see whether it's the right moment to make their entrance.'

'Exactly. Whereas if we arrive too early, we'll look utter fools, all by ourselves – except for three cats and a calf – in that enormous room!'

'Oh! You're simply maddening, Claudine! Look? if there's nobody there, we'll go up the little staircase and rout out the boarders and we'll go downstairs again when the dancers have arrived!'

'All right. In that case, I'm quite willing.'

To think I had feared that this great room would be a desert! It was already more than half-full of couples who were gyrating to the strains of a mixed orchestra (mounted on the garlanded platform at the end of the room); an orchestra composed of Trouillard and other local violinists, trombonists and cornet-players mingled with sections of 'The Friendly Club of Fresnois' in gold-braided caps. All of them were blowing, scraping, and banging, far from in unison but with tremendous spirit.

We had to push our way through the hedge of people who were looking on and cluttering up the main doorway. Both the double doors were flung open for it was here, you realize, that a self-constituted vigilance committee took up its station! It was here that disapproving remarks and cackles were exchanged about the young girls' dresses and the frequency with which certain couples danced together. 'My dear! Fancy showing as much of one's skin as that! What a little hussy!'

214

'Yes, and showing what? Just bones!'

'Four times, *four times* running she's danced with Monmond! If only I were her mother, I'd give her what-for to teach her a lesson, I'd send her straight home to bed!'

'Those gentlemen from Paris, they don't dance like we do here.'

'They certainly don't! You'd think they were afraid of getting themselves broken, they exert themselves so little. Now, our boys here, that's something like! They enjoy themselves without minding how hard they go at it!'

It was the truth, even though Monmond, a brilliant dancer, was restraining himself from doing flying leaps with out-spread legs, 'with reference to' the presence of the people from Paris. A dashing young spark, Monmond, over whom there was fierce rivalry! A lawyer's clerk, with a girl's face and black curly hair, how could you expect anyone to resist him!

We made a timid entrance, between two figures of a quadrille, and we walked slowly and deliberately across the room to go and seat ourselves on a sofa against the wall – three model little girls.

I had been fairly sure, in fact, I had seen for myself that my dress suited me and that my hair and my wreath made my little face look very far from contemptible – but the sly glances and the suddenly rigid countenances of the girls who were resting and fanning themselves made me quite convinced of it and I felt more at ease. I could examine the room without apprehension.

The 'dress-suits', ah! there weren't many of them! All the official group had taken the six o'clock train; farewell to the Minister, the General, the Prefect and their suite. There remained some five or six young men, mere secretaries, but pleasant and civilized, who were standing in a corner and seemed to be prodigiously amused at this hall, the like of which they had obviously never seen before. The rest of the male dancers? All the boys and young men of Montigny and its neighbourhood, two or three in badly cut evening clothes, the rest in morning-coats; paltry accoutrements for this evening's party that was supposed to be an official occasion.

The female dancers consisted entirely of young girls, for, in this primitive countryside, a woman ceases to dance as soon as she is married. They had spared no expense tonight, the young ones! Dresses of pink muslin and blue muslin that made the swarthy complexions of these little country girls look almost black, hair that was too sleek and not puffed out enough, white cotton gloves, and, in spite of the assertions of the gossips in the doorway, necks that were not cut nearly low enough; the bodices stopped their décolletage too soon, just where the flesh became white, firm, and rounded.

The orchestra warned the couples to set to partners and, amidst the fan-strokes of the skirts that brushed our knees, I saw my First Communion partner, Claire, languid and altogether charming, pass by in the arms of the handsome assistant-master, Antonin Rabastens, who was waltzing furiously, wearing a white carnation in his buttonhole.

Our lady mistresses had still not come down (I was keeping assiduous watch on the little door of the secret staircase, through which they would appear) when a gentleman, one of the 'dress-suits', came and made his bow to me. I let myself be swept off; he was not unattractive; too tall for me, but solidly built, and he waltzed well, without squeezing me too tight, and looking down at me with an amused expression . . .

How idiotic I am! I ought to have been aware of nothing else but the pleasure of dancing, of the pure joy of being invited before Anaïs who was staring at my partner with an envious eye . . . and, yet, during that waltz, I was conscious only of unhappiness, of a sadness, foolish perhaps, but so acute that I could only just keep back my tears . . . Why? Ah, because . . . – no, I can't be utterly sincere, I can only give a hint or two . . . I felt my soul overwhelmed with sorrow because, though I'm not in the least fond of dancing, I should have liked to dance with someone whom I adored with all my heart. I should have liked that someone there so that I could relieve my tension by telling him everything that I confided only to Fanchette or to my pillow (and not even to my diary) because I so wildly needed that someone, and this humiliated me, and I would never surrender myself except to the some-one whom I should completely love and completely know – dreams, in short, that would never be realized!

My tall waltzer did not fail to ask me:

'You like dancing, Mademoiselle?'

'No, Monsieur.'

'But then . . . why are you dancing?'

'Because I'd rather be doing even that than nothing at all.'

We went twice round the room in silence and then he began again:

'May one observe that your two companions serve you as admirable foils?'

'Oh, heavens, yes, you may! All the same Marie is quite attractive.'

'You said?'

'I said that the one in blue isn't ugly.'

'I . . . don't much appreciate that type of beauty . . . Will you allow me to ask you here and now for the next waltz?'

'Yes, certainly.'

'You haven't a dance-programme?'

'That doesn't matter: I know everyone here, I shan't forget.'

He took me back to my seat and had hardly turned his back before Anaïs complimented me with one of her most supercilious 'My dears!'

'Yes, he really is charming, isn't he? And you'd never believe how amusing it is to hear him talk!'

'Oh! Everyone knows *your* luck's right in today! *I've* been asked for the next dance, by Féfed.'

'And me,' said Marie, who was radiant, 'by Monmond! Ah! Here comes Mademoiselle!'

Here, in fact came both ladies. They stood framed in turn in the little doorway at the far end of the room; first, little Aimée who had only changed into an evening top, an all-white, filmy bodice from which emerged delicate dimpled shoulders and slim, rounded arms; in her hair, just above the ear, white and yellow roses made the golden eyes look more golden still – they had no need of them to make them sparkle!

Mademoiselle Sergent, still in black, but trimmed with sequins this time, wore a dress that was cut only very slightly low at the neck, revealing firm, amber-tinted flesh. Her foaming hair cast a warm shadow over her ill-favoured face and made her eyes shine out; she really looked quite well.

Behind her came the serpentine train of the boarders, in white, high-necked dresses, all very commonplace. Luce rushed up to tell me that she made herself 'décolletée' by tucking in the top of her dress, in spite of her sister's opposition. She had been right to do so. Almost at the same moment Dutertre entered by the big main door; red, excited, and talking too loud.

On account of the rumours that circulated in the town, the whole room was keenly watching these simultaneous entries of the future Deputy and his protégé. But neither of them fluttered an eyelash: Dutertre went straight up to Mademoiselle Sergent, greeted her and, as the orchestra was just beginning a polka, he boldly swept her off with him. She, flushed and with her eyes half-closed, did not talk at all and danced . . . very gracefully, upon my word! The couples re-formed and attention was turned elsewhere.

Having conducted the Headmistress back to her place, the District Superintendent came up to me – a flattering attention, very much remarked. He mazurkaed violently, without waltzing, but whirling round too much, squeezing me too tight and talking too much into my hair:

'You're as pretty as a cherub!'

'In the first place, Doctor, why do you call me "*tu*", like a child? I'm practically grown-up.'

'No, have I got to restrain myself? Just look at this grown-up person! . . . Oh, your hair and that white wreath! How I'd love to take it off you!'

'I swear that *you* won't be the one who'll take it off!'

'Be quiet, or I'll kiss you in front of everyone!'

'No one would be surprised – they've seen you do it to so many others . . .'

'True. But why won't you come and see me? It's not fear that stops you, you've got thoroughly naughty eyes . . . You see, I'll catch you again one of these days; don't laugh, you'll end up by making me lose my temper!'

'Pooh! Don't make yourself out so wicked – I don't believe you.'

He laughed, showing his teeth, and I thought to myself:

'Talk as much as you like: next winter, I'll be in Paris and you'll never run into me there!'

After me, he went off to whirl round with little Aimée, while Monmond, in an alpaca morning-coat, invited me to dance. I didn't refuse, certainly not! Provided they're wearing gloves, I'm very willing to dance with the local boys (the ones I know well) who are charming to me, in their way. Then I danced again with my tall 'dress-suit' of the first waltz up till the moment when I took a little breather during a quadrille so as not to get flushed and also because quadrilles seem to me ridiculous. Claire joined me, gentle and languishing, softened tonight with a melancholy that became her. I questioned her:

'Tell me, is everyone talking about you because the handsome schoolmaster's so assiduous?'

'Oh, do you think so? . . . They can't say anything, because there's nothing to say.'

'Come on! You're not going to pretend to make mysteries with me, are you?'

'Good heavens, no! But it's the truth – there really is nothing! . . . Look, we've met twice, tonight's the third time. He talks in a way that's absolutely . . . captivating! And just now he asked me if I ever went for walks in the evening in the Fir Plantation.'

'Everyone knows what that means. What's your answer going to be?'

She smiled, without speaking, with a hesitant, yet longing expression. She would go. They're odd, these little girls! Here was one who was pretty and gentle, docile and sentimental, and who, from the age of fourteen, had got herself deserted by half a dozen lovers in succession. She didn't know how to manage them. It was true that I shouldn't have the least idea how to manage them either, in spite of all the magnificent arguments I put up.

A vague giddiness was coming over me, from spinning round and, above all, from watching others spin round. Nearly all the 'dress-suits' had left, but Dutertre was whirling round with tremendous enthusiasm, dancing with all the girls he found attractive or who were merely very young. He swept them off their feet, turned their heads, crushed them nearly to death and left them dazed, but highly flattered. After midnight, the hall became, from minute to minute, a homelier affair; now that the 'foreigners' had gone, everyone was among their own friends again, the public of Trouillard's little dancing and drinking place on holidays – only one had more room to move in this big, gaily-decorated room and the chandelier gave a better light than the three oil-lamps of the *cabaret*. The presence of Doctor Dutertre did not make the boys feel shy, very much the reverse; already Monmond had stopped restraining his feet from sliding over the parquet floor. They flew, those feet, they sprang up above people's heads or shot wildly apart in prodigious 'splits'. The girls admired him and giggled into their handkerchiefs scented with cheap eau-de-Cologne. 'My dear, isn't he a scream? There's nobody like him!'

All of a sudden, this enthusiastic dancer shot past, as brutally as a cyclone, carrying his partner like a parcel, for he had betted a 'boocket of white wine', payable at the buffet installed in the courtyard, that he would 'do' the whole length of the room in six steps of a galop; everyone had gathered round to admire him. Monmond won his bet, but his partner – Fifine Baille, a little slut who brought milk to the town to sell, and something else too, for anyone else who wanted it – left him in a furious temper and cursed him:

'You great clumsy b—! You might easy have gone and split me dress! You ask me to dance again, and I'll clout you over the ear!'

The audience was convulsed with laughter and the boys took advantage of their being jammed together to pinch, tickle and stroke whatever was within reach of their hands. It was becoming altogether too gay; I would soon go home to bed. The lanky Anaïs, who had at last vanquished a lingering 'dress-suit', was promenading about the room with him, fanning herself, and giving high, warbling laughs, rapturous at seeing the ball warming up and the boys getting excited; there would be at least one of them who would kiss her on the neck, or somewhere!

Where on earth had Dutertre got to? Mademoiselle had ended by driving her little Aimée into a corner and was making a jealous scene; after leaving her handsome District Superintendent, she had once more become tyrannous and tender; the other was listening, shaking her shoulders, her eyes far away and her brow obstinate. As to Luce, she was dancing desperately – 'I'm not missing one' – passing from arm to arm without getting breathless; the boys did not think her pretty but, once they had asked her to dance, they came back again; she felt so supple and small, melting into their arms, light as a snowflake.

Mademoiselle Sergent had disappeared now, vexed perhaps by seeing her favourite waltzing, in spite of her objurgations, with a tall fair counter-jumper who was squeezing her tight and brushing her with his moustache and his lips without her objecting in the least. It was one o'clock, I wasn't enjoying myself a bit any more and I was going home to bed. During the break in a polka (here, they dance the polka in two parts, between which the couples promenade arm in arm round the room in Indian file), I stopped Luce as she was passing and forced her to sit down for a minute.

'Aren't you getting tired of all this business?'

'Be quiet! I could dance for a whole week on end! I can't feel my legs . . .'

'So you are thoroughly enjoying yourself?'

'I've no idea! I'm not thinking about anything at all, my head's in a whirl, it's simply marvellous! Still I like it awfully when they hold me tight . . . When they hold me tight and we're doing a fast waltz, it makes me want to scream!'

What was that we suddenly heard? The trampling of feet, the shrill cries of a woman who was being hit, screamed insults . . . Were the boys fighting among themselves? But no, the noise definitely came from upstairs! The screams suddenly became so shrill that the couples stopped their promenade; everyone became anxious and one good soul, the gallant and absurd Antonin Rabastens, rushed to the door of the inside staircase and opened it . . . the tumult grew louder and I was thunderstruck to recognize the voice of Mademoiselle Sergent's mother, that harsh old peasant-woman's voice, yelling quite appalling things. Everyone listened, nailed to the spot, in absolute silence; their eyes fixed on that little doorway from which so much noise was coming.

'Ah! you bitch of a girl! It serves you right! Yes, I've broken my broom-handle on his back, that swine of a doctor of yours! Yes, I've given him a good whack on the bum all right! Ah, I've smelt a rat a good long time now! No, no, my beauty, I'm not going to hold my tongue, I don't care a f—, I don't for the fine folk at the ball! Let 'em hear, they'll hear a nice thing to be sure! Tomorrow morning, no, not tomorrow – this very minute – I'm packing my bag. I won't sleep in such a house, I won't! You dirty little beast, you took advantage of him being drunk and incapable (*sic*) to get him into bed with you, that fellow that'll grub in any muckheap! So *that's* why you got a rise in pay, you bitch on heat, you! If I'd made you milk the cows like *I* did, you'd never have come to this! But you'll suffer for it, I'll shout it everywhere, I'd like to see them point their fingers at you in the streets, I'd like to see you a laughing-stock! He can't do nothing to me, your dirty dog of a District Superintendent, however much him and the Min'ster's in each other's pockets; I gave him such a whack that he ran away from me. He's frightened of me, he is! Comes and does his filthy business here, in a room where I make the bed with my own hands every morning – and doesn't even lock the door! Runs off he does, half in his shirt and nothing on his feet, so that his dirty boots are still there! Look, there's his boots – take a good look at 'em!'

We could hear them being thrown down the stairs, bumping against the steps; one fell right down to the bottom and lay in the doorway, in the full glare of light, a patent-leather boot, all shining and elegant . . . No one dared touch it. The infuriated voice grew less loud, retreated along the passages to the accompaniment of banging doors, and suddenly ceased. Then everyone looked at each other; no one could believe their own ears. The couples, still arm in arm, stood there perplexed, keyed-up for what might happen next; then, little by little, sly smiles appeared on mocking lips and ran all through the room, gradually turning into bantering laughter till the band on the platform caught the infection and laughed as heartily as everyone else.

I looked round for Aimée and saw that she was as white as the bodice of her dress, her eyes were stretched wide, staring at the boot, the focal point of the entire room's gaze. A young man charitably went up to her, and offered to take her outside for a little to recover herself . . . She cast panic-stricken glances all around her, then burst into sobs and rushed hurriedly from the room. (Weep, weep, my girl, these painful moments will bring you hours of even sweeter pleasures.) After this flight, no one hesitated to restrain their wholehearted amusement; everyone was nudging each other and saying: 'I say, did you see *that*!'

It was then that I heard just beside me a hysterical laugh, a piercing, suffocating laugh, vainly stifled in a handkerchief. It was Luce, who was writhing, doubled-up, on a sofa, crying with pleasure, and wearing such an expression of unmitigated bliss on her face that *I* was overcome with laughter too.

'You've not gone out of your mind, have you, Luce, laughing like that?'

'Ah! Ah! . . . oh! let me alone . . . it's too good . . . Oh! I'd never have dared to hope for that! Ah! Ah! I can go now, that'll keep me bucked for ages . . . Lord, how that's done me good! . . .'

I took her off into a corner to calm her down a little. In the ballroom, everyone was chattering hard and no one was dancing any more . . . What a scandal there would be in the morning! . . . But a violin launched a stray note, the cornets and trombones took it up; a couple timidly began a polka step, two others imitated them, then all the rest followed suit; someone shut the little door to hide the scandalous boot and the dance started up again, all the gayer and wilder for having witnessed such a comic, such a totally unexpected interlude! As for myself, I was going home to bed, completely happy at having crowned my schooldays with such a memorable night.

Farewell to the classroom; farewell, Mademoiselle and her girl friend; farewell, feline little Luce and spiteful Anaïs! I am going to leave you to make my entry into the world; – I shall be very much astonished if I enjoy myself there as much as I have at school.

VINTAGE CLASSICS

Vintage launched in the United Kingdom in 1990, and was originally the paperback home for the Random House Group's literary authors. Now, Vintage is comprised of some of London's oldest and most prestigious literary houses, including Chatto & Windus (1855), Hogarth (1917), Jonathan Cape (1921) and Secker & Warburg (1935), alongside the newer or relaunched hardback and paperback imprints: The Bodley Head, Harvill Secker, Yellow Jersey, Square Peg, Vintage Paperbacks and Vintage Classics.

From Angela Carter, Graham Greene and Aldous Huxley to Toni Morrison, Haruki Murakami and Virginia Woolf, Vintage Classics is renowned for publishing some of the greatest writers and thinkers from around the world and across the ages – all complemented by our beautiful, stylish approach to design. Vintage Classics' authors have won many of the world's most revered literary prizes, including the Nobel, the Man Booker, the Prix Goncourt and the Pulitzer, and through their writing they continue to capture imaginations, inspire new perspectives and incite curiosity.

In 2007 Vintage Classics introduced its distinctive red spine design, and in 2012 Vintage Children's Classics was launched to include the much-loved authors of our childhood. Random House joined forces with the Penguin Group in 2013 to become Penguin Random House, making it the largest trade publisher in the United Kingdom.

@vintagebooks

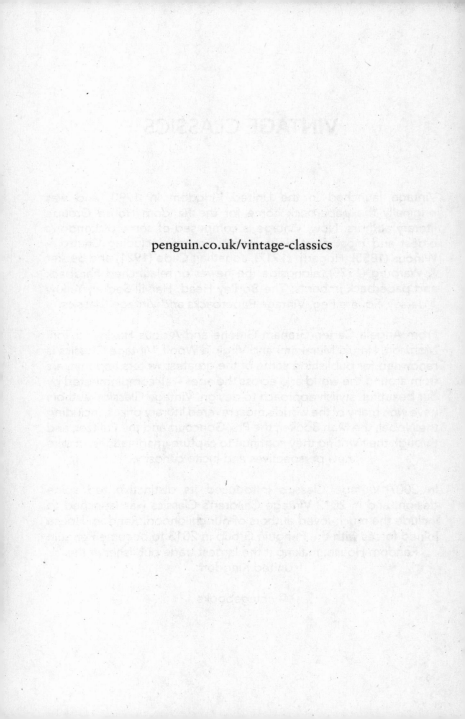

penguin.co.uk/vintage-classics